THE HOUSE OF THE WITCH

CLARE MARCHANT

Boldwood

First published in Great Britain in 2024 by Boldwood Books Ltd.

Cover Design by JD Design Ltd

Cover Photography: Shutterstock

A CIP catalogue record for this book is available from the British Library.

Paperback ISBN 978-1-83603-037-9

Large Print ISBN 978-1-83603-038-6

Hardback ISBN 978-1-83603-036-2

Ebook ISBN 978-1-83603-039-3

Kindle ISBN 978-1-83603-040-9

Audio CD ISBN 978-1-83603-031-7

MP3 CD ISBN 978-1-83603-032-4

Digital audio download ISBN 978-1-83603-033-1

Boldwood Books Ltd
23 Bowerdean Street
London SW6 3TN
www.boldwoodbooks.com

Daddy, my Daddy

PROLOGUE

1646

The silhouette of a church stands against the night sky, fragile waning moonlight casting shadows across uneven ground. A person stumbles over the muddy, disturbed space towards a dark void, gaping wide. There is a smell of damp, freshly dug soil, mixed with that of sweat and fear.

Short irregular movements: a body is rolled into its final resting place. A warmth still rises, even though there is no life left within. Climbing down beside the corpse, jagged iron spikes are pushed through limbs as though anchoring them to the earth. Whispered words, spoken to prevent the dead from rising.

The mud piled high to one side is pushed in, until all is hidden. Bracken and brambles, piercing dirty skin with sharp thorns, cover the mound, ensuring it remains unseen in this barren piece of land.

Placing the nearby stone, already engraved, on top of the grave, a sharp piece of flint still slick with blood is used to complete the letters upon it. Everything has led inexorably to this, it could only end this way. The death administered here was no crime, it was just and needed, to save those who need protecting from evil.

The fingers of daybreak pierce the horizon, a reminder that there is little time left for the final task. The one which will complete this story.

1

2024

'Good grief, Addie, did you actually look at the pictures of this place before you signed the rental agreement? It's a complete mess.' Rick dropped her suitcases on the hall floor and screwed his nose up at the cobwebs and dust which greeted them. 'And I've just noticed there are some roof tiles loose on the front left corner. Be careful when you go outside, they could fall and cause you an injury.'

'Of course I saw the pictures,' Adrianna replied. 'I know it hasn't been occupied for a while. The letting agent explained everything to me, but that's why it's cheap. I can't run two properties, even for six months, unless one of them is a budget option. Guess which one we're standing in?' She sidled past him and wandered through the small lounge with its sloping floor, exposed beams and pale, powdery lime-plastered walls, into a large kitchen situated in what looked like a later extension at the rear. Through the dirty windows festooned with yet more cobwebs, she could see the garden stretching towards an orchard in the distance, the trees already sprinkled with the beginnings of blossom. Beyond that, on the horizon, the soft buff of sandy dunes and a glimpse of a shining strip of sea beckoned to her. 'It will be lovely when I've sorted it out, I'll soon get it ship-shape,' she added as Rick joined her, opening cupboards and peering inside.

'I know you will, my little house-mouse.' He pulled her in for a hug and ruffled the top of her hair. 'Now, let's have a quick look around and I must use the bathroom, but then I'm afraid I need to be getting back to London. Busy day at the coalface tomorrow. And not too much housework for you, please. Remember this is supposed to be a sabbatical, a rest from everything? Don't start giving yourself too much to do.'

'Of course,' she replied, 'but this won't be taxing my brain, will it? No deadlines here. I'm going to sit in the garden or in front of a fire in the living room and read books all day.'

'You'll need the chimney swept first,' Rick warned. 'Chimney fires can reduce a house to a burning pile of rubble in a very short time. You need to stay safe, darling.'

'I'll be careful,' she reassured him. 'Now let's go and have a poke around upstairs. We could test the bed?' She raised her eyebrows suggestively. With a grin, Rick caught her hand and they ran up to find the bedrooms.

* * *

'I still don't understand why you don't just let me have your car whilst you're up here,' Rick said as they drove to King's Lynn later. 'It's going to be a pain for me having to travel on the tube for the next six months. Besides, there's no off-street parking at the cottage so you'll have to leave it on the lane. I know how precious you are about it, and it'd be much safer in the car park beneath the flat.'

'I won't be able to get anywhere without it,' Adrianna pointed out. 'At least you have decent public transport. You've just got used to using my car because I live so close to work in London.' She'd bought her Range Rover with her previous year's bonus and Rick had been very enthusiastic. It was no wonder, because it seemed to be him who'd put most of the miles on it.

'If I have an emergency, or I need to come back to London, I can't be waiting three days for a bus to turn up,' she said.

'I do think you'd be fine,' he started again as they pulled up on the station forecourt, hunching his shoulders up and pouting whilst fluttering his eyelashes at her.

'It's still no,' she said, laughing. Getting out of the car to kiss him goodbye, she leant into him as he wrapped his arms around her. She loved how safe and protected he made her feel as he gathered her to him. With a lingering kiss and, 'Love you, let me know when you've got back,' she waited while he walked into the station. This stay in Norfolk was a six-month respite from her busy and demanding role as a financial project director in the city and all that the strain had led to. She'd ended up in a place she never wanted to go to again and she placed her palm on her chest, reminding herself to keep calm. Having a difference of opinion about who kept the car, as if it was a pet in a custody battle, wasn't the way she'd envisaged her break beginning.

The drive back to the cottage was more relaxing and Adrianna hummed along with the music on the radio, drumming her fingers on the steering wheel. Rick always pulled a face at the classical music she sometimes put on, but she found it soothing. There were signs of the burgeoning spring along the hedgerows as clumps of daffodils, their buds now unfurling to reveal their vibrant yellow, huddled beneath blackthorn and beech, the wintery, black, spiky silhouettes flecked with green leaves hinting at the warmer days to come.

When she arrived back at the cottage, a fog was beginning to roll in from the sea and she could no longer see the horizon. The heavy swirling white covered the ground two feet deep and she could see nothing below her knees. In the churchyard next to the cottage, the tops of the gravestones rose from the milky pallor. Keeping her eyes averted, Adrianna quickly let herself back inside.

Inside it felt colder than it had earlier and, rubbing her hands together, she found her gilet and slipped it on before going to the kitchen and holding the kettle under the tap. She held her breath and waited to see if the water would flow and thankfully, after several splutters and a shower of droplets, it arrived. Making herself a cup of coffee, she carried it into the living room.

Kneeling at the hearth, she wondered whether to risk lighting a fire, despite Rick's warning still echoing in her head. It was the only heating in the cottage – other than the Aga in the kitchen – there was no central heating. Brushing away the dirt and ashes still evident there, her hand slowed as she uncovered a large dark discolouration across one corner. It was crimson and ochre, almost brown, and it looked suspiciously like a bloodstain.

2

1646

A loud banging at the door stopped Ursula's hand, and in a single motion the half-skinned rabbit she held between her knees was under a sack beneath the table. She kicked some of the straw scattered across the floor over the pool of blood at her feet. Poaching carried a death sentence and although, like her neighbours, Ursula considered the fields around her cottage to be common land, the local squire did not. He'd enclosed them and declared them his own.

'Ursula, thank our Lord in heaven you are here.' The young girl on the doorstep anxiously jigging from foot to foot was in her early adolescence and the eldest of seven children belonging to the blacksmith. Her face carried the pinched, hollow look of a child who rarely got enough to eat and, beneath the knitted blanket she wore around her shoulders, her frame was all angular bones. Behind her the haar, the sea fog which had edged it way across the land overnight, now lay heavy and damp, suffocating the sun and silencing any noise. Experience told Ursula that it was unlikely to lift all day and they'd enter darkness under the same dank mantle. It hung in the air sucking the smell of wood smoke from the chimneys down to the ground.

'I would not be out in this weather,' Ursula replied, adding, 'Is the babe on its way?' The blacksmith's wife, Ruth, was due to deliver her eighth child and, as local midwife, Ursula had been expecting to be called.

'Aye,' the girl nodded, 'she is near her time now; she has been labouring since last night. This baby is taking its time.'

'Wait while I get my bag of herbs and I will walk back with you,' Ursula said. She quickly damped the fire down to ensure no stray spark could set her cottage ablaze whilst she was out, and after tying her shawl on, she picked up a leather satchel. It contained all she'd need for a birth.

She slipped her boots, the left one with a split at the front but not yet ready to be discarded, inside a pair of wooden pattens. They'd been made for her by the local carpenter in exchange for a remedy which had saved the life of his young son when fever struck.

The young girl was almost running, so concerned was she to get home and Ursula hurried after her. Although Ruth was experienced and capable at giving birth, they both knew there was always a risk something could go wrong. Women – and their babies too – often died in childbirth.

Approaching the smithy, the flickering orange and yellow flames from the forge were just visible and Ursula could smell hot metal as the ring of hammer on horseshoe rang out. There was no possibility that the man would be inside looking after his wife or his family, she thought, as she stepped up her pace. The sooner she was there, the better.

Inside the house, which was larger than her own, Ursula could immediately hear moaning from above her head. A group of children with the same thin, impoverished faces as their sister looked towards her with relief as she entered. Only the youngest two continued playing on the floor with some pieces of smooth stone, oblivious to the noise upstairs.

'Get me some hot water,' Ursula instructed the girl who knew the procedure and immediately collected a pot and began to fill it. Ursula hurried up the stairs as she heard her patient calling out to her.

'I thought I heard the door.' Ruth was holding onto the end of her rough wooden bed, swinging her hips from side to side. There was no fireplace up here but the room was warm from the fire downstairs and her dark hair was plastered to the beads of sweat on her face.

'It looks as though I am just in time.' Ursula smiled as she took the pile of clean linens from the press in the corner and placed them on the floor. She knew Ruth didn't like to be laid down, nor seated on a birthing chair. When the time came, she'd lower herself to her knees and deliver the baby straight onto the floor covering, unless Ursula was there to catch it. Any way a woman wished to deliver was acceptable as far as Ursula was concerned. She herself had never given birth – nor did she have any intention of doing so – and she felt it was right to be entirely led by what the mother chose to do.

Ruth's moaning became louder and she knelt, still holding onto the bed. Crouching behind her Ursula could see the baby's head already crowning.

'Slow your pushing.' She spoke calmly. 'Let me ease this little one into the world carefully.' She held onto the baby's head to take its weight in her hands and inch by inch drew him out until finally Ruth gave one loud yell which seemed to go on forever before a slippery, bloody, and wet baby slid out into Ursula's waiting hands. She laid it on the bed of cloth she'd arranged on the floor.

Picking up the edge of one of the linens she rubbed the baby, a boy and a big one at that, briskly until his face screwed up and an indignant wail filled the room. It was only at that moment she saw the baby was not right. His legs were bowed, both feet curled inwards so they lay along the ankles at an unnatural angle. Gently she tried to ease them out to where they should be but they barely moved before resuming their original position.

Ruth swung her leg over him as she turned and lowered herself to the floor whilst Ursula tied a piece of clean twine around the cord and cut it.

'This babe is not normal,' she warned before handing him to his mother. There was a sharp intake of breath and a pause as Ruth took in what she was looking at.

'Why is he like this?' she whispered. 'Why are his legs bent so?'

'I do not know,' Ursula admitted, 'but do not worry at present, put him to the breast and let him feed.'

Ruth did as she was bid and the baby began to suckle.

'What will you call him?' Ursula asked, as quietly she delivered the afterbirth. She wrapped it up to put on the fire downstairs.

'Given that John insisted we call the first-born boy after him I think it is fair that I choose a name this time, and I shall name him Henry, after my own father.'

From below they heard John's voice calling up the stairs.

'I was fetched,' he said. 'They told me they heard a baby cry and I do not hear my Ruth still hollering and screaming,' he laughed as he spoke. 'May I come up?'

'You may,' Ruth replied. Quickly Ursula passed a swaddling linen but not fast enough and, as John arrived in the small room, he looked silently at the both of them before drawing back the cloth. Tears welled in Ruth's eyes and wordlessly she passed him the baby.

'What have you done to him?' Immediately John handed him back. 'Why does he not have proper legs? Why do they twist like this, like serpents?'

'Not all children are born perfect, we know this,' Ursula said. 'And not all babies are born with breath in their bodies. We should be thanking the Lord that Henry does.'

Ruth was now crying noisily, holding the baby to her chest.

'Nay, it would have been kinder to this baby to have not taken his first breath, for he shall have a very hard life if he cannot walk. He will be a burden on us as parents.' John's face was red, his fists clenched. He turned and walked out and they listened to the thump of his boots as he ran downstairs. The door slammed, making the timber-framed walls shudder. A moment later they heard hammer on metal start to ring out again.

'He is just upset, he will get used to how Henry looks,' Ursula reassured as she placed the baby in the oak cradle beside the bed, its edges dark and shiny from the years of hands rocking it, before she helped Ruth into a clean linen shift and onto their hay-stuffed mattress. No wonder she preferred to give birth on the floor, this would be laborious to replace if it was soaked in blood.

Handing over some yarrow for Ruth to chew, she reminded her to use it sparsely. 'It will help return your womb to normal,' she said, 'but too much will give you pains and much bleeding. Just one leaf a day is sufficient.'

Downstairs in the kitchen, the eldest girl was handing out steaming bowls containing bread soaked in a watery pottage, with pieces of parsnip and leek floating on top. No wonder the children looked so thin and ill, perhaps their father should look to feeding the ones he already had, rather than bringing more into the world. There were herbs to prevent babies, if he was agreeable, but she bit her tongue from saying anything. He would likely tell her it was none of her business and he needed more children as surety against the future, if any were to die. She suggested that one of the children took some pottage up to their mother.

Going outside she went to find John, wanting to explain to him that Ruth needed to be treated kindly and not blamed for their new son's physical ailment.

'I do not need your advice, midwife,' he said, dropping a small pile of coins into her hand. 'She is my wife and I shall deal with this how I wish.'

Ursula knew there was no point arguing and, putting the money in her satchel, she left. She wasn't looking forward to walking home alone in the fog and she set off along the village street keeping close to the buildings and using them as landmarks through the shadowy haze until she saw the familiar flint-built cottage that was her own. Some repairs the previous year had been done with new red bricks, several in slightly different sizes, but she much preferred the dappled grey and white patterns of the local stone. She tilted her head, but all was still silent; the soothing sound of the waves crawling across the stones and sand in the distance were hushed. It was the background noise to her entire life, the horror she'd endured and seen, all that she could never wipe from her memory. But no more, she'd broken the cycle and it would always remain so; the past was trapped in a box in her head and the lid was kept closed, it was best kept that way. It didn't do to reminisce. This was her life now and she was thankful for it.

3

1646

Later that same day as Ursula walked to the well in the centre of the village, her empty leather bucket swinging from her hand, the sound of raised voices from one of the fishermen's cottages made her raise her eyebrows at her friend, Katherine, who was already cranking the wooden handle round to bring the heavy bucket, water slopping over the sides, to the surface. Ursula helped her lift it and pour the contents into a receptacle similar to her own.

'Spent all his money on beer,' Katherine said. Ursula nodded, wincing as the shouts increased, followed by the thump of something heavy and what sounded like the splintering of wood. There was a small high-pitched scream and then silence. Both women knew better than to interfere, what was occurring behind that door happened often at other houses in the village. Men with coins in their pocket drinking all night and then waking up with a sore head and delivering the marks of their excess on their wives.

Ursula had seen the results of a big, powerful man in his

cups who cared not one jot for his wife and family and talked through his fists with the punches he threw. It had been the story of her childhood, watching her father's violence towards her mother, herself, and her brothers. She still bore the scars from being thrown across the room at the age of four, and was lucky to have survived. Her mother wasn't so fortunate, meeting her end by her husband's violence.

He'd known that the moment word got out that he had killed his wife, he'd be in the gaol at King's Lynn to hang from the gibbet. Taking just minutes to snatch up some food and ale, he fled. There had been not a moment's thought about his three children, leaving Ursula to raise her brothers. His moment of brutality had changed her life.

She'd dragged her mother's heavy body from the parlour so as not to upset her brothers when they returned home from where they were searching for driftwood at the beach. Days later there had been a pauper's funeral at the church next door and Ursula had remained in the cottage with her brothers. She was old enough to look after her siblings until each of them found work and moved away. Her youngest brother, Peter, now worked as a cow hand near Norwich and had returned to visit twice in recent years but of Richard, she had no idea. Perhaps he was fighting in the civil war. She included them in her prayers every night.

Returning home she threw some logs on the fire. The remains of a pottage she'd cooked with the rabbit she'd snared was starting to bubble. The rich meat scent was now weaker but with the addition of turnip and barley she could eke it out for another few days. One of the village lads was missing a hand after being caught poaching earlier in the year, and he was lucky not to swing for it. The estate manager was a hard man, but Lady

Mayling was more lenient and thankfully she had intervened. Perhaps if she'd also got involved when her husband had enclosed the common land which surrounded the village, then the locals wouldn't be quite so poor now, with nowhere to graze their sheep and forced to steal rabbits and pheasant. It was a meagre, wretched existence for many.

As Ursula had expected, Jane, the fisherman's wife who'd been in an argument arrived at her cottage door later that day. Her face was a swollen, purple, blotchy pulp, like bread soaked in blackberry juice; her nose, dried blood crusted around the nostrils, was pushed to one side. She ushered the woman inside and sat her on a stool beside the fire whilst she busied herself with a wash of rosemary and feverfew and a poultice of pennyroyal to try and reduce the swelling.

Working quietly, she bit her lip to stop herself from saying anything to the battered female in front of her. There was no point, many men abused their wives and used their fists freely, but what escape was there? These women had nowhere else to go. Killing a spouse would result in the death sentence, but bruises or a broken bone would mend and were easily hushed up by both the perpetrators and their victims. People simply turned their faces and looked the other way.

The actions of her father had had a profound effect on Ursula. Never would she put herself in the position her mother had been, a piece of meat for a man to use and ill-treat as he wished. Because he owned her. She lived alone possessed by nobody, making ends meet with her herbal remedies and her work as a midwife, and her proficiency at mending the broken, like Jane sitting in her room now sipping warm spiced ale, through swollen lips, caked in blood. A tooth was now loose in the front of her mouth.

Passing over a scrap of linen wrapped around a paste of alder leaves she'd soaked in hot water and then crushed with her pestle and mortar, she told Jane to hold it across her eyes, both so puffed-up they could hardly be opened, and the top of her nose.

The two women sat in silence for a quarter of an hour. Occasionally Ursula would get up and potter about tidying things but there was nothing else she could do but be a voiceless companion. After a little while, Jane stood up and went to pass the cloth back to Ursula, but she shook her head and told her to keep it.

'You can warm it up several times,' she said. 'It will last for a day or so and continue to help with the swelling. If you need to dispose of it quickly, then throw it on the fire, I have other scraps of cloth. Do not let your husband see it if it will rile him further.'

Her patient nodded, a tear rolling down her cheek to drip off her chin onto the poultice she was holding. They both knew there was no more to be said, and Ursula opened the back door and let her slip out. It was better that she wasn't seen leaving in case her husband were to hear of it and think she'd been telling tales. That may lead to another beating.

Kneeling beside the fireplace in her parlour, Ursula prised up a loose floorboard beneath which she kept her purse of money together with a sheaf of parchment leaves she used as a journal, her quill and some ink she'd made with oak galls, copperas and gum arabic. Nobody knew she was able to read and write, and she kept the knowledge to herself. A woman who chose to live on her own was already an anomaly. One who was also known to read and write would cast suspicions where there were no grounds for them.

The village priest, incumbent before the current one, had taken pity on her. He'd probably heard the violence and screaming when he was in the churchyard alongside her cottage, and he offered her some small pieces of mending work at the manse. Whilst she was there sewing, he started to teach her some letters. With the Bible now in English, she was able to learn to read and she'd been leant a small, printed book of psalms with which she practised her reading when the house was quiet and she was able to escape to the beach, the book tucked into her pocket.

She remembered how she used to run across the common, skirting around the tall grasses and bog weed which indicated where the ground was swampy, until she reached the dunes and beyond that, the sea. Away to her left was the harbour at Brancaster, the small fishing boats either bobbing on the water with sails flapping, or away at sea. There was a permanent smell of rotting fish drifting in the air, the innards discarded so that the incoming tide would take them back from where they'd originated. At the water's edge, women sat mending nets whilst chatting and laughing together. It was hard work, but there was a sense of camaraderie in their joint hardships. For a while, her father had laboured with the men on board the fishing wherries and her mother had been there too with the other wives, and Ursula could remember as a small child being told to mind her brothers while her mother worked. But then their father had chosen to prevent her mother from leaving the house, and that was the end of that.

And now, Ursula made sure she wrote up everything she did. It was useful sometimes to be able to check which medications had been helpful, or how a previous birth had gone. Sitting at her table she entered the birth she'd attended the previous day. She remembered John's reaction to his new son and her mouth turned down at the edges. Henry would not have a life sailing on calm waters, that was immediately obvious.

She replaced the journal from where she'd retrieved it.

Everything about her life involved stealth: keeping herself inconspicuous because she lived on her own and other people were wary of that. Hiding her abilities. It was a secretive life, but one she chose, and would choose again. Silent and safe was all she wished for.

4

2024

After a restless night during which she couldn't settle, Adrianna was up early the next morning. It hadn't occurred to her that night in the countryside would be so much darker than in London where the flash of blue lights and a cacophony of sirens would often puncture the hours of darkness. Once she turned off the bedside light, the room was plunged into a black abyss that closed in as if suffocating her, and she'd ended up sleeping with the lamp on.

In the kitchen, after several sharp tugs, Adrianna managed to pull open the back door, the bottom of it catching on the quarry tiled floor where the wood had swollen during the winter. She'd made a coffee intending to take it into the garden, but what greeted her made her realise that idea would have to wait.

There was a clear space of approximately two metres around the door and beyond that, a wilderness. Tall grasses, battered and wet after overnight rain, wrestled with a labyrinth of brambles, nettles and dead, brown weeds. Only the time of year stopped it being a complete jungle, but sharp green fronds of unfurling bracken glanced from within the undergrowth, taunting anyone with the idea of attempting to clear them. A scent of wet earth mixed with rough salty sea air settled on her tastebuds.

The wall separating the next-door church and surrounding graveyard from the garden was covered in ivy, spilling over like boiling milk in a pan. Far away beyond the overgrown orchard, the grass almost as tall as the lower boughs of the trees, was a dry-stone wall. And then the enticing glimpse of pale ochre sand and a narrow stripe, a knife edge of deep grey, where the sea lay past the dunes. Adrianna looked forward to early morning swims once the weather warmed up.

Her knowledge of the difference between flowers and weeds was negligible, but she had plenty of time to find out. It would be nice to have a garden to sit in during the summer. When she'd imagined having a break from work, that had been the mental image she'd clung on to. Halcyon days with no worries, no pressure, no stifling anxiety. How hard could gardening be? She'd add some tools to her shopping list.

Back in the living room there were a few pottery ornaments on the mantelpiece, but the rest of the room was empty of homely details, just an old sofa with scratched wooden arms and an armchair with the seat dipping in the middle, defying anyone to be able to get out again once they'd sunk into its depths.

Collecting a duster and polish from the kitchen she cleaned the room, carefully lining up the now clean trinkets so they were precisely the same distance apart. Pleased with the tidier aesthetic she then turned her attention to the fireplace. It looked neglected, ash still laying in the grate, but she couldn't draw her eyes away from the large stain she'd discovered the night before. She hoped it was just paint, because if it was blood, then it must be a recent spillage and she wondered what had happened before the previous occupant left. She'd been told the old lady had died in hospital, but Adrianna didn't know the details of how she'd got there.

A sudden and unexpected clawing and tapping noise made her pause. In her grandparents' old house, the pipes used to bang and make her jump, but this was different. It sounded like something was inside the pipes trying to get out. Going into the kitchen she kicked the Aga, vainly hoping it might release some air, but it did nothing.

'Be sensible Addie,' she said out loud. 'It's just going to be a bird caught in the chimney, or a mouse.' She remembered the mice in the wall space at a hotel she and Rick had once stayed at. Or attempted to, he'd made a scene and got a refund and their weekend away was abruptly cancelled. She'd add traps to her shopping list.

After she'd showered and with nothing in the house for breakfast, Adrianna drove to King's Lynn in search of shops. The village and her garden were waiting to be explored, but before that she needed to stock up.

* * *

Once home, having found a supermarket and spent a long time at the garden centre, she was unpacking her purchases from the car when she was interrupted by a woman hurrying across the street. She was wearing jeans and a striped top, her steel grey hair cut into a bob with a sharp fringe. Her face was split in two by a wide smile.

'I thought I saw a light on in Church Cottage last night,' she called as she trotted over. 'Have you bought it? I'm Louise by the way, the landlady at the King's Head.' She waved her hand behind her towards the village pub.

'Hi, I'm Adrianna,' she introduced herself. 'I haven't bought it though, I'm just renting it for six months from Mrs Murray's grandson, Jason. I gather that he's working in South Africa and can't decide what to do with the place, so I'm staying here in the meantime.'

'Blimey, I bet it's in an awful state, isn't it? Since Mrs Murray went into hospital, nobody has been near the place.'

'Well, it does need a good clean,' Adrianna agreed, 'but I've got plenty of time. And I thought I'd tackle the garden too.' She indicated the tools she'd just removed from the boot of the car.

'That's going to take a lot of work – you do know how big the garden is, don't you?'

Adrianna admitted she had no idea, the information from the agency had been scant. No wonder they'd been so keen to get her deposit and contract signed.

'It wasn't always so big,' Louise continued. 'Mr Murray, may he also rest in peace, bought some paddocks to increase the land to at least two acres. Goodness knows why. You see that wall?' She pointed into the distance to the one Adrianna had spotted earlier, 'That's the boundary.'

'Hmm, I don't think I'll get that much cleared,' Adrianna admitted, 'I was thinking more about enough space for a garden chair where I can drink my morning coffee, with perhaps a few flowers in the summer, if there's anything still lurking beneath the weeds. Or I can buy some bedding plants.'

'Well, best of luck with that! And are you working whilst you're here? I know you youngsters all seem to work from home these days.' Louise asked.

'Um no, not at present. I usually work in London,' Adrianna could feel tears prickle the back of her eyes as she thought about it, 'but I'm taking a break for six months, a sabbatical.'

'A sabbatical, that sounds posh. So, what is it that you do?'

Adrianna explained as briefly as she could about how she

made sure that big, million-pound projects were delivered on budget.

'Ooh, very high-flying.' Louise raised her eyebrows and pursed her lips. 'You must be extremely smart to have a job like that,' she said.

'No, no I'm not really,' Adrianna laughed as she replied, feeling a little embarrassed, 'I was just in the right place at the right time, I kind of fell into what I do. I'm not that clever at all.' Even thinking about the office made her feel wobbly these days.

She was the only woman in the department and, from her initial confidence that she could do the job, she now realised she'd been fooling herself. Over the past year she'd disintegrated, gone from a self-assured city worker to someone who was afraid to walk the few hundred yards from her flat to the office. She was burned out at the age of thirty-five and wondering what she was going to do with the rest of her life. Not just burned out, 'unhinged' was what Rick had jokingly suggested, and he was right. She was a fraud thinking she could juggle those big projects; one mistake, one set of figures supposedly missed off a report and she'd tipped from high-flying and super confident into a dizzying plummet to an abbess of anxiety and stress. She'd lost all control, doubting everything, and her projects had fallen like dominoes: once one began to falter, they all followed.

'If you've got time on your hands, you must come over to the pub one evening and I'll introduce you to the locals,' Louise said. 'I have a daughter, Jess, she works behind the bar and lives with me; she's got a three-year-old little boy, Malachi. His dad was a nasty piece of work, they're both better off without him and I love having them here with me.'

'Thank you, I'd like that. I must get on now, but I'll see you later.' Adrianna picked up her shopping bags and took them inside. Even talking for that short while had exhausted her and she was glad to be able to escape into the silence of the cottage. Her hands were trembling, and she sank down on the sofa for a moment. What was happening to her? How had she become this person, a shell, her self-confidence dissolved. Work had beaten her into a tiny ball and thrown her in the bin. She'd lost her grip on everything. In fact, she hadn't even been able to go to the office for the final two weeks before her sabbatical and had relied on Rick to meet up with her boss and relay their inevitable disappointment back to her. She was lucky, he'd told her, that they were prepared to allow her to take this time off.

Walking upstairs, she slipped off her shoes and climbed beneath the duvet. Curling up in a ball, she hoped that hiding from the world would make things feel less overwhelming. She waited silently for a sense of solace that didn't come.

5

1646

'Hello, Ursula, are you home?' A woman's voice called through from the scullery, waking Ursula from where she was dozing beside the fire. She'd been kept awake during the night by a screaming vixen which finally stopped its eerie, ghostly howls just as the room began to brighten and sunlight beckoned the day.

'In here,' she called back, recognising the voice of one of the young village girls, Rebecca Thorpe, who'd been married the previous year at the church beneath whose shadow Ursula lived. Rebecca and her husband, Samuel, were living with his family in an already overcrowded cottage. 'Can I help you with something?' she added as the girl walked into the main room. Her face was pallid and strained and she'd lost the new bride soft pink bloom she'd had, the shiny-eyed expectation of a happy married life ahead. Though she was one of the lucky girls, one who'd married a lad she loved.

'I hope so.' Rebecca pulled the stool over and sat down beside Ursula. 'Would you read the future for me please? I have been married for nigh on eight months now and yet I have my courses again this morning, there is no sign of a babe.'

'Some babies take a little while to arrive,' Ursula reminded her, 'but I can look and see what your hand tells me. It will cost you a piece of silver though.'

Rebecca handed over the coin and Ursula slipped it into her pocket. She'd still been a young girl, perhaps twelve or thirteen when she'd realised she had a gift to see the future in people's hands. Not simply the reading of lines as others did, but sometimes as she watched, fleeting glimpses of lives not yet lived. Love and laughter, and often pain which took her breath away, as though she were living it too. It only happened when she looked into the future of other women but thankfully it was rare that a man would ask her to use her powers.

It was a legacy from her mother. Just as she'd inherited the colour of her skin, a soft brown akin to the young leverets in spring, her dark eyes with long lashes and her glossy black hair wound up beneath her cap. Her mother used to tell her stories of how as a small child she'd journeyed with her family from a country far away.

Taking Rebecca's rough hand in her own she could feel the ingrained, hard calluses in the skin, those which every villager over the age of ten possessed. The sign of a hard physical life, the only one they could look forward to. Looking at the lines weaving their way across the palm Ursula slowly rubbed the side of her thumb over them. She could feel the sweat there, Rebecca was more worried than she was allowing herself to show, which Ursula understood. A barren wife would often lead to a husband straying, for every man wanted a brood of children, especially sons.

As she let herself relax and her eyes stare into a world that did not yet exist she watched as she saw Rebecca holding a small baby with three other young children at her feet. Her face was alight and she was laughing at someone whom Ursula couldn't see. But then the picture swirled and went dark and Ursula saw Rebecca kneeling beside a pallet, clutching Samuel's hand. His face was dark and blotchy, the skin stretched over sharp angled bones. He was close to death, if not already there. Ursula looked up quickly and tried to clear her mind of what she'd just seen.

'Four children,' she stated, squeezing Rebecca's hand. She was rewarded with a big smile as Rebecca put her hands to her face. When Ursula's mother had realised Ursula had the sight into the future as she did, she'd emphasised it wasn't imperative to tell everything seen and she should choose when to speak out and when to keep quiet.

'Praise the Lord,' she whispered through her fingers, 'I was so worried. Now I know the babes will come, I can stop fretting. One day we shall have a family to cherish. Thank you, Ursula.'

'I am always happy to read what is in your future,' Ursula replied, whilst thinking to herself that whilst she may have seen it, today she wouldn't divulge the truth. But after Rebecca left, Ursula added her predictions to her sheaf of papers.

6

2024

The sound of rain being blown against her bedroom window woke Adrianna up a little later, a loud tattoo, as it seemed to try to gain entry. A high-pitched whistling was accompanying a wet splattering noise as she watched the curtains wavering and dancing in the draught. The wind was infiltrating the room, sliding through gaps in the wooden frame, the view beyond a distorted swirl of green and brown. Mostly brown. The rain had temporarily put a halt on her plans to attempt any gardening, and feeling as dismal as the weather outside, she pulled on jogging trousers and a sweatshirt and padded downstairs.

In the living room she looked around, expecting to find puddles where the water had found a way in through the loose tiles Rick had pointed out when they'd first arrived. She hoped they were sufficiently attached not to let any bad weather in. So far so good, she thought, everywhere looked dry. Despite the large, thick-piled rug on top of the wide, polished floorboards in the living room floor she could feel the wind making its way into the cottage through every space it could, chilling her feet. She found her sheepskin boots and pulled them on.

Having barely started on the cleaning she decided to continue giving the downstairs rooms a thorough blitz. Thankfully the scratching, scrambling sound from earlier was now silent, whatever causing it probably now asleep in a nest somewhere. She needed to set the traps she'd bought at the garden centre.

All the while she was conscious of the dark patch on the hearth and despite her concerns, she found herself drawn to it. Kneeling down she took a scouring pad and hot water and began to scrub at it until her face was flushed and sticky. But her efforts had done nothing, it was still there as dark and foreboding as before.

Sitting back on her heels she looked at the old built-in cupboards which flanked the fireplace. To fit in with the uneven walls and ceiling they both appeared a little crooked and asymmetrical. When she tried the door of the one on the left of the chimney breast, it opened easily to display a stack of beautiful bone china plates decorated with deep yellow roses, gilded around the edges, together with delicate tea cups and saucers, though everything was covered in grime. Carefully Adrianna carried them to the kitchen sink to wash later.

The rest of the cupboard was empty other than old pieces of wallpaper lining the shelves, the edges curled and yellowing. Getting to her feet, Adrianna brushed her knees off and turned to the other one. Perhaps more of the tea set was stored inside. She'd love to find a teapot to match, so she could lay out afternoon tea as a treat when Rick next visited. There might also be evidence of her suspected mice, and if so, she could put some traps down in there.

As she took a step towards it she felt a sudden jolt, a push from behind as though propelling her forwards. Putting her arms out to stop herself falling, her hands came to rest on the second cupboard door. It felt hot and snatching her hands away, Adrianna jumped backwards. Perching shakily on the arm of a chair she looked towards the fireplace but it was cold and empty, as she knew it would be. There was nothing to have created the heat she'd just felt.

Her fingertips were tingling and her heart beat quickly as she tried to work out what had just happened. Tentatively she touched the wooden door again ready to pull her hand away, but there was nothing. No change in temperature, no disturbance in the air, nothing.

This door, however, refused to open and she wondered if it was locked, although there was no keyhole. Now intrigued, after looking through the drawers in the kitchen for a suitable knife to use as a lever and not finding anything, she went out to the brick shed beside the back door. Although easing off slightly, the rain was still falling and over the garden in the distance, the horizon was a sullen blur of violet cloud, the rain laying close to the ground.

Pulling open the shed door she took a step backwards waiting to see if there were any visible spiders. It was the only thing that had put her off renting an old ramshackle cottage, she hated anything with eight legs. Her eyes roved across what had been left in there. She wasn't expecting to see a rack of tools, there was no reason why old Mrs Murray would have needed anything like that, but she hoped there was something which would help her prise open the stuck cupboard door. What had happened inside when she'd approached it had shaken her, and her resolve hardened to finish what she'd started. She silently congratulated herself. This person, this tenacity, was a tiny shard of who she used to be.

There wasn't anything resembling a crowbar in the shed, but an old rusting hammer lay on a shelf and she picked it up with two fingers and held it at arm's length whilst inspecting it for creepy crawlies, sighing with relief when she saw there were none. Beside it, an old piece of flint with a sharp edge looked as though it may work as a lever, so taking that too, she squelched back inside, removing her boots in the kitchen.

The old, uneven wood of the hammer's handle was rough against her hand as she gripped it, knocking the thin wedge of the flint between the edges of the closed doors. Once it was in slightly, she twisted it trying to prise the doors apart. The more they refused to shift, the more determined she was to open them. Pushing against the stone, she levered it to both the left and the right in several places, feeling a satisfying crack as the doors shifted slightly against each other. Eventually, she was able to push in a longer piece of the sharp, smooth plane and with a nasty splintering sound finally the wood separated. With a gap wide enough to push her fingers in she gave a sharp jerk and tugged the door open, wincing at the sound of more wood fragmenting. She told herself she'd repair it later.

The cupboard was empty. No china, no evidence of rodents, the shelves coated in a thick layer of dust. It smelled different to its partner though, a pungent scent of earth and herbs immediately filled the air around her, swirling and dancing, tiny motes of summer breath. Welcoming her as though she were expected. Taking a step forwards Adrianna leant her head in to look at the ceiling and see if there were any forgotten bunches of herbs hanging there, but there was nothing. Her movement though made the floor dip slightly and rasp and she realised that the board was shifting because it was loose. Kneeling, she pushed one end with her left hand which lifted the other enough for her to reach her hand underneath and pull the wood up. She appeared to be becoming proficient at taking the cottage apart, one piece at a time.

It came away more easily than she'd envisaged, leaving a hole and dusty flagstones beneath. No wonder there was a spiteful breeze cutting into her ankles and making the floor so cold if there was no insulation between the boards and the stone.

Leaning forwards, she switched on her phone torch and shone the light into the hole. Something seemed to have been directing her here and although she wasn't expecting to find anything, it seemed the most logical thing to look before she replaced the board and surveyed the damage she'd caused to the cupboard doors. The space below wasn't empty though; she could see a package and reaching down she gingerly lifted it out. Backing out of the cupboard on her hands and knees she sat back to look at what she was holding.

The aromatic scent of lavender and spices she'd noticed when she'd opened the doors was much stronger now, catching in her throat. In her hands was a thick folded piece of dark brown leather, dull and stiffened with age, tied with matching narrow thongs that cracked as she opened them. Breathing out slowly she unveiled a stack of old, yellowed parchment, sewn together with brown waxed thread.

Closing the cupboard she gently placed the package on the coffee table. The edges appeared to be stuck together which was hardly surprising given where it had been hidden. Although the proximity to the fireplace must have helped to prevent the damp seeping in. Was it hidden? What did it contain that was so important that it needed to be left where it may never have been found? And why, she questioned herself, had she had felt an overwhelming urgency to open the cupboard as though she was meant to find it?

As she carefully eased the papers apart, a misty gloom slowly began to creep across the room from the corners, a splintering cold stillness prickling her skin and making her look up. Gasping, the freezing air rushed into her lungs and the air shifted slightly as if disturbed by someone drifting past. Something at the window knocked. She looked around the room expecting the door to have swung open and let in the weather outside, but all was still. Quickly folding everything up, her cold hands unable to move as rapidly as she needed them to, she pushed it all into the cupboard and slammed the doors shut. Whatever was written on those papers, she suddenly had no desire to find out.

7

1646

Ursula crept into church as the bells were ringing their final peal to ensure that all the villagers were present. She preferred to sit quietly at the back of the nave where the shadows dwelt, where the light from the tall stained-glass windows didn't reach and no candles were lit.

Her relationship with God was complicated, she'd never understood why he'd allowed her mother to be murdered and she mostly attended church because it was expected of her, not out of devoted belief.

The pew in front of her, which was usually empty, was today occupied by two people: a man and a woman. From their backs, Ursula didn't recognise them, but she could see their apparel was of good quality, both wearing coats of fine damask, hers in a deep red and his in black. Ursula tugged her warm but ragged shawl around her shoulders and put her hand to her coif, a thin linen one, not starched and pristine like the one being worn by the lady in front of her.

As the service started and Ursula rose to her feet, she accidentally knocked against the pew in front and the man looked around, frowning at her. He paused for a moment too long before turning back to the front. Despite just being a couple of seconds of inadvertent eye contact, Ursula noticed a lot about him. She felt safer knowing as much as possible about those she encountered and she'd trained herself to be observant. His eyes were a pale, insipid blue, his blond hair was cut short – he was a supporter of Cromwell then, not a Royalist, which explained the plain dark coloured coat. Not like Lord Mayling, who was for the king and supposedly wouldn't hear a word against him, although he hadn't gone to fight in the war. At least not yet, for he was sitting in his box pew at the front of the church as he did every week with his wife Lady Arbella and their son, Edward. Three other sons had died during childbirth or within weeks afterwards, their tiny gravestones lined up in a row in the family plot outside, beside their grandparents. Ursula saw babies not survive birth, but to lose three sons like that must have been heartbreaking.

After the service, the congregation waited until the Maylings had left before they all proceeded to file out. Ursula sat quietly looking down at her hands until the church was empty before getting to her feet. Ordinarily her neighbours had dispersed by the time she left, but as she walked outside, she immediately noticed the couple who'd been sitting in front of her, still talking with the rector. The man turned to watch her as she scuttled past, keeping her head down yet conscious of his eyes following her.

Almost at her front gate, Ursula paused as a horse pulled up beside her, kicking dust from the street into her face. She turned away as the fine particles scratched her eyes and made them water. The rider dismounted and stood in front of her so she had nowhere to go, forced to confront him. She knew immediately who it would be, and indeed the gentleman from the church was

looking down at her. His female companion was no longer
with him.

'Good day to you, mistress. My name is Oliver Bruton,' he
introduced himself. Ursula was quite sure he already knew who
she was. 'My sister and I have lately moved to Great Mayling.' He
mentioned a village two miles from Finchingham, then continued, 'I am a physician, trained at Cambridge. I am told you are
the local wise woman, a purveyor of medications and also a
midwife?'

Was he worried she was in competition with him? 'Aye sir,
just for the poor folk in the village and surrounds,' she replied.
Nobody that he might treat would be arriving at her door for
help.

'Do not fear me.' He put his finger, in its dark brown soft
lambskin glove, under her chin and tipped her face up so she
had no option but to look at him. His light eyes she'd already
seen and now she could see what a large, square head and
colourless complexion he had. Although he was smiling and
showing surprisingly decent teeth through a short, clipped
beard, there was no warmth in his eyes. He carried an aura of
superiority and confidence about him and it was making her
heart race.

'You and I may have patients who could benefit from both of
our attention. I should like to discuss with you the ailments
which occur locally with the proximity of the sea and marshes. It
is a special interest of mine. Please allow me to visit you another
day and we can discuss it further.' He ran his finger down her
face and along her jawline and Ursula couldn't prevent a
shudder of revulsion ripple through her as she leant away. His
eyes narrowed and she knew he'd noticed. She had no desire for
him to visit again and discuss the diseases common to the people
living in the wetlands, but she knew she couldn't refuse him.

Without a word and dropping the merest hint of a curtsey, she turned and hurried around to the back of her cottage and in through the door.

Once inside, she poured herself a cup of strong beer and drank it straight down, waiting for her heart to stop pounding. During her adult life living here on her own, she'd managed to remain mostly unseen other than by those who needed her, but she knew why the doctor had approached her.

Just as some of the men in the village had also come sniffing at her door as she'd grown into womanhood. Her heavy black hair, her large, deep-brown eyes and her well-rounded curvaceous figure was attractive and men considered she must be in want of a husband. They couldn't be further from the truth. More than once she'd cursed the fact that she'd inherited her mother's dark, sultry, foreign looks, which drew men like bees to summer flowers. Because she'd seen what husbands did and she wanted no part of it. It had been easy to deter the village men who, rebuffed, had sought out the more compliant and malleable young girls wanting a ring on their finger and a brood of children. If Oliver Bruton was thinking he might cajole her with his talk of their shared work, he'd have to realise that he may as well leave her be too. Taking her papers from their hiding place she added an entry.

8

2024

Adrianna, her hands shaking, poured some of Rick's malt into a glass. She didn't care that it was still only mid-morning, she drank it straight down, coughing and spluttering as it scorched its way through her gullet but immediately, she poured another generous measure, and sipping it a little slower, she sank down onto one of the kitchen chairs and kept on drinking.

As the heat stole through her, warming her up and she began to feel a little more relaxed, she wondered if she'd imagined what had happened in the other room. It was probably just a draught from where she'd removed the floorboard, a gust of wind from outside. She looked out of the window but all was still. And that didn't explain the heat on the cupboard door when she'd laid her palm on it before. Whatever had been in there had disturbed the air surrounding her. As if a veil between her and someone or something else had thinned, allowing them to reach out to her. She was too frightened to go back and look, terrified of what she might see.

Instead, she leant against the kitchen table looking out at the wilderness beyond. The rain had finally eased and she glanced across at the new tools propped up beside the back door. Unless she took a grip of herself and got on with something, they'd remain in their lustrous burnished steel glory for the whole six months and never see any mud or weeds. She needed to be outside, away from the cupboard and its secret papers, doing something physical to stop her mind turning over what she'd just experienced. To add some rationality into the day.

By the time she'd eaten some thick doorsteps of toast dripping with butter as she tried to soak up the alcohol she'd drunk, a watery sun was finally breaking through the clouds. She decided to venture outside. This sabbatical might be about resting, but she still needed something to occupy her time and stop her flighty, buzzing brain from churning. Now, not only did she have work to worry about, but also the fear that something may be occupying the cottage with her.

From the pictures she'd seen on Instagram, it looked fairly simple to create a gorgeous garden. Taking her spade outside she swung it around at the closest weeds in an attempt to decapitate them and in doing so almost toppled over sideways. She hadn't reckoned on the unbalanced weight, battering the vegetation into submission wasn't going to work.

Beneath her feet lay a thick layer of brown and yellow leaves, and below them wet and slippery paving slabs, one of which wobbled as she stamped down, soft mud squelching out the sides. Taking another step forwards, she kicked out and brought her foot down only to discover she was at the edge of the patio, as abruptly she stepped into a muddy puddle. Her foot slid away from under her, and she sat down with a thump.

'Shit,' she muttered under her breath.

'Hello, are you okay?' A voice seemed to float towards her, and scrambling to her feet she looked around but could see no one. Had she imagined it? The church was next door, hence why she was now residing in Church Cottage. Was it some spirit or the good Lord himself checking in on her? Rick was right, she was going mad.

'Are you hurt?' the voice came again. As she looked around above the weeds and towards the house, it added, 'I'm here, in the churchyard.' Peering over, she realised she could see the head and shoulders of a man by the wall which divided the two properties.

'Sorry, I didn't see you there,' she called back, 'I'm fine, thank you. I thought I was on the patio and discovered at the last minute that I wasn't, as I slipped off. I look a mess, but I'm all right.'

'I was just doing some weeding and I saw you go down. It looks as though you're attempting some, er...' He paused and Adrianna suspected he'd seen her swinging the spade as if she was an Olympic hammer-thrower. 'Gardening,' he finished.

'Well, I was trying,' she admitted, 'but I have no idea what I'm doing. That's probably obvious though.' She gave a wry smile.

'I shall not say another word,' he laughed. 'I'm Tom, I keep the churchyard tidy and dig the occasional grave. I'm also married to Roger, the vicar. If you need any assistance, I'm happy to help. I've got a heavy-duty strimmer which could sort out those weeds, I'll drop it round if you like.'

'Thank you, I definitely need some help! As you can see, I'm a complete novice,' Adrianna said. 'I'd better go and get out of these muddy clothes now.' With a wave goodbye she leaned the new, and what she now considered treacherous, spade against the cottage wall and went into the kitchen where she stripped off her clothes, pushing them into the washing machine. Running upstairs, she quickly showered and put on some clean clothes.

As she moved around the cottage, she was constantly alert, aware of what had happened in the living room and the papers she'd pushed back into the cupboard. She still wanted to examine them properly to discover what they were, despite her fear. Slowly, she edged towards the doorway but the room was empty and also warmer, the temperature no longer the breath-stealing cold it had been earlier.

'Whoever you are, I'm not afraid of you,' she announced. 'I don't believe in ghosts.' Her shaking voice belied what she'd just said, her conviction that there were no such things feeling less unwavering than previously. This was an old cottage, perhaps it harboured someone who was unable to leave? She stood and waited for something to happen, but whatever had been there with her was no longer occupying the space.

Sitting down on the edge of an armchair she eyed the cupboard. Although she didn't want to open it again, she knew she was going to. She *had* to. Her hand slowly moved towards the door which now, after her battering, didn't close properly.

This time it felt cool and pulling it slowly with shaking hands she paused for a moment and looked around the room again. Everything remained quiet. Reaching in she removed the package and placed it quickly on the coffee table. Even holding it made her heart beat faster. Opening out the folded leather once again she took out the parchment document.

There were dark lines where creases had engrained themselves into the sheets. Across every inch was tiny archaic looking writing, the ink now pale brown with occasional blotches amongst the words. Beneath the written pages were two printed pamphlets with woodcut illustrations on much thinner paper. Immediately she could see these were very old, maybe even centuries old, and she began to wonder about what she now had in front of her.

It was difficult to read what was written there with the lack of contrast between the sepia-coloured paper and the dirty, ochre-tinted words. The first piece was loose, not sewn in with the others, and appeared to be written on a torn piece of parchment. It only had a couple of lines surrounded by several ink spots as if penned hurriedly. The writing was scratchy and it took her thirty minutes of copying out every letter to work out what it said in its barely comprehensible old English.

Always look for that which seeks you out to do you harm, for it watches you. Harness that which is concealed deep within you, as I have. Our strength and might shall overcome evil.

She dropped the paper on the table again. Was it a warning of some sort, or a curse? And who had it been directed at. She didn't want to read any further but she chided herself for being frightened when there would obviously be a simple explanation. She'd tell Rick when she next spoke to him, he was very good at being logical.

Opening the booklet, she turned to the first page and slowly began to decipher each word, heaving a sigh of relief as she realised that it was simply a recipe for an old herbal medication for toothache. It was followed by several more lists of herbs for various ailments, then an account of attending an elderly man with a weak heart. What she'd found appeared to be the journal of a herbalist. The date at the end of the entry when the author had visited the old man was 1645, and Adrianna let out a slow, long breath. These papers were far older than she'd imagined and should really be in a museum.

Her back had stiffened up whilst she'd been hunched over and she stretched gingerly. The lack of manual work in her everyday life was apparent, as after her attempt at gardening, the muscles in her back and arms were now complaining. Loudly. Carefully she folded the papers back and returned them to the cupboard. She was at once thrilled with such an historically important find, and yet frightened by the warning on the slip of paper she'd first read, and by what she'd experienced when she'd first taken them from the cupboard.

Right now, she wanted someone else to give her a rational explanation, and pulling on her trainers, she walked across to the pub to seek out some company.

9

2024

Adrianna paused for a moment outside the pub door. Going into somewhere public on her own was no longer the easy thing it once was. A year ago, she'd have marched in without a second thought, but she was a different person then. She hesitated, wondering whether to return home and put a ready meal in the microwave but before she could turn around a voice behind her called, 'Hello again,' and turning, she saw Tom walking across the road towards the pub, accompanied by a black spaniel, who he introduced as Apollo.

'Are you in search of a libation to keep out the chills too?' he asked as reaching around her, he pushed the door open. She had no option but to walk in.

Inside it was everything she'd imagined it would be. Rough flagstones under her feet and a low ceiling criss-crossed with dark beams which also crawled up the walls mimicking the trees they'd originally come from. The building appeared to be of a similar era as Church Cottage. The tables were shiny dark oak, the seating made up of a mix of stools and wheelback chairs with the occasional pew. Lamps and fairy lights created a cosy atmosphere and behind the bar, lit by an incongruous fluorescent strip light, a young woman smiled at them.

'Hi Tom,' she greeted him. A pint appeared almost immediately on the bar for him, as he asked Adrianna what she'd like to drink.

'Just an orange juice please,' she replied, reminding herself that she didn't need any more alcohol after what she'd consumed earlier.

'I'm Jess,' the young woman introduced herself as she held the card scanner towards Tom. 'My mum said there was a new resident in Mrs Murray's old cottage. I assume that's you?'

'Yes,' Adrianna confirmed, 'I'm just staying for six months.'

'So I gather. Taking a break from work?'

'I'm, um, just having a pause.' Before she could cause any more chaos, she thought to herself. She could feel Tom's eyes on her as he digested this information.

'That sounds like an excellent idea,' he said, 'more people should do it. Although I can't imagine Roger's flock being very impressed if he took time off, his job is somewhat defined by his availability for hatches, matches and despatches. And providing guidance for the lost souls of Finchingham. So how are you settling in? Is this your first visit to Norfolk?'

'No, I used to come and stay for school holidays,' she explained. 'My mum grew up near to Hunstanton, and she met my father who was in the US Air Force when he was stationed at Mildenhall. After we moved to America, we returned each summer to visit my grandparents and it always felt like I belonged here. As though it was home. When I finished school, I decided to attend university over here, and I've been here ever since, although I like to think I have roots in both places.'

'I thought I detected an accent,' Jess said, and Adrianna smiled in acknowledgement. She was used to being questioned

about the twang that had never left despite spending half her life
on this side of the pond.

'As for how I'm settling in,' Adrianna added, trying to sound
casual, 'I did want to ask if any of you knew of any strange
happenings in the cottage?'

Before anyone could answer, Tom was joined by another
man – the dog collar peeping above his burgundy jumper the
only indication of his profession – whom he introduced as his
husband, Roger.

'Adrianna was just asking if anyone had heard of anything
peculiar connected with Church Cottage,' Tom explained.

Jess leant on the bar, stretching forward so she could also
hear. 'What sort of odd happenings?' she asked. 'There have
been all sorts of rumours over the years. Have you found another
mummified cat? One was found bricked up in the cottage back
in the 1970s. There's a framed article from the local paper in the
village hall.'

Adrianna paused for a moment, unsettled by what she'd just
heard. She hoped it was a joke, although a ghostly cat might
explain the feeling that she was sharing the cottage with something else, but whatever was there, she didn't think it was an
animal.

'Er no, it's papers, a journal of some sort,' she explained.
'They look very old, the parchment's thick with brown edges. I've
transcribed the first two pages, the entries are dated in the seventeenth century, which will be incredible if it's for real.'

'Goodness. And you just discovered them in the cottage? I
wonder if they belonged to Mrs Murray?' Roger said.

Adrianna felt her face flush. She couldn't explain what had
happened to draw her to the floorboard beneath which they
were hidden, and she just said she'd found them accidentally.
Not that they had found *her,* which was closer to the truth. 'I'm

not sure if anyone even knew they were there, given that I lifted the loose floorboard,' she added.

'Then this is the person you need,' Roger indicated towards Jess. 'She's the one who studied history and archaeology at university.'

Adrianna's heart lifted at the thought that maybe she had someone properly knowledgeable on her doorstep. She was hoping to get to know Jess, a new local friend, and this was a perfect situation.

'There's something that looks like a curse or a premonition on a piece of torn parchment with them. It's quite creepy, actually.' She didn't want to admit exactly how disturbed it had made her feel.

'It's probably just someone's idea of a joke,' Roger said. He smiled and Adrianna got the impression he was just reassuring her, not that he believed that there was anything awry. He was probably right, saying it out loud now made her feel a bit ridiculous.

'Yes, of course, I expect it is,' she agreed, although she could hear the doubt in her voice.

Before she left, she remembered to ask if anyone had the number for a chimney sweep, and with the number of the local company saved in her phone, Adrianna walked back across the road. She'd double check with the letting agency that she was allowed to go ahead and get the work done.

It was starting to get dark and the street lights glowed dimly, so sparce their beam didn't reach as far as the edge of the village where she was. Even the fifty yards from the pub drew her into a dark and shadowy space and she made a note to leave a light on if she went out in the evening again. Beside the cottage, the church on its slight hill was a dark outline against the opaque skies. She kept her eyes averted from the churchyard in case she saw any movement there. There was an eerie atmosphere, as though something was stirring, something she had woken.

Quickly opening the front door she stepped in, flicking the light on, reprimanding herself for her ill-founded fear. She called Rick and was surprised when it went to voicemail but she left a message telling him how much she missed and loved him and without waiting for a reply she went to bed. It had been a long day.

10

2024

Drinking her second cup of coffee of the day after another uneasy night where she'd abandoned any hope of sleep as the sun began to rise, Adrianna was disturbed by a loud banging at the front door.

'Morning.' Tom was standing on the doorstep, a broad grin on his face. 'As promised. I know it's a bit early but the forecast is good so I thought you might be getting on with your garden clearance today.' He lifted the strimmer he was holding.

'Thank you. I wasn't expecting you so soon, come in.' She ushered him in, and he followed her through to the kitchen, opening the back door and leaning the tool outside.

He looked around the compact downstairs. 'I've never been in here. We didn't know Mrs Murray very well. She wasn't particularly enamoured of the church apparently, told Roger that God isn't all that he's cracked up to be. It's lovely though, isn't it? This is reputed to be the oldest house in the village. Have you seen the inscription above the front door?' he asked. Adrianna admitted she hadn't and she followed him outside.

'Look here.' Tom stepped outside and pointed up, holding

the wisteria with its pale purple buds already emerging, away from the wall. '1587. That was probably the year it was built, isn't that amazing?' Adrianna agreed that it was. Offering him a cup of tea, they went back inside.

'You'll have to give me a demonstration, I'm afraid,' she told him as she passed him a cup, putting a plate of biscuits between the two of them. 'I've never done any gardening and that piece of equipment looks lethal.'

'Of course, it's simple when you're used to it.' He took two chocolate digestive biscuits from the plate, pressing them together, before dipping them in his drink and biting half off. 'My special hack,' he explained as crumbs fell from his mouth onto the table. 'If you have two at the same time they don't disintegrate. Roger won't let me have biscuits,' he added. 'I'm supposed to be watching my weight.' With a small grin he dipped the other half of his biscuit sandwich into his tea and consumed it.

'Do you work?' Adrianna said.

'Not these days. Used to work at a National Heritage Park; it was lovely but it's hard graft and better suited to the young folk. They needed to make some redundancies a couple of years ago, I was in my mid-fifties so I snatched it with both hands. And now I'm a man of leisure.' He took another two biscuits. 'Roger wasn't as happy as I thought he'd be, though. He says I get under his feet now while he's trying to work. He even suggested I take up golf, but I don't have any intention of wasting my time pushing a trolley full of clubs for hours and whacking a stupid little ball into a hole. I'd spend the whole time looking to see how well they'd done their mowing. So, I'm available for gardening advice any time you need it.'

'Thank you, that's really helpful.' Adrianna beamed, making a mental note to add *biscuits* to her shopping list.

'Right.' He rubbed his hands together, crumbs showering onto the floor. 'Let me show you how the beastie works and then I'll let you get on, I'm sure you've got lots of things you need to be doing.'

Outside, warm sunshine was beginning to dry the previous day's rain. Tom held the strimmer out and explained how to use it, suggesting that she waited for the weeds to dry further first.

Once he'd left, Adrianna decided to have another look at the paperwork again. Although she wished she was imagining it, something was inexplicably drawing her back to it.

Standing in the doorway, she scanned the room, waiting for something to happen as it had before, but everything was still. With a sigh of relief that she couldn't sense any other presence, she took the papers out, quickly putting the top piece at the back so she didn't have to read it again and instead began to transcribe the next entry. It was an entry about a small boy with a fever followed by a description of various plants concealed close to some rhubarb. The following page was more interesting though.

Birth of a baby boy to Ruth and John Blacksmith. Baby born with legs and feet that curl unnaturally inwards but he is healthy. May our Lord protect him, for life is hard.

Written this day the twenty third day of March in the year of our Lord 1646.

So the author of these papers was a midwife as well as a herbalist. But there were other forces too, still clinging to the papers, she could feel them. And now she had disturbed them. What had she done?

11

1646

If Ursula had believed her rejection of Oliver Bruton's attention was to be the end of the situation, she soon discovered she was wrong.

The morning after the church service she arrived home from a walk collecting samphire from the beach, where it grew alongside the rock pools. It was now visible as the tide flowed back out displaying more and more of the pale gold sand as the water inched away. Immediately she recognised the doctor's horse tethered outside the inn opposite.

She hoped he was simply thirsty for ale after a ride out and it was a coincidence he was in the village, but she wondered if he may be watching her cottage waiting for her to arrive home.

Doubling back on herself she crouched down and skirted across the former common, hoping he wouldn't see her in the distance. Her dull coarse brown hemp gown concealed her well and, arriving at the church wall, she scrambled over, careful to ensure she didn't spill the plants she'd just harvested. After dodging through the churchyard, hiding behind the tilted gravestones which had sunk into the earth, she climbed down onto the piece of land between her cottage and the church. She bent low, trusting that the tall grasses, now at their full height as summer approached, would continue to shield her until she reached her back door.

Ursula never locked her doors. Her fellow villagers would not enter if she was away from home and to pay for a lock was an expense she didn't need. But the moment she walked into the scullery, she regretted that decision, because immediately she could tell someone had been there. That Doctor Bruton had been in her home. A musky male scent of sweat, tobacco and horse overpowered the usual sweet aroma of dried herbs which drifted down from the bunches hanging from the beams in both of her downstairs rooms. The house hadn't smelled this way for a long time, not since her father left. Ursula felt her stomach lurch and her heart beat faster. There was no place here for a man, and if she had to be more forthright in telling him, then so be it.

Placing her basket on the scullery table she stepped into the parlour. She knew he wasn't there any longer, she would have felt the stirring of his breath in the air. Nothing went past her. Slowly she turned around in a circle, looking for anything that had been tampered with. There was nothing obvious, no wanton destruction but she could see that some items had been moved. Her pestle and mortar, which always sat on the end of her work bench, was now on the floor beside the wooden chair she sat in at night. And the fire that she'd damped down before she left was extinguished, splashes of water spilling out onto the stain on hearth, shining droplets across the bloodstain from the murder it witnessed all those years ago, a mark which did not age. Where her mother had fallen, hitting her head on the hearth and killing her instantly, a look of fury forever etched on her face. Her eyes had stared at Ursula's father as if cursing him from wherever she had gone to, and no amount of scrubbing with sand and horsetail plant could erase it.

Ursula stood, wondering why he'd come into her house like that, perhaps some sort of subtle message to frighten her. Then there was a knock at the front door and the light in the room darkened as, without waiting to be bid entry, it opened to admit him. By thinking about him had she somehow conjured up his presence?

'Mistress Beal,' he said, removing his tall conical hat, 'I was hoping to see you whilst I was in the village conducting business.'

For a moment Ursula was thrown by his greeting; nobody called her Mistress Beal, and least of all would a superior usually do so. If he was trying to put her at her ease, he couldn't have been more wrong. Nevertheless, she dipped a slight curtsey and although she wanted to point out she knew he'd already been into her home whilst she was absent, she kept quiet. If she'd had any doubts it was him, they disappeared as she breathed in the same smell emanating from him that she'd noticed the moment she'd walked into the cottage.

'Doctor Bruton, I am surprised to see you again. Surely you do not have need of my medicines?'

'Of course not.' The man frowned as if such a notion was too ridiculous to imagine. 'Instead, I come with a proposition. I mentioned yesterday that I believe we can be of benefit to each other.'

A prickle started along Ursula's spine, a crawling against her skin. Inch by inch, the feeling continuing down her arms. It was the uncanny sensation whenever she knew there was an undercurrent of words being unsaid. Just like the tide which sometimes pulled one way and yet beneath was pulling another. It could haul a person into its depths and never let them go. A small girl from the village, collecting seaweed with her mother in the shallows, had disappeared that way the previous year, dragged suddenly below the water by unseen arms and then swept out to sea. Her mother could do nothing to save her. A stealthy unseen movement which hid below the obvious, but she could detect it, and it was happening here. Would she, too, be drawn down and not let go? It didn't matter how clever Oliver Bruton thought he was, she had a special sight and she knew everything about his visit was not as it seemed. It was an untruth. And untruths, she could expose.

'If you do not have need of my medicines or assistance with a birth, I do not understand why you seek me out,' she said. Already he'd ensconced himself in her chair beside the fire, although as he'd doused it, there was no heat. She could only perch on the stool in front of her work bench, but instead she decided to remain standing from where she had the strength of a height advantage. Wordlessly she leant down and picked up her pestle and mortar and placed them back where they normally sat. She watched him through her dark eyes, unwavering, and he looked away.

'I have an interest in the ailments that people who live beside the marshes develop. I expect you have had to provide remedies to help and I think with the ideas I have brought from Cambridge, we may find a way to cure those people who suffer,' he said, rubbing his hands along his breeches. He was more nervous than he wanted to appear, Ursula thought.

'The ague is a killer,' she told him. 'There are few medications to prevent a person who has it from going early to their grave. I am surprised you have not come across this whilst at Cambridge, it is a common sickness for those who live in the Fens.'

'Indeed I have seen the illness, hence why I wanted to discuss it with you now I am living in these wetlands. If you are called to someone who ails, you must invite me to accompany you so I too may examine the patient.'

'The people who call upon me for concoctions are not those who would have need of a physician,' Ursula pointed out, folding her arms. 'Nor would they welcome a stranger into their home. Villagers are poor people with no money for your ministrations.'

'And you, Ursula, are you poor too?' He suddenly changed the subject, taking her by surprise.

'I manage on what I can earn,' she replied. 'People will always have sicknesses and the women will always give birth and require my assistance.'

'There are ways you can earn more than a handful of groats.' Oliver got to his feet and in one stride he was standing in front of her. Ursula stepped backwards, the edge of her workbench pressing into her thighs. With his height and breadth of shoulders he was like a wall in front of her. 'I could visit you during the evenings when the moon is high and the streets are empty,' he said, his voice lowered, 'and keep your bed warm.' He ran his hand up her thigh and waist until he reached her breast.

Ursula darted to the side away from him and walked, keeping her back straight, to the front door which she wrenched open. She wouldn't show him how scared she was, even though, beneath her skirts, her legs were shaking. If she screamed no one would hear, her cottage being a little way from the other houses in the village. And her neighbours wouldn't intervene anyway. It was the way they all lived: men did what they wished and women had no way of retaliation. As her mother had learned.

'You are not welcome here, Master Bruton,' she told him. 'Please leave and do not return. I do not wish to work with – or for – you.' Although her heart was racing, she kept her eyes on his, her teeth clenched together as she spoke through barely parted lips. Around her body her blood sang, pulsating as it fuelled her anger. Her fingertips were prickling. Now she knew her suspicions about him when they first met were just.

Oliver laughed slowly, the sound coming from deep in his chest as he placed his hat on his head and walked to the door. 'I have never worried about where or not I am invited,' he assured her, his voice dropping, the words clipped, 'so you can expect to see me again. I am sure I shall find a way of helping you to realise how advantageous my protection of you could be.' With this warning, he dipped his head under the door frame, striding out without a backwards glance.

Ursula slammed the door shut the moment he'd left and pulled a wooden bar down across it leaning her back against it, her legs still quaking as if they were made of calves' foot jelly. Holding onto her workbench she made her way back to her chair which was still warm, revoltingly, from where Oliver had been sitting on it. Clearly he was intent on a physical relationship whether she desired it or not. She hoped he had no thoughts to force himself on her if she didn't concede.

Clearing the hearth of cold and damp ash, she laid a new fire, her hands trembling as she struck the tinderbox over and over until it finally produced a spark to catch on the rough piece of fleece in the fireplace. Quickly she piled sharps sticks of kindling on top and the last two of her peat bricks.

Walking outside to the back garden, she picked up her axe and began chopping logs. Each one she placed on the stump she used as a block she imagined it to be Oliver's head as she whipped the axe down and split it neatly in two. She needed to make him realise she wasn't interested in any sort of relationship with him. Yet, at the same time, she couldn't afford to have him as an enemy. If he chose, he could spread rumours and potentially leave her with no customers and thus, no income either.

Once the fire was re-lit, Ursula poured herself a potion to calm her anxiety and sipped it as she sat at the bench preparing a tonic for Ruth who hadn't recovered from the birth as quickly as she would have hoped. She was unable to feed Henry and a wet nurse had been found for him, whilst Ruth's sister was looking after her younger children. Ursula knew all the villagers and their ailments, having lived and grown up amongst them her whole life. They trusted her, but the new doctor was a man of learning, clever with words. A few whispers in the ears of men in their cups could change everything.

Going to the cupboard beside the fireplace she retrieved her bundle of parchment and wrote an account of her day.

12

2024

Despite its somewhat lethal look, Adrianna decided to try the strimmer. The sun had been shining all afternoon and the weeds were dry. Pulling on a long-sleeved top and jeans, she wound her long, almost-black hair into an untidy bun. Together with her olive skin, which always looked as though she'd just returned from a week in the sun, she was the double of her grandmother. As though the strongest of genes ran fast through the family line.

Finally, after several attempts, it roared into life and slowly she began to make her way across the garden, increasing the patch of cleared ground as she went. She avoided the brambles with their sharp spines looking lethal, deciding she'd attack them later with her new shears. Instead, she continued with the cow parsley, willow herb and tall grasses, their seeds flying about as the fan from the strimmer whipped them up into a whirlwind.

An hour later her hands were vibrating so much the jittery feeling had crawled up her arms and switching the machine off, she laid it down for a moment. Despite no longer holding it, her hands were still shaking. Turning in a circle she surveyed what she'd managed to achieve. The patch she'd cleared was larger than she'd realised, however it wasn't remotely symmetrical as she'd wandered about haphazardly swathing through the undergrowth. She was sure she could neaten it up so she'd have a nicely proportioned garden she could use by the time she finished. A sense of achievement that she hadn't felt for a long while flushed through her.

After a hastily eaten sandwich, she was back outside with her shears and spent a further hour hacking away at the brambles, pleased she'd had the foresight to buy some large leather gardening gauntlets to cover her forearms. She still managed to get several big scratches on the top of her arms, but working was making her hot and she didn't want to wear a coat for protection.

As she'd worked with only the sound of birds to accompany her, Adrianna began to feel a calm settle upon her. As though the ground, the plants she was surrounded by were welcoming her. Had been waiting for her to arrive. Expecting her. She'd never gardened before and yet it was as though she had always been meant to be here.

By the end of the day, she'd collected enough cuttings and branches to create a sizeable pile. If it dried out she could have a fire, but in the meantime she needed somewhere to dump it away from where she was attempting to create her garden. Screwing her eyes up she looked at the trees in the distance. She wasn't going to clear a path down to there, it would take her weeks. If she was going to build a bonfire, or even a compost heap, it would have to be nearer to the house.

That would have to wait for another day though because dusk was already beginning to fall, darkening clouds starting to edge across the sky from beyond the dunes and the shining light from the kitchen window was drawing her back inside. She remembered the bottle of Merlot in the cupboard and decided a bath and a large glass of wine, followed by an omelette to fortify her, was a good idea. Her shoulders now more relaxed, she put the garden tools away.

Checking her phone, which she'd left on the kitchen table, there was a new message from Rick.

> Hope you're having fun and don't tire yourself out with that gardening. I've been paid today so I've transferred your rent, hope you get it okay. Xxx

Quickly Adrianna checked her banking app which confirmed the money was in there.

She and Rick had been together for a year since meeting at a mutual friend's wedding, and after six months dating he'd moved in. It had been a strange situation, they hadn't actually had a conversation about living together, he began to stay more frequently until eventually he was there all the time. She'd barely had time to realise what was happening before his own flat had been sublet, his expensive coffee machine was in her kitchen and his PlayStation was plugged into her television. His rent, a contribution to the utility bills, would help cover her expenses at the cottage. He was right when he'd told her his moving in would benefit them both. He was always right.

13

2024

After her exercise and a large glass of wine, Adrianna slept all night without waking. Even the impenetrable darkness no longer worried her and she was awake and feeling refreshed at seven o'clock. Ready to tackle more of the garden, and ready to examine more of the papers.

In the light from an angle poise lamp brought down from her bedside table, Adrianna opened the package up again. She quickly turned the first page over and laid it face down on the table. It didn't seem to matter where she hid it in the pouch, it was always on top when she returned to them.

Taking a deep breath, she laid the large sheets of thick, rough journal out. She carefully copied out the next entry and transcribed it, finding it a little easier now she was more used to the way the words were written.

Rebecca of Oak Tree Cottage visits for a reading. Her future will not run smoothly, I believe the babes she wishes for will come, but I have seen her first love will not be her last. Some-

times my gift, my sight, is also a curse. Written this day the
fourth day of April in the year of our Lord 1646.

Adrianna sat back in her chair. It appeared the original owner of this journal also read palms, but the mention of a 'gift' was unsettling. Adrianna had always been sceptical of people talking of having special or psychic powers but it seemed this person believed they could see happenings in the future.

She was interrupted by a knock at the back door and swearing under her breath she folded the papers together and put them back in the cupboard before going to see who was there. For a moment she thought she caught the scratching, tapping sound of before.

Despite her annoyance at the interruption, she was pleased to see Tom standing on the doorstep, surveying what she'd done the previous day.

'Roger said I should check you hadn't killed yourself with the strimmer,' he laughed as he relayed the grim message. 'I told him that I reckon you're made of steel. And I'm not wrong, you've achieved a lot out here.'

Adrianna smiled. If only he knew how little steel she'd actually got inside. A year ago, she would have described herself as being strong, but now she knew she was weak and feeble. A smart, sassy career girl who'd fallen from her tower and now couldn't undertake what was expected of her. Couldn't climb back up.

She ushered him into the kitchen and made him a drink, piling yet more of her biscuit stash onto a plate.

'It took me most of the day to do all that,' she said. 'My problem is that now I have a huge pile of rubbish which I need to move away from where I've cleared here by the house, but I don't know where to put it. It's not dry enough to burn,' she explained.

'Clear down along the wall against the churchyard and leave it there,' Tom said. 'When it's dry, I'll collect it from the graveyard side and stick it on my bonfire, I have a patch in the back corner where I put grass cuttings and dead flowers and burn it all every so often.'

'Thank you, that's a great idea, if you don't mind?' Adrianna said.

'No of course I don't, I'm happy to help. And I like a blaze so extra rubbish to throw on is a bonus. Now I know you're alive and well, I'll leave you to it.' He stood up and brushed the biscuit crumbs – Adrianna noticed the plate was unsurprisingly empty – from his trousers.

After leaving a quick voice note for Rick, she went outside to carry on with what she'd started the day before. The sun darted out between the banks of clouds which still dominated the sky but there was a definite warmth in the air and Adrianna was determined to finish the first part of her new garden.

Stomping over to the church wall she could see where it bordered her garden for about three hundred and fifty yards, although it was six foot deep in brambles. They were going to take a lot of manhandling.

By the time she paused for lunch the sharp thorns had left her arms resembling those of a lion tamer. Taking a kitchen chair and putting it outside the back door, Adrianna sat and consumed a toastie and a mug of tea. She looked at her drink as she contemplated that she'd been drinking coffee for ages because it was the only hot beverage Rick drank, but in fact she'd always preferred tea. She'd be buying more teabags next time she went to the supermarket.

Already the garden was transformed from how it had been a

couple of days ago. Who'd have thought she could do that? She might be washed up where work was concerned, but this week she had achieved *something* and a small frisson of warmth opened out like emerging flower petals inside her.

After another hour working it was just beginning to spit with rain and she decided to finish for the day when, once again, she stepped backwards and almost went flying. Luckily this time she was able to get her balance and looking down at her feet she realised that there was a random piece of rock sticking up out of the ground, surrounded by grasses as if placed there specifically to trip her. Bending down she brushed the grass surrounding it away.

It was a pale grey, with patches of rough yellow and green moss between the splashes of white lichen creeping across. Despite the rain, which was now beginning to increase, Adrianna knelt down to look closer, wincing as a thorn stuck into her leg. Using the pads of her thumbs she rubbed away at the stone where she could see marks in places as if it had been decorated in some way. She couldn't remove it all, some of the moss was stuck too firmly, but from what she could see there were several circles with partially eroded lines inside.

Getting to her feet, she brushed down the front of her jeans and with the rain starting to plaster her hair down, she turned to hurry back into the house. A sudden sharp gust of wind blew the rain into her face momentarily blinding her and almost taking her feet from under her. Putting her head down she ran into the kitchen and shut the door, only for it to blow open a moment later. Swearing under her breath she pushed on it with her shoulder and turned the key. The wind seemed to have come out of nowhere, but as she looked out through the rain spattered windows it had just as suddenly dropped again, the trees in the orchard now still, their leaves dancing beneath the downpour.

Looking down at her muddy legs and sodden shirt, it seemed the only immediate option was to jump in the shower. Then, she'd go and see if Tom or Jess had any knowledge of what she'd just found.

* * *

'Just the person.' Tom hailed her as she walked into the bar, and Adrianna smiled to herself. She'd only been at the cottage for a week and already she felt as though she was part of the community. There was no such thing in London, and it made her feel warm, and welcomed. 'We were just talking about your discovery, have you brought them with you?'

'No, um, I think the papers are too fragile to take anywhere, I was going to ask Jess if she'd like to come and have a look?' raising her eyebrows she looked across at Jess whose face lit up.

'I'd love to,' she said, 'I was hoping you'd ask, they sound fascinating. And good call about not moving them more than you need to.'

Adrianna extended her invitation to Tom too, guessing he was just as invested in the mystery as Jess was. 'Actually though, I haven't come across to talk about those, because the cottage, well the garden, has thrown up another surprise this afternoon.' She took a sip from the glass of wine Roger passed her before putting it on the bar and explained about the solitary stone in the middle of the garden, and its strange markings.

'It's quite weathered,' she explained, 'but I could make out something engraved on top, a circle and some lines, a bit like a daisy. I need to get a hard brush and get rid of the rest of the moss and see if I can decipher anything. Is it something either of you know about?'

'Nope,' Tom said. 'Mind you, Mrs Murray couldn't deal with

all that garden so a lot of it has been overgrown for decades, probably longer. And depending how far it is from the house, you might be in the part that was originally common ground.'

'Maybe it's someone's pet grave?' Jess suggested. 'If you can find any letters, they'll read *Fido*.'

'I could come and take a look,' Tom suggested, 'although Jess is probably right.'

Adrianna nodded, but she wasn't so sure. The cold wind that had whipped up as she'd stepped away from whatever she'd discovered had sliced through her. Not only was there something inexplicable in the cottage, but there was also something in the garden which had wanted to be found.

14

1646

A soft knock came at the door and Ursula stopped stirring the posset she'd made with two of that morning's fresh eggs and cocked her head on one side, unsure if she'd heard anything. A few seconds later it came again, and opening the door, she found the lady she recognised as Oliver Bruton's sister on the doorstep.

'Mistress Ursula?' she asked, and Ursula nodded silently in reply. Given her brother's visit, then surely he had told her who lived in this cottage beside the church. 'My name is Anne Bruton. May I come in?' the woman asked. Checking that she was on her own, Ursula stood to one side, opening the door fully.

The floor in the cottage was swept daily, but the herbs hanging from hooks in the beams above her head dropped a constant filtering of dust and dried leaves to cover the floorboards in a carpet of sweet-smelling debris and this was now being caught up and swept along by the hem of Anne's black grosgrain dress, its sleek ribbed weave giving it a rigid structure. It had a crisp, white, square puritan's collar, and her head was covered in a goffered white cap, stiff with starch. In her hand she carried a pair of leather gloves that looked as soft as silk, and Ursula hid her own rough, peeling hands in the folds of her skirt.

'Please, sit down.' She offered Anne the chair in which her brother had been sitting only days earlier. Perching on her stool opposite, she guessed that Anne was maybe five years younger than herself. Despite the difference in their lives and the colour of her own skin from the years of working beneath the summer sun, neither of them had any lines around their eyes.

'Would you like a cup of ale?' she asked.

'Thank you, I would, the dust gets in my throat when I ride. Ale would be most welcome. I am sorry that I am disturbing your work,' Anne apologised, indicating the workbench which was covered in small posies of dried rosemary, 'but I believe Oliver came to call and I knew I must speak with you.'

'If you are here to persuade me to accept your brother's offer,' the corner of Ursula's lip quirked upwards in a sneer as she said the word *offer*, 'then you have wasted your time. I have no desire to be any man's mistress, nor his wife. You may assist me by telling him to stop visiting, to leave me alone to live my life as I wish to.'

'He will not be asking for your hand in marriage,' Anne said, 'for he has a wife in Cambridge.'

This did not surprise Ursula. A clever man with a good living, of course he was married. And he hadn't made any mention of a ring when he visited, he wanted her for her body, until he tired of her. To support her financially, he'd already mentioned that, and to warm her bed when he fancied it, possibly leaving her with a baby growing inside before he left her to poverty and shame. Whether she were a possession of marriage or not, a man could take her for what he wanted and use his physical power if he chose to. As God was her witness, she would not live like that.

'He has children?' she asked, even though it made no odds to her.

'Two daughters,' came the reply, 'but my sister-in-law is frail and sickly and Oliver cannot cure her. She has the white plague and now coughs up blood.'

'He has left her there to die on her own?' Ursula's eyes widened.

'She is not on her own, her mother stays with her and she has servants. My brother visits, but he prefers to live close to the sea, which he believes is beneficial to his own health. I find it too wild and desolate, but he is my guardian so I must go where I am told.'

'And yet he didn't bring his wife, so she too may benefit from the sea air?' Ursula asked. 'Why, pray, have you come here today to tell me this?'

'I came to warn you.' Anne looked into her eyes and Ursula could see fear there, reflecting her own. 'My brother is relentless when he decides he wants something, and if he desires you, then I must tell you that you are in grave danger. He will not stop until he has whatever he wishes. The real reason we have left Cambridge is not to do with living close to the sea, but because he used a young woman, a dear friend of mine who was found dead. Strangled. She was not a doxy, nobody would have questioned if that were so.' Ursula nodded in agreement, the girls who plied their trade on the streets were considered nothing more than rats. 'She was the daughter of a merchant, and a frequent visitor to our home. Oliver drew her in with words of love and then one day I heard her in his parlour. There was shouting and talk of a baby. The next day she was dead. I urge you to stay away from him, for he is dangerous. He will use you, then dispose of you.' The last of Anne's words came out in a rush as if she couldn't hold them in any longer. The truth of what she'd come to say.

The situation was worse than Ursula had envisaged. She'd thought that after being rejected, Oliver would leave her alone, as the boys and men in the village had done over the years.

'I have told your brother I have no interest in him,' she told Anne, 'and you may convey the same message. Please tell him to bother me no more, for I will not change my mind. I have my own reasons to live here as a single woman and I shall remain true to my choices. If he comes using violence, I will protect myself.' She knew she was not as physically big as Oliver, but she was strong. There were items in her cottage which could be used as weapons, and she'd start to carry her small knife when she went out. But she also knew if needed she had other ways to protect herself.

'That is why I have come today whilst he is in Norwich and will not know where I am. I fear he will not pay heed to your refusal of him, because he does not accept being told no. He will not use force, he says that doing so makes him as one with the animals or the low-class men. There are other ways though, for he states that he can use his cunning to gain whatever he wishes. That is what makes him so dangerous. If you have a relative you can live with, now is the time to go,' Anne said.

Ursula shook her head. 'I have no one,' she said, 'but even if I did why should I leave my home, my friends, and my work? No, I shall remain here and rebuff your brother however many times he comes to my doorstep. He will tire eventually I am sure of it.'

'I hope you are right, but I know him better than anyone and he never backs away from a fight. The more you say no, the more he will try to claim you for his own.' Having said her piece, Anne finished her ale and bade Ursula goodbye.

Ursula watched her being almost lifted onto her horse, a fine palfrey, by the stableman who'd accompanied her and waited patiently, until they rode away, their mounts kicking up the dust behind them. When she'd first arrived Ursula had been displeased to see Anne, but now she was glad she'd allowed the other woman to speak, even though she didn't like what she'd been told.

Sitting back beside the fire, Ursula gripped her hands together until they were scored with red marks where her short nails were pressed into the flesh. The air she was breathing felt heavy, too thick to pull into her lungs. For the first time in many years, she was fearful of a man, and she had no means of escape. And, she argued with herself, why should she? This cottage was her home, her protection. This village was hers, the occupants her neighbours. She would not run.

15

2024

'No, honestly I'm feeling fine.' Adrianna had her phone wedged between her ear and shoulder as she made her way around the kitchen tidying the worktops and lining up the electrical items so they stood sentry against the tiles. Life was calmer when everything was neat and tidy. 'Well, I'll have a rest tomorrow then. I've seen the weather forecast and it's not looking good, so I probably won't be able to get outside anyway. I'll have a day going through the papers I found and see if I can transcribe them.'

She'd been looking forward to giving Rick an update on her exploits, excited about all she'd achieved, but he was more concerned with her getting too tired. And although she felt bad lying to him, she hadn't actually checked the forecast because a bit of rain wasn't going to stop her.

'Remember you're there to have some time out,' he reminded her, his voice soft. 'You need to slow down, darling, and chill out. Are you still taking your medication? The garden doesn't have to be pristine and you won't be able to accomplish a lot in six months anyway. Perhaps it would be better if you passed the historical artefacts to a local museum, someone who actually knows what they're doing? You might inadvertently do some harm if you're blundering about with them.'

'No.' She could hear a pleading tone in her voice and she cleared her throat before continuing, trying to sound firmer, 'I'm going to show them to Jess who lives at the pub. She used to study history and she may have some ideas, plus she's going to look at what I've found outside. I'm enjoying doing something different with my brain. I promise I won't exhaust myself though, I'm taking plenty of breaks.' She thought of the pills which were still in their packet in her handbag, remembering the doctor who prescribed them suggesting that she should step away from work with its capacity for stress and enjoy a quieter time somewhere she could find a slower pace of life. Already the cottage, the garden, were bestowing on her a calm she'd forgotten was possible. It was starting to get under her skin, and, dare she think it, imbibing a kind of magic, a peace in her, through the earth and plants she handled.

'Good. I'm looking forward to seeing you at the weekend, perhaps you can arrange some nice weather please?' Rick said. 'We could go to the coast and eat somewhere in the evening?'

'I can't organise the weather, but we can certainly go out for dinner,' Adrianna agreed. 'Perhaps to the pub across the road from me? You can meet Jess and the other friends I've made.' She realised how proud she felt as she said the words, that she'd overcome some of her anxiety to get out and meet people.

'Well, yes, but it might be nice to try somewhere different. I'll do some research online and book a table, shall I?'

Adrianna agreed trying a new restaurant would be lovely, even though she was disappointed he hadn't wanted to go to the Kings Head. They said goodbye and she ended the call. Despite what she'd told Rick, she was feeling shattered. She'd felt tired for months but this was different, this was a physical exhaustion, not a mental one, and she welcomed it. The fog that had swamped her thinking, her very being for so long was still there, but it was beginning to thin, just a little. She didn't have the energy to try and battle her way through it though, to see what it was hiding.

* * *

The chimney sweep arrived unannounced the following morning. He explained that Louise had seen him in the village and suggested he called by. Adrianna was delighted because she'd been looking forward to lighting a fire since she'd arrived, and she left him swathing the room in dustsheets and assembling the poles and brushes while she walked back across the garden to the stone she'd found the previous day.

Seeing it without the rain running down and obscuring the marks on top, it looked quite different. She'd found an old brush under the sink, it smelled musty and sour and the bristles were already worn down, but it was exactly what she needed.

The moss and lichen were still a little damp, a woodlouse crawling through the coarse green, however some brisk scrubbing quickly removed the rest. She looked at what she'd now revealed, and immediately she could see this wasn't a pet grave, although she had no idea what it actually was.

The top of the stone was flat and engraved with several circles. In the middle of some were the petals of crudely carved flowers. She began to ponder – they looked like a group of daisies – perhaps this was simply an ugly garden ornament that Mrs Murray had bought which had just worn away over the years. In one top corner was a star with eight points and crisscrossed across the middle. Below the symbols she could see something else which she thought were possibly initials, but definitely not the name of a dog as Jess had suggested.

She sat back on her heels not noticing the damp of the cut grasses and bracken around her. This made no sense at all, these just looked like the sort of things that a child might do with a penknife on a hot summer day when bored. In the days before non-stop screen time. Had Jason done this? She had his email address for emergencies, which this certainly wasn't, but she was going to ignore the voice in her head telling her he didn't need to be bothered, because her interest was piqued. This cottage was throwing out more intrigue, more questions she needed answering.

As she turned to go back into the house, she saw the sweep's brush appear out of the top of the chimney, scattering pieces of vegetation and twigs.

'Looks like you had a bird's nest up there,' he explained as he vacuumed up a heap of old dried foliage from the hearth. 'That's the trouble with living so close to the coast, the gulls will set up home anywhere. Get a fire lit and it will stop them coming back.'

Perhaps the occupant of the nest had been making the noises she'd heard. She knew there had to be a simple explanation, just as there doubtless was for the creeping cold feeling of not being alone that she'd felt before. Before she did anything else, she'd email Jason and ask him what he knew about the stone in the garden and the documents she'd found. She might also broach the subject of whose responsibility it was to pay the chimney sweep.

* * *

Adrianna sat in the car in the station car park. She'd already checked her inbox three times but there wasn't yet a reply from

Jason. It was ridiculous expecting an instant response, but she couldn't help herself.

A knock at the passenger window pulled her from her musing and she grinned at Rick, who was peering in, smiling back. His teeth were so straight and white they looked as if they'd been created by AI, but she knew the pain and cost he'd gone through in Turkey to get them and how much he valued his appearance. He'd told her when they first met that he considered first impressions to be extremely important, especially when he was meeting wealthy clients who expected a level of class and sophistication. He certainly had that, his high cheekbones and strong chin were always clean-shaven and his blond hair was cut so it had just the right amount of 'flop'.

'Hey, gorgeous!' After throwing his overnight bag on the back seat he slipped in beside her, leaning in for a kiss. He smelled of a sharp citrus aftershave and mints. And just a hint of cigarette, so subtle she almost missed it. She hated the smell of stale smoke and wouldn't have dated him if he smoked. He'd assured her he didn't, but this wasn't the first time she'd thought she could taste it when he kissed her.

'Good journey?' she asked, laughing as he rolled his eyes and pulled his hands down his face. Even dragging the skin down, nothing could mar his good looks.

'I decided to travel first class,' he said, 'to make sure I could get a seat. I've got some reports that need completing and I thought I'd get them done on the train. But some woman arrived with her two kids and they whined and screamed the whole way. I'm sure she should've been back in cattle class but the guard didn't question her tickets when he checked.' Adrianna winced at his comment about 'cattle class', given that she always bought a standard ticket. She might earn a decent wage but she was happy to sit with anyone, even children, who were, after all, designed to be noisy.

'Never mind you'll be able to chill out at the cottage,' she soothed. 'It's so wonderfully quiet there. Apart from the occasional car along the main street all I can hear are the birds and the wind in the trees. And if it's in the right direction you can even hear the sea.'

'Sounds a bit too quiet for me, I'm used to sirens and people shouting at all hours.'

'So was I this time a couple of weeks ago,' she reminded him, laughing, 'and yet now I feel like I've been living in the wilds for years.'

'Don't become too much of a country bumpkin,' Rick said, 'you're a city girl at heart, you belong – with me – beneath the bright lights.' She refrained from pointing out that until she could do her job again, she was neither one thing nor the other.

By the time they got to the cottage it was already dark, so Adrianna couldn't show Rick the work she'd done in the garden. Instead, they carried her shopping and the small bag of logs she'd bought into the house and within an hour they were eating steak and salad, snuggled up on the sofa in front of the fire. She was pleased she'd had the forethought to buy some food before she picked him up; she wanted to spend the evening cuddled up with him. She'd missed him and tonight, she was pleased to have him all to herself.

16

1646

Ursula chose not to go to church that Sunday. There was every likelihood Oliver would attend, and she didn't want to remind him of her presence. Despite what Anne had told her, she still held onto a thread of hope that maybe he'd find another woman to bother and would forget about her.

Whilst the rest of the village were at church she decided to go and harvest the wild tansy and yellow archangel now emerging in the hedgerows; splashes of pale flowers the colour of soft sand amongst the sharp fresh green of new leaves and shoots. Mixed with meadowsweet and chamomile, which she grew in her garden, she could make a remedy which would help with the ague, the shaking and fever that often killed, especially in older people. It seemed that once caught, it lay dormant only to reappear in the winter months. And it was usually contracted after harvest time, when the wet weather came and the marshes began to flood.

She set off towards the far side of the common where the hedgerows were ablaze with blackthorn and mayflowers. Despite the early hour of the day the sun was already warm and she rolled her sleeves up above the elbow. The fabric of the simple russet gown she wore over her shift and petticoat caught the seeds from the swaying grasses as she brushed against them. Butterflies the colour of cornflowers danced from plant to plant and the drone of bees hummed as they made their way around the clover and celandine. She had her own bee skep, a woven inverted basket on stilts beneath a roughly made thatch cover and she hoped it was her bees collecting the pollen, the clover giving it an added piquancy. Honey was an ingredient she often used in her remedies to disguise bitter medicines and was also a welcome sweetening to milk puddings.

Out here was where she felt most alive. Where she was a part of the earth and the plants, as though they were a part of her. A warmth and stirring rose from beneath her feet that only she could feel.

Breaking off some wild garlic leaves she laid them in her basket and turned to make her way back across the common. It had been usual in years gone by to walk amongst the villagers' sheep, she'd even had two of her own at one point, but now that Lord Mayling had enclosed the common land for his own, nobody had grazing space. Everyone had chickens, at least when the fox didn't come calling, and some villagers occasionally bought a pig to fatten up for the Christmas and New Year celebrations. Sometimes she'd be called to an ailing person during the festivities and be paid with a platter of hot, juicy meat and sharp scraps of blackened crispy skin. She'd broken one of her back teeth biting into a particularly hard piece, but it was still one of her favourite foods, and a rarity.

As she approached her cottage, she was dismayed to see the church service had finished earlier than she'd expected and a group of people were chatting with the rector at the church door. Taller by far than most of the congregation, Oliver was very noticeable and for the final few yards before she reached her back door she stared at her feet so she wouldn't accidentally catch his eye. She walked through her garden until she couldn't stand the panic any longer and began to run, pushing open the door and then pulling down the wooden bar behind her. She hurried through to the front of the cottage and bolted that door as well, realising as she did so that she'd left her basket with the greenery she'd just collected outside. It would have to remain there until she was certain he'd left.

Climbing the steps into her bedroom she huddled down. It was the only place in the house where she couldn't be seen and there wasn't time to close all the shutters on the windows downstairs. Five minutes later, as she'd guessed would happen, the house shook as a heavy fist banged on the front door. She heard Oliver call out her name, then a few seconds passed, before the back door rattled as well. He didn't seem to believe she wasn't at home and she listened to the thump of his heavy boots as he walked around the building stopping occasionally to peer through the windows.

Eventually it went quiet, and holding her breath, Ursula slowly edged her way down the slatted rough wooden steps trying not to make any sudden movements in case he was watching the cottage from across the road. Finally, content that he'd left, she went to the back door and drew back the bolt to retrieve her basket, only to find it halfway across her garden, the contents strewn everywhere. There was no wind to have done that, she guessed it had been kicked in frustration. Quietly she picked the cuttings from amongst her vegetable beds and took them inside. It seemed her request to Anne, asking her brother to end his pursuit, had failed.

She spent the rest of the day making up some of her most popular herbal remedies, the ones she needed to always keep available. Nobody could avoid going out to work in the midday sun, and before their pale winter skin turned brown there were always a few weeks of red tenderness and blistering which needed soothing. Ursula depended on the stupidity of the men who stripped their smocks off when they got too hot and would subsequently need a cooling ointment.

The coins her medicines earned her were the only income she had other than her midwifery skills and the occasional request for her to read a palm. She still needed to buy flour for bread and hops for ale, even if she could grow or catch everything else she consumed. Her gown was ragged and torn around the bottom mostly from brambles or sharp branches when she collected berries, but there was rarely enough money to replace her clothes. Better though, to live with few resources and alone than to be beholden to a man with no say in how her life was lived.

She would not be a woman who hid her face behind the swathes of a shawl to cover the misshapen lumps where it had been beaten to a bloody mess. A husband would speak sweet words when he was wooing you, but once you wore his wedding ring there was no saying how he may change. Especially years when food was lean and money tight. There were plenty who weren't violent, John the blacksmith and Katherine's husband, Paul, were both good men, but there was no way of knowing for certain and it was a risk she wasn't prepared to take. Her home was her security.

A noise in the scullery caused her to jump up from her stool, knocking over a small bottle of oil she had open on her bench. Cursing, she set it upright again. Was he back? It was hours since Oliver had been snooping around her house but he couldn't be trusted, already she knew that. She was certain she'd left her doors bolted, but picking up the iron poker from beside the fire, she crept through to the back of the house, where everything appeared to be as she'd left it.

Except... perched outside on the window ledge was an enormous speckled brown herring gull, watching her through small beady black eyes whilst tapping his yellow beak against the thick, almost opaque, glass. When the bird saw her, it opened its beak and let out a loud squawk, making Ursula jump. She'd never seen such a huge sea bird. As she tentatively opened her back door the bird hopped down to the ground and began to walk in as if invited.

'No, no, you cannot come in here,' Ursula said, kicking her foot out to scoot him back out again. The bird flapped his wide wing span, making a draught and wafting the hop husks on the floor from where she'd been making beer that morning into a small cloud.

Continuing to walk forwards waving her arms, Ursula finally made the bird step back outside and she quickly shut the door again. She'd never seen a bird be so tame and it unnerved her. A loud screech from outside alerted her that it was still there, but she ignored the noise, knowing it would soon fly back to the sea.

Retrieving her parchment bundle from its hiding place she wrote an entry to record Anne's visit adding the strange bird with its unusual behaviour, together with a crude sketch of the gull beside what she'd written. She considered adding a line about the persistence of Oliver carrying the scent of danger with him but she hoped he might have now accepted her decision.

17

2024

Adrianna slid her feet into her slippers and pulled on the shirt Rick had taken off the previous night, rolling up the sleeves before doing up enough buttons to cover her modesty. The cottage wasn't overlooked, other than by the inhabitants in the graveyard next door, but she'd been hijacked in the garden by Tom once before. Just in case he was about early, she didn't want to give the poor man a heart attack.

It had been lovely to sleep in Rick's arms again. He'd been horrified at the scratches on her arms, but she was sure when he saw everything she'd achieved outside he'd see they were a small price to pay. She may have faltered in other areas of her life but this was one thing she could feel proud about. If she'd listened to her inner voice, the one that now whispered that she couldn't achieve anything, she'd have decided there was no point starting.

Making a pot of coffee for Rick – although she'd reverted to her favourite tea, he'd still expect the strongest, most bitter coffee – she opened the back door. The day was already bright, a dusting of pale eau-de-nil night cloud streaked in broad brush strokes across the sky as the day pushed its way onto the stage, the sun holding the promise of spring warmth. High above the church a kite was drifting, its forked tail rocking from side to side like a rudder. Perhaps that was what she needed to steer herself through life.

'I thought I could smell coffee.' Rick's voice behind her startled her.

'I was about to come and wake you,' she said. 'We don't want to waste the day.'

'No,' he agreed as he wrapped his arms around her and pulled her in, leaning his chin on the top of her head. 'First though, I need to get those reports written. If I do them this morning then we'll have the rest of the day to do something together.' He poured himself some coffee and blew her a kiss before sitting at the kitchen table with his laptop, which had appeared as mysteriously as he had.

'Oh, I didn't know you'd have to work this weekend.' She tried hard not to show her disappointment.

'I did tell you,' he reminded her, 'the last time we spoke. It won't be for long, I promise, but this is important.' He turned back to his screen.

He hadn't mentioned the garden, or the stone and documents she was keen to show him, but she knew his job always came first and he needed to be up to date with paperwork, so leaving him to it, she put the kettle on again and went to see if Jason had emailed back. With the excitement of Rick arriving, she'd forgotten to check.

To her delight there was a reply waiting in her inbox, and she took a deep breath as she read it. He started by explaining that the cupboard door was always stiff and a little warped, and his grandmother had preferred to leave it empty. She felt a twinge of guilt as she glanced over at the door, now constantly ajar where she'd split the wood. She needed to find a joiner at some point.

What he said next made the hairs along her arms stand up. His mother, now dead, had grown up in the cottage, but hated it. She'd said there were often icy cold spaces in the living room, which his grandmother accepted as part of the building's atmosphere, saying there was a history that should be left to lie, and when the right person arrived it would show itself.

He also explained that although he'd visited as a child, he could only remember his grandparents having a lawn and flower beds close to the house, and nowhere near the church wall. His grandmother had never felt easy with the graveyard next door. He concluded by saying that if he could remember anything else he would let her know.

She replied thanking him and promising to keep him updated and send some photos of what she'd done. What he had just told her had spooked her. Was she the person that his grandmother had alluded to? She'd found the journal, but she wasn't family; she couldn't work out why it may have been waiting for her. Her excitement was piqued once again, and she decided to translate some more of the journal whilst Rick was finishing his work. If he saw her with it, perhaps he too would be interested.

A new physic has arrived in Great Mayling and attended church with his sister this morning. He has turned his attention towards me, and I have told him it is unwanted. I shall never suffer at the hands of a man as my mother did. Written this day the eighth day of May in the year of our Lord 1646.

Adrianna screwed her face up as she finished reading. Whatever had happened to the owner of the journal, and her mother, it must have been serious if it was enough to put her off all men.

* * *

It was another hour before they were ready to go out. Rick was having trouble getting the numbers on a spreadsheet to add up and she didn't feel she could offer any assistance, given how her own statistical analysis had almost caused a catastrophe at work.

Instead, she went out to take the photos she'd promised Jason. Standing outside the back door she was conscious of a slight, warm breeze lifting the ends of her hair and a robin singing in a nearby rowan tree. She turned her head towards the stone standing proud of the coarse cut vegetation. The sun was shining across the garden, and yet the stone was in shadow. As she walked towards it, Adrianna became aware that the breeze was dropping and an eerie silence hung in the air. The robin had gone. She looked to see if there was a cloud partially covering the sun which might explain why she was still in sunlight but the stone was not. There was nothing marring the now cerulean blue though as it stretched above her, other than faded vapour trails criss-crossing the sky.

She could see Rick still working on his laptop and she opened her mouth to ask him to come outside, and then shut it again. He'd told her she was going mad when everything had started to fall apart at work and the words had stung, she wasn't going to give him the chance to pin that label on her again. As she continued to approach the stone the temperature steadily dropped and her footsteps slowed, her breath coming in shallow puffs in front of her face as her heartbeat increased. She could feel it, hear it, pulsing in her ears.

As she drew closer, the air felt charged, vibrating as though a storm was coming, humming with tension. The sky above her stretched to the horizon, still as clear as it had been two minutes previously. The weather wasn't responsible for what she was sensing.

'Who are you? Please tell me what you want,' she whispered.

Whatever was happening was being orchestrated by someone, or something. Whether it was a spirit from the past, or, she thought fleetingly, an evil presence, she wasn't alone. Leaning down she put her hands on the icy stone. A singing in the air was getting louder like the noise of a wet finger around the rim of a glass and making her whole body tremble along with it, and she could hear again the scratching noise she'd previously heard inside the cottage.

Then, as instantly as it had grown cold, the sun flooded across the area once more engulfing her in warmth, and she let her breath out slowly. Whatever had been there with her had left, the air suddenly light and clear and she could hear the birds again. Bending over she put her hands on her knees while she tried to make sense of what had just happened. She'd felt drawn to the stone as if it, or someone, was trying to tell her something. She stretched her fingers out, the tips tingling as they had before. What on earth had she started?

A sudden loud caw from the church wall made her jump, and looking across, she spotted the culprit: a huge, brown speckled sea bird. It turned its head to one side and watched her. Being so close to the sea, Adrianna was already used to the number of seagulls that wheeled in the sky overhead, calling to each other in mournful tones, but she hadn't seen one as close as this one was and certainly wasn't expecting it to be so big.

'What do you want, eh?' She thought that by speaking it would fly off again, but instead, it took two very measured steps towards her. 'Go on, shoo!' she laughed but could hear a shake in her voice. She wondered if it was possible to be attacked by a gull because this was big enough to do some damage.

'Addie, what are you doing?' Rick's voice carried across the garden and immediately the bird took flight, flapping away across the churchyard and out of sight. As it lifted in the air, its feet against the stone wall made the familiar scratching noise she'd heard before.

Her heart, which she hadn't realised had been thumping so hard in her chest, started to return to normal and she waved as she walked back to where Rick was standing at the back door. By the time she got to him she'd already made her mind up not to mention what had just happened. He wouldn't believe her and anyway, she had no words to explain it.

'Just taking some photos of what I've done out here to send to Jason, my landlord,' she explained, holding up her phone. Kissing him, she breathed in the warm citrusy scent of his after-shave. 'Have you finished with work?'

'I have. Why on earth are you bothering this Jason chap about what you're doing? He probably isn't even slightly interested. Forget about that and let's get out and find something to do for the rest of the day.' Catching her hand, he led her back into the kitchen and locked the back door behind her. Whatever was out there, she considered, wouldn't be dissuaded from its purpose by a locked door. In fact, she knew it was already in the house too.

It was five o'clock by the time they got home and Adrianna suggested they spent the evening at the pub. She still hadn't introduced him to the locals she'd met. There was no guarantee anyone other than Louise or Jess would be there, but her new friends were becoming increasingly important to her.

'Not tonight, eh?' Rick wrapped his arms round her pulling her in for a kiss. 'I'd like it to be just the two of us, if that's okay? I have to go back tomorrow and I want to enjoy our time together on our own.' Adrianna was disappointed, but she decided not to insist. She knew from experience that forcing him to do something he didn't want to would just culminate in a sulk and spoil an evening out. And she'd been the one who'd wanted to stay in and enjoy an evening, just the two of them, the previous night. So why shouldn't he want the same again? It was only fair they did what he wished. After all, she'd left him in London to take a break, she reminded herself with a stab of guilt.

'Of course, you're right. We can just chill out here. That sea air has made me sleepy.' As if on cue she yawned and they both laughed. She got out a bottle of wine together with some cheese and a baguette she'd bought the previous day. She'd even remembered Rick's favourite vegetable crisps and his rather bizarre penchant for cocktail sausages.

'A carpet picnic, perfect.' He grinned at her as she sat down beside him feeling warm and happy. The effects of taking this leave of absence from work were beginning to ease the knots that tied her insides together.

* * *

The following morning Rick was quiet. He assured Adrianna that it was just the 'Sunday Blues', the thought of having to return to London later and work the next day.

'You don't know how lucky you are,' he said, giving her a squeeze which threatened to evict all the air from her lungs. 'Nothing to get up for tomorrow morning.' She didn't feel lucky, what she'd been through at work was still haunting her, but she chose her words carefully in an attempt to not engage in the conversation.

'How about a full English?' she suggested, changing the subject. 'And then you must come and see all my work outside.' Rick still wasn't as enthusiastic about the garden as she'd hoped, but once he'd finished eating and she'd washed up he came out to admire her hard work.

'You've cleared a huge space,' he said, raising his eyebrows as he looked around. 'Remember you're only here for six months, you can't hope to do a lot more than keep the grass down. Is there a ride on mower?' he asked, suddenly beginning to sound excited. 'I could give you a hand if there is, get the rest of the weeds. How far does the garden extend to?'

'Nope, no ride on, I borrowed a strimmer to do this. Do you see that wall in the distance beyond the orchard? That's the other end of the garden. Really, I've barely scratched the surface.'

'Seriously? That is probably well over an acre of land,' he said.

'Apparently, it's about two. It's enormous, isn't it?'

'You could build another couple of houses out the back here, make a killing.' Immediately Rick was estimating ways of making money out of the beautiful old property.

'Well as it isn't mine, I don't need to consider that,' she said, without adding that, if the cottage *was* hers, she wouldn't be building anything more than a greenhouse. She already loved the view from the kitchen window and that would be lost if someone was greedy enough to build houses on the land.

'Anyway, come and see what I found.' He followed her across the garden to the stone she'd uncovered.

'It's just a rock, isn't it?' he said, the disinterest immediately apparent in his tone. 'Probably some kids graffitied it at some point and that's what these marks are.'

'No, I don't think they are.' Adrianna tried to keep the disappointment from her voice; she really wanted Rick to share her excitement. 'See here? There are circles interlinking with flower petals inside, like daisies. Where they meet in the middle, it's like a Venn diagram and there's something else there, but I can't work it out. And look, a star here. It feels a bit odd for a teenager's graffiti. Plus, according to Tom, the local folklore suggests this was originally common land, then it was owned by the local squire, but at some point, Mrs Murray's husband bought it, although he didn't go on to cultivate it. So it could genuinely have been overgrown for centuries.' She looked at him willing him to show some interest and agree with her suppositions, not mentioning that she thought she'd been drawn to uncover it.

'I still don't think it's anything special.' Rick shrugged and looked at his watch. 'Anyway, I just need to send a quick final email and then I should be heading back to the station. I don't want to be getting back late or I'll be exhausted for work tomorrow.'

Five minutes later he was cursing, banging his fist on his laptop. 'This thing is useless,' he growled. 'There was loads of charge in it earlier but now it's completely drained. If I use my phone to forward something to your email, can I quickly borrow your laptop to alter a spreadsheet and send it to my boss?'

'Of course,' Adrianna said. Booting it up, she left him to it and went upstairs to pack his belongings back into his weekend bag. She'd loved having him close to her at night and it felt as though he'd only just arrived. The week ahead stretched lonely and long.

'All done?' she asked, pasting a smile on her face that she didn't feel inside as he arrived upstairs.

'Yup, everything sorted and ready for tomorrow morning.' He pulled the zip of his bag shut. It was a Louis Vuitton one she'd bought him for Christmas the previous year. She wasn't keen on the monogrammed leather, but he loved it and had been ecstatic when he'd opened the wrapping paper. 'Do you mind if I drive to the station?' he asked. 'I haven't had a chance behind the wheel this weekend and you know how I love driving your car.' Adrianna did know, he told her often enough.

Her return journey from King's Lynn took a little longer as – instead of racing along the narrow country roads pretending they were at Silverstone – she drove sedately and enjoyed the burgeoning countryside around her. In the short time since she'd arrived, it had burst into life, the previously stark hawthorn trees and blackberry bushes now a bubbling mass of vibrant, snowy blossom, the trees speckled with new glossy, acid green leaves as they began to unfurl and flutter in the breeze her car created. Flocks of sparrows flitted in and out of the hedges making them alive with movement. It all reaffirmed her recent musing that the world kept revolving and perhaps her problems would eventually drift away, as winter had.

Letting herself into the cottage the atmosphere felt charged, awaiting her return. She hoped it was just her overactive imagination, but she knew it wasn't when she looked across the room to the cupboard. The piece of parchment with the warning inscribed on it lay on the floor. Her fingers began to tingle once more. And, as she held them out in front of her, the tips started to vibrate.

18

1646

Ursula had received a message asking her to visit one of Lord Mayling's tenant farmers. Two of the children were ill with fever and now one of them was reportedly covered in a rash. Fevers in children were nothing unusual and often went away as quickly as they came, but one that was accompanied by spots could be something more dangerous. And there was always the worry it could be a contagion which may spread to other members of the family, and beyond.

Packing her basket with a bunch of septfoil leaves she'd harvested from where it grew amongst the broom trees in the hedgerows, Ursula left at first light, walking the three miles to the farm. The sun was creeping up into a cloudless blue sky and high above her she could hear the trilling of a skylark, whilst swooping across the skyline swifts called to each other. It was truly summer when they arrived. She had an uncomfortable feeling as she walked that she was being watched, but although she turned around several times and scanned the hedgerows and thickets of trees as she passed, she couldn't see anyone. That didn't mean they weren't there though.

Despite the early hour of the day, by the time she arrived Ursula was already hot, having walked briskly. Sweat trickled down the side of her face and she took off her cap to fan herself for a moment before pulling it back on and knocking on the door.

'Come in, Miss.' The child who opened it looked no more than five years old, but he was obviously expecting her and she followed him to a small truckle bed in the back corner of the room that she'd stepped in to.

'Where is your mother?' she asked, shocked to see that both children in the bed, one of about three and the other even younger, looked worse than she'd been expecting. They were pale, their skin clammy and very hot to the touch, as she lay her hand on each of their foreheads.

'She is in the dairy,' he replied.

'Then go and get her please,' Ursula snapped. She knew the cows needed to be milked but these children were too ill to be left alone. It often appeared to her that animals on a farm were treated as more important than the children.

Pouring some water onto a piece of linen Ursula began to swab both children's faces and necks.

'So, Ursula, what do you think is wrong with them? They are going to be all right, are they not?' Behind her the children's mother, Betty, bustled in, the sour scent of milk curds following her.

'I do not yet know,' she replied. 'They both seem very unwell. Where is the rash?'

Betty pulled up the shift on the older of the children and showed her his torso, completely covered in raised red spots.

'They are both the same,' she said. 'The little one only started with the spots this morning. Is it smallpox?'

'No, I do not believe it is,' Ursula replied, realising that Betty, unlike herself, hadn't seen many ailments. 'The pox would have big pustules that weep. I think this is measles, it is usual for the rash to be beneath the skin as this is.'

'Will they be all right? Will they live?' Betty sat on the edge of the bed and took the cloth that Ursula was bathing the children with and began to swab them. Her voice sounded tremulous and Ursula realised she was more worried than she was admitting.

'I cannot say. Some recover quickly and do not have much of a rash, but sometimes weak children die. Or they sleep for a long time and do not wake properly, they do not leave their beds again. I cannot tell you what will happen but I can give you medicine. And keep that one,' she nodded at the small boy who'd opened the door to her and was standing in the corner watching them, 'out of here. Measles spreads quickly and you do not want him succumbing too.'

'Alfred, you heard the lady, get out of here.' Betty flicked her head towards the back door and the boy ran out into the yard. There was a loud clucking as he disturbed the chickens which had wandered in through the open door scratching their feet against the flagstones searching for scraps and grain.

'If you can send someone down to my cottage later, I will make up some saffron linctus for them too, in case it is needed.' She was lucky that several years previously she'd been given some crocus corms as part payment. The saffron they now produced was a helpful addition to her medicines. 'And a flask of wormwood and rue with which to cleanse this room thoroughly to prevent any infection spreading. I cannot guarantee the outcome, but with God's grace they will survive,' Ursula said as she got to her feet and picked up the satchel she'd brought the medicine in. She didn't like the glassy look in the smaller child's eyes as she gazed unseeing into the distance. Wherever the child was, it wasn't in the room with the rest of them.

Saying her goodbyes, now with a truckle of cheese and her purse – hidden in the folds of her skirt – full of coins which knocked against her thigh as she walked, Ursula began to head home. She'd need to make a fresh batch of medicine as soon as she got back. Those children may need several doses, and if they did indeed have measles, then it was possible that other people in the village were already infected.

Walking home along a track between two hedges, the tall trees now wearing their summer plumage met above her, their canopy of leaves making a soaring roof like that of the church. It was cooler here and Ursula would have liked to forage for herbs but was aware she needed to be at her workbench. She had a busy day ahead of her.

A pounding of hooves from behind made the dry track beneath her vibrate and Ursula skirted to one side pressing herself into the hedge and almost losing her balance, the spines on the hawthorn tearing tiny holes in her skin where blood bloomed like flowers and spread across her clothes. It was necessary though before she was crushed beneath the hooves of the galloping horse. As it pulled up in a flurry of dust, she wasn't remotely surprised to see Oliver mounted. How had he known she was here? He must be having her watched, someone spying on her every movement.

She clambered upright, taking leaves and twigs from her hair where her cap had come off. Retrieving it, she pulled it back onto her head trying to capture the hair which had escaped its bun beneath the crumpled linen. Pushing his horse alongside her, Oliver leant down in the saddle and ripped it off again.

'You have beautiful hair, Ursula,' he said. 'I should like to see more of it.'

'You shall not.' She snatched her cap back. 'I have given you my answer to your proposal,' she reminded him, her hands on her hips. Her palms were stinging but she was so angry she barely noticed. 'I told you to leave me alone, nothing will change my mind. I have no interest in you, Doctor Bruton. Perhaps you should return to your wife and children in Cambridge.'

By the way his eyes widened she knew he was surprised she was already availed of that knowledge and hoped she hadn't got Anne into trouble. He was not a man to cross and even as she'd said the words, she knew she should have kept her mouth shut. Not a trait she was very good at.

'I can only assume my sister has paid you a visit.' He spoke the words through gritted teeth, his brows close over his eyes. 'However, my home situation is none of your business.'

'And yet mine is to you?' Ursula spat. 'You came into my house and made comments about how I live my life, even though it is of no concern of yours, either.'

'Indeed, because you are a villager, a pauper, and you need protection. If you do not have it from me, then anyone could come into your cottage and take advantage of you. You are no match for a man, Ursula. Despite the danger growing at the end of your garden, I have seen with my own eyes what you have there. Plants that could kill a man if desired. Ones that your neighbours surely do not know about.'

'I am not afraid of any man,' she said. 'I have looked after myself perfectly well thus far and I shall continue to do so. Now please do excuse me, I must return home and prepare some medication for two children who are ill with measles.' She inclined her head and walked away along the track. She measured her steps carefully, determined not to let him see how afraid she was and that her legs were shaking as she stepped around the tufts of grass that grew between the cart tracks so as not to trip on them.

It was several minutes before she heard the horse move off

again and she stopped herself from turning around to ensure he'd really gone as the noise disappeared into the distance behind her. Eventually when she did look, she sighed in relief that she was alone once more. Except she wasn't on her own, because walking silently behind her was the gull she'd seen before. She assumed it was the same one as last time, bigger than a cockerel and watching her silently. When she stopped for a moment, the bird also paused. When she set off again, it followed her.

'Go. Away.' She stamped her foot at it to make it fly but it just jumped back and waited until she started walking again.

Increasing her pace until she was almost trotting, she was eager to be back in her cottage. She'd never felt unsafe or nervous on the paths and tracks she traversed across Norfolk, but now she did. Her mind kept mulling over Oliver's throwaway comment about dangerous plants. What would he say if he knew exactly which plants were at the end of her garden, concealed behind the rhubarb. Had he already been snooping out there?

If he were to discover what she grew, he could potentially use that information against her. All wise women occasionally needed more powerful plants and those herbs and bushes she grew were for specific medications that needed something strong, in the same way that she used the archangel for the ague. Small amounts of hemlock, wolfsbane or foxglove could revive a person on their death bed. But too much could send someone to their eternal rest, and only someone as proficient as she knew the difference. But she didn't tell those she treated when she needed those special plants and the information of what she was growing felt far more dangerous if Oliver knew about them.

19

2024

'Right,' Adrianna said to herself as she pulled her wellingtons on, 'let's go and see what I can discover about the village and its previous inhabitants at the church.' How the cottage had felt when she'd arrived back the previous day was still disturbing her and not having Rick and his solid dependability there made her feel worse. She hadn't realised how much she was missing him. Her life and his felt as if they were drifting separate ways and she didn't want that. She loved him; he made her laugh, and feel safe. He was her rock, her everything.

Being positioned on a slight hill meant the church could be seen not only from the whole of the village but with the land so flat, it was visible for miles around. It felt odd looking down at her own cottage from a different vantage point, and seeing the garden from this angle made her realise she'd cleared far more than she'd intended. The stone she'd discovered was close to the wall, so not visible from the church door.

Turning the heavy, metal, looped handle she was pleased to discover it was open and she stepped in quietly, unsure if there would be a service going on, but all was quiet, the only sound being the slight squeak of her wet boots against the ancient slabs on the floor. She looked around to see if anyone was there, but she was all alone.

Outside the clouds were an oppressive grey and despite there being numerous windows depicting bible scenes in tiny panes of flamboyant coloured glass, with no sun shining through them, the building was cavernous and dark. A musty atmosphere of old books, dust, and ancient prayers filled the hushed space.

Her musing was interrupted as a grating sound came as someone pushed the door open. Adrianna gave a start, the sudden noise making her jump and her heart begin to pound until she realised it was Roger. Not wanting to give him the sort of shock he'd just given her, she immediately called across to him. His face lit up when he saw her.

'Hello, this is a nice surprise,' he said. 'Are you here to talk to the Big Man, or just having a look around?'

'I came to explore, I hope that's okay?'

'Of course, this is God's home and open to all at any time. Well not between the hours of darkness and dawn because I lock up then.' He laughed at his own joke and Adrianna found herself joining in. 'If I've interrupted you in silent prayer then I apologise. I can just scoot through to the vestry and leave you in peace.'

'No, please don't. When you have some spare time, I'd love it if you could tell me a bit more about the church.'

'I'm always happy to show people round this beautiful building, so how about now? And I also have something outside to show you which you may find interesting.'

'That sounds intriguing,' Adrianna raised her eyebrows.

After a tour they finished outside the door. 'This is what I thought you'd like to see,' Roger said. 'When you described what you'd found in the garden it reminded me of these, see if you recognise them.' Beside the huge wooden frame, bleached pale grey by centuries of the sun and rough with the salt air, there were marks etched into the wall. Symbols which matched those on the stone in her garden. Around her all fell silent, before it was rent by a loud caw from the wall, alerting her to the herring gull standing like a sentinel, watching her.

* * *

As soon as she'd seen the carvings on the church wall, Adrianna insisted Roger followed her to her garden to see what she'd uncovered.

'It's just here.' She felt her feet sinking a little on the vibrant green spongy moss as she made her way across the newly exposed ground. She hoped she wasn't preventing him from anything urgent he had to do, given that she had rather hijacked him. 'There seem to be flowers and stars. Rick, my boyfriend, thinks they're just graffiti, but now I've seen the same things on the church wall I'm sure they aren't. Plus, this at the bottom looks like initials.'

'No, no, you're right, this isn't graffiti. As I thought they might be from your description, they match the church markings.' Roger crouched down, his knees cracking as he did so, and wiped a hand across the carvings, looking closer. He stood up again, wobbling for a moment but then steadying himself.

'How did you know they'd be the same?'

'Because these, Adrianna, are witch marks. They're called hexafoils, and I'd hazard a guess that if we stand at the wall now,' he was already striding across the wet grass and Adrianna hurried to keep up. 'Yes, there look,' he announced in triumph, pointing at the church. 'In a direct line. Whoever carved your witch marks did these too. I'm not sure why, but I would guess to protect the church and its boundaries from what they thought were witches, or someone colluding with the devil.'

'Witch marks? What does that even mean? I've never heard of such a thing.'

'Back in the sixteenth and seventeenth centuries when there were witch hunts, these marks were used to try and ward off evil spirits. Hence why they're sometimes found by church doors. Given that they're here and next door too, I imagine someone who lived in these parts was very frightened.'

Adrianna couldn't decide if she was more pleased that she'd been correct about the marks not being scrawled by a local delinquent, or that there was some real history sitting here in her garden. But remembering the sheet of parchment with the warning on it and the occasions she'd experienced something eerie and uncomfortable, she wondered exactly how happy she should be about this discovery.

'Ask Jess if she knows anything about witch hunts around these parts,' Roger suggested as he turned to go. 'There were definitely some in King's Lynn, you could look up Margaret Read. But I warn you it's a bit gruesome. And one of my parishioners, Jack Miller may have some knowledge of any local tales. He's in his nineties, he lives at Mayling Farm and his family go back generations, hundreds of years according to him. I can speak to him if you want.'

'Thank you, that would be great,' Adrianna said. She needed all the help she could get.

Within minutes of Roger leaving, she had her laptop open, searching online for Margaret Read and soon realised why Roger had warned her about it being somewhat unpleasant. A tale of the woman being burned at the stake in King's Lynn for being a witch and her heart bursting out of her body to hit the wall of a building opposite. Whilst it was, of course, just folklore, she made a note to go and have a look at the building when she next visited the town and see the brick which supposedly marked the spot.

There was nothing online about a witch hunt local to Finchingham, but the minutes turned into hours as she read more and more about the East Anglian trials in the seventeenth century and how many innocent women were simply convicted on the hearsay of men. And in particular, one man, Matthew Hopkins, the Witchfinder General. Not only did he pick on poor, vulnerable women, but he employed other women, often their neighbours and friends to undertake the examinations and torture until they gained a confession and sent the defenceless to the gallows. Because who could have said no to a man in that era? No female could.

There was no way of knowing why the witch marks were here in her garden but she was sure there had to be some connection with the ones at the church. And whatever it was, she was going to discover it. From the first time she'd arrived in the village Adrianna felt a belief that here was something she *could* do. Getting out the journal she began to read the next entry, feeling herself shiver as she did so.

Tonic of Clove and Gilliflower prepared for Ruth Blacksmith. The baby fares well but his mother does not. I shall add birthwort which is not without its dangers but I believe is needed in this case. And a visit again from the new doctor, Oliver Bruton. He means me harm if I will not let him have his way with me but I shall never endure that which my mother did at the hands of my father. Marriage or the carnal knowledge of a man is not what I choose, I shall live my life in safety. I told the doctor to leave but I fear he will return. Written this day the nineth day of May in the year of our Lord 1646.

It seemed that one woman had decided she would say no to a man.

A sudden tapping made her jump, and looking up, she saw the same gull as before knocking its beak against the window as if demanding admittance.

20

2024

Adrianna decided to do as Roger suggested and ask Jess if she knew of any myths about witchcraft in the village or its surrounds, so in the early evening she wandered across to the pub. Across the fields, the round globe of an orange sun seemingly balancing on the horizon slowly sank, touching everything that lay before it with fire. Lengthening shadows crept over the ground.

With a glass of wine in her hand and some food ordered, she explained everything Roger had told her about the strange stone in her garden, but Jess didn't know of any local witchcraft folklore.

'Why not check if there's any history about where you're living though,' Jess suggested, 'because, going by its date, it's sixteenth century. I wouldn't be surprised if it's listed. Start by finding out if there are any deeds stored anywhere, they might even be in the cottage. You may at least discover who owned the property before the Murrays.'

'I did wonder if it's listed. I'll ask Jason, and also whether there are any deeds, see if they turn anything up.' She was pleased to have a plan, even though it didn't point her towards anything specifically about the witchcraft which she increasingly believed was something to do with what she was experiencing.

As soon as she got home, she emailed Jason, as planned. Whilst doing so she realised she hadn't messaged Rick other than her usual *'good morning'* WhatsApp and, checking her phone, she noticed that he'd read it but hadn't replied. She glanced at the clock but it was only ten o'clock so she called him. He was a bit of a night owl, so he wouldn't be in bed yet.

The phone rang several times and she was about to hang up when he answered. Immediately she could hear a lot of background noise and she guessed he was in a bar.

'I was just calling to say hi,' she told him, 'but I can hear that you're out so I won't bother you now.'

'It's fine, I've stepped outside for a moment,' Rick said. 'We're having birthday drinks for one of the girls in the office. If you were here, instead of holed up in the wilds, you could have joined in. We're having a good laugh.'

Adrianna frowned and paused before she answered. Rick had been encouraging when she'd decided to take a sabbatical somewhere quiet, and yet now he kept implying she'd made a mistake leaving London behind for a few months.

'Well life out here in the wilds, as you call it, hasn't been dull,' she said. 'I've discovered those marks on the stone in my garden are called hexafoils and were supposedly used to ward off witches. I'm going to try and do some research and see if I can find out why they're there. It gives me something to do, and I'm finding it fascinating.'

'Research?' he questioned. 'You're not a historian, will you even know where to start? It takes years and a university degree to do proper historical investigations. I think you might be aiming a bit high, darling.'

Adrianna felt her heart sink a little. He was right, of course he was. She had not one ounce of expertise, her degree had been in informatics and she'd then started straight from university at her current employers, first as an intern before quickly climbing the corporate ladder. Except now she was near the top, the view didn't look as wonderful as she'd thought it would. All she knew about was numbers and computers.

'I know,' she admitted. She could hear how small her voice had become. 'But it gives me something to do when I can't be outside.' He'd already given his opinion about her gardening but whatever he said, she couldn't deny how being amongst the plants made her feel. At home, at one with the earth. Unlike any way she'd felt before, an energy from the ground running through her.

'Just take a break and chill out,' Rick said. 'You're supposed to be resting your brain, not giving it something else to worry about. Now, I've got to go, it's my round next and I can hear some heckling from inside. We'll chat tomorrow, okay? Love you loads.' Adrianna just had time to say goodbye as the call was cut off. She put her phone on charge and went around the house making sure the doors were all locked. Rick was right of course; she had no experience in anything historical and she was doubtless just wasting her time.

* * *

The next day Adrianna woke early to sunlight filtering in around the edges of the curtains in her room. Summer was waiting in the wings and she could expect more early awakenings.

Checking her phone, she could see there were no messages from Rick, but she did have an email from Jason. She had forgotten she'd messaged him, and despite Rick's derisory comments about her historical know-how, she felt a frisson of excitement as she opened the email. Jason had no idea where the deeds were, but he could confirm the era of the house was as the stone above the door insinuated, and it was indeed listed. He told her she had carte blanche to do anything she wished in her historical investigations.

With the day looking fine, Adrianna wanted to do some more gardening, but she was also keen to continue reading the journal. She decided to do that first because she couldn't risk getting any ingrained dirt from her hands on the document.

The next two entries were lists of plants needed for remedies, one for 'sore winter skin' and another for a remedy for excess blood loss after childbirth. Then there was another journal entry, longer than the previous ones and it took a while to transcribe it but eventually she managed to read what was written.

I did receive another visitor. Anne Bruton, sister of the new physician whom I have seen in church, called upon me. She told me of his two daughters and his ailing wife, left behind in Cambridge to die. And also of a girl murdered when she became with child. I know now my decision to spurn him is the right one and I pray he will not call again. My second visitor brought some light to these dark days, a mighty herring gull in tawny brown speckles who entered my home as if invited. Written this day the fourteenth day of May in the year of our Lord 1646.

Beneath the entry was a crude outline of a seabird which looked uncannily like the gull which she'd seen outside. A bizarre coincidence, but one that made her swallow hard.

The doctor sounded a nasty piece of work, expecting to take everything he wanted and being violent when he couldn't. She felt an uneasy stirring in the pit of her stomach, a fear for this woman she'd never actually known. Just as before, the temperature in the room began to feel cooler and the hairs down her neck started to prickle.

From the corner of her eye, a movement at the door made Adrianna jump to her feet, looking around, but although she could see she was alone, it felt as though she wasn't. There was a shift in the air, a fine opaque shadow suspended in the middle of the room. There and yet not there. A dusting of dry lavender husks spun across the floor. They hadn't been there before; she'd vacuumed that morning. After a couple of seconds, although to Adrianna it felt like several long minutes, the darkness began to recede and slowly the temperature returned to how it had been previously. Hastily she returned the documents to their hiding place. The sheet with the warning was on top of them. What were the powers it alluded to, and the evil? She'd given up hiding it behind the journal because it was always on top when she opened the wallet.

21

___

1646

Ursula wasn't sleeping well. Since she'd been apprehended by Oliver on her way back from the farm, she was certain she was being watched. There were no physical signs, nothing in her cottage had been moved as before, but she felt a prickling sensation creeping up the back of her neck whenever she was out in her garden or the village. Even when she stood beside the small windows in her home, she was certain that eyes were observing her every movement. Someone was out there. She'd told herself she wouldn't let Oliver change how she lived her life, that she wouldn't be crushed by him. And yet despite her resolve she found herself avoiding her windows and only venturing outside at dawn and dusk when it would be difficult to see across the common.

After church on Sunday, which she'd avoided again, there was a gentle knock at the door.

'Who is it?' Ursula called out.

'Mistress Beal, are you there? This is Lady Mayling, I have need of your help.'

Frowning and wondering if one of her neighbours was playing a trick on her, Ursula opened the door, to be met with the sight of a lady in a fine, pale green, velvet gown. Behind her Ursula could see a small carriage and a groom and she realised this woman was indeed who she said she was. Curtseying, she stepped to one side to allow the visitor into her cottage. Suddenly her home seemed very small, although as Lady Mayling sat down and smiled warmly, Ursula felt less uncomfortable.

'May I offer you a drink?' she asked, unsure of how to behave with such an illustrious person.

'No thank you, I must return to the hall as soon as I am able,' she said. 'I have come to ask if you have a medication for the measles? My son, Edward, has succumbed and is most unwell. He has a fever and does not recognise me when I sit with him. I asked the new physician at Great Mayling to attend, three times he has let some of Edward's blood but it has achieved nothing, indeed my boy is now weaker and he seems to have deteriorated over the past day.'

Ursula pursed her lips. She had feared that the contagion would spread and it seemed it was beginning to do so. Leeches would not help, she knew that.

'I have seen other cases of measles recently,' she said, 'I have given those children septfoil and saffron, I have more medicine and I can come and visit your son if you wish. What age is he?'

'Just six years old.' Lady Mayling's voice broke and she dabbed at her eyes with a pristine white lace-edged handkerchief. 'I cannot lose him, we have not been blessed with any other living children. We have lost three babies before their first birthday.'

'I should see him to ensure it is the measles he ails with, if you will allow me to?' Ursula said.

'Yes, please come immediately,' Lady Mayling replied, her hands twisting together as though she were washing them. 'My carriage waits outside.'

Ursula gathered together all the medications she thought she may need before damping down the fire. Picking up her satchel which now emanated a pungent aroma of rosemary and rue, she followed Lady Mayling to the street. It was the first time she'd ever travelled in something as luxurious and, in her haste to climb in, she didn't notice she was being watched from the doorway of the inn.

Although she could understand Lady Mayling's sense of urgency as she instructed the driver to take them home as quickly as possible, Ursula was disappointed she didn't have longer to enjoy the opulent surroundings in which she found herself, the soft pile of the deep red velvet seating felt like moleskin as she pushed her fingertips in the material closing around them.

The speed they were travelling at made the ride bumpy as the wheels caught and leapt over the deep ridges in the road. And seeing the countryside outside the window moving past so quicky began to make her nauseous so it was with a sense of relief when, with shaky legs, she alighted outside the front entrance of the hall.

It was an impressive building made of red brick in a herringbone design, rows of stone mullioned windows with thin, even panes of glass, so different from the thick semi-opaque ones she had. Lady Mayling ascended the front steps to where the wide oak door, with black iron ornate hinges which stretched from one side to the other, was being held open. With no instruction to the contrary, Ursula followed. She was looking straight ahead eager to see inside this magnificent building, although without checking, she was aware of the servants narrowing their eyes in disgust that one as lowly as she was walking in through the front door.

'This way, please follow me.' Lady Mayling swept across the inner hall. Despite the many windows it was a dark space, the burnished dark oak panels appearing to crowd inwards. A fire was burning in a wide stone fireplace, soot staining the beam above it. Ursula would have liked to have explored further but Lady Mayling was already halfway up the stone staircase and she hurried after her.

They seemed to walk for miles along corridors which were sometimes strewn with fresh, pale rushes, sweet with the scent of lavender and warm summer meadows, and sometimes with thick rugs of intricate designs. Eventually after a further staircase, they arrived in the nursery where three maids darted about as if trying to appear busy. Given that the room was immaculately tidy and their charge lay beneath crisp linen covers in his four-poster bed, Ursula wondered to herself what they did all day. A bright fire popped and crackled in the fireplace.

Lady Mayling hurried straight to the bed and sat beside it, picking up the limp hand of a small boy, almost invisible amongst the bedding piled up on him. Ursula walked to the other side of the bed, past the three maids who were now standing in row in front of the window.

'Is there any improvement?' Lady Mayling asked.

'No, mistress,' the eldest of the three maids replied. 'He has barely opened his eyes and would not take any food or drink.' At this news Lady Mayling let out a low moan and lay her forehead down on the tiny hand she was holding.

'No, no my sweet boy,' she crooned. 'You must eat and get better. I cannot lose you too.'

Ursula turned back the blankets and gently lifted up the

small boy's night shift. As she suspected his entire body was covered in the measles rash, dark red against his skin, what little there was of it not covered in spots. He was breathing rapidly, his sunken chest working hard and she could see in the crook of his elbow three small marks where the leeches had been attached. It had merely weakened the boy further.

Lifting the items she'd packed in her satchel she held out some rosemary to the nearest maid, together with a stoppered bottle of clear liquid.

'Burn the rosemary in dishes,' she instructed, 'and use this lotion to wipe down every surface in the room. It will help the contagion from spreading.'

Taking a clean piece of linen and another bottle from her satchel she soaked the cloth and dabbed it against the livid rash.

'His skin is burning,' she explained as she worked, 'this should help to take some heat from it and make the rash calmer.' She handed a twist of paper containing septfoil and saffron to the same maid. 'Add two big pinches to a cup of small beer,' she said, 'spoon it slowly into his mouth a little at a time, and then repeat every four hours, day and night.'

'Will he live?' Lady Mayling whispered. Her face was streaked with tears and Ursula could see them settle in the lines of sorrow and worry that each passing baby had wrought. And now her only surviving child at death's door.

'I cannot foresee what our Lord in heaven has decided for him,' she said, 'but I hope I can save him. He is very ill though,' she warned. 'May I attend tomorrow and see how he fares?'

'Of course, I shall send my carriage in the morning,' Lady Mayling replied before telling one of the maids to take Ursula back to the front door and inform the groom he was to take her home.

The drive back was slightly more comfortable as it wasn't at the breakneck speed of the outward journey, although she still felt every bump in the road. Two of her neighbours were in the street as she pulled up in front of her cottage, their mouths hanging open as Ursula opened the door and scrambled out. Neither of the footmen moved to help her alight as they had when their mistress had been with her. She hurried into her cottage, well aware that there would be gossip whipping around the village within minutes.

She returned to the hall twice more. The first time she could see a small improvement, Edward still propped up on his pillows with his mother looking as though she hadn't moved, beside him. His eyes were open and he watched her as she checked his rash, not as vivid as the day before, his breathing more normal. She handed over additional medications and suggested posset and coddled eggs if he was able to eat.

The carriage came for her one final time, a week later, when she found Edward sitting beside the fire playing with a selection of painted wooden horses. His eyes were bright and his skin bore a slightly pink bloom where the rash was fading fast. She curt-seyed to Lady Mayling who also appeared much happier, dressed in a pale-yellow gown embroidered with bluebells.

'I believe now he will make a full recovery,' Ursula told her.

'I can never thank you enough for what you've done,' Lady Mayling replied. 'I have informed Lord Mayling that only you shall treat Edward if he ails. Doctor Bruton will never again set foot in the nursery. He was here yesterday with my husband and I told him of my decision.' Ursula's heart sank. The last thing she wanted to do was antagonise the doctor further.

'This is for you.' Lady Mayling removed a velvet purse from her gown and handed it over. It was weighty with coins and Ursula felt the heaviness of her heart lift a little. She would face

Oliver's displeasure at least knowing that she'd been paid handsomely.

As the carriage took her home for the final time, she tipped the contents of the purse into her lap, the shine of the gold and silver it contained making her face glow.

22

1646

Ursula barely had time to enter the details of Edward's recovery in her journal and hide it away before there was another knock, this time at the back door.

'Tis just I, Katherine,' came a voice and Ursula hurriedly unbolted the door and let her friend in. As soon as the door was opened a few inches, the gull appeared and with a loud cry it slipped through the gap and ran across to the fireplace where it stood in front of the warm embers.

'What is this?' Katherine shrieked as she jumped back. 'Where has this bird come from?' She flapped her skirts towards the gull. 'Out you horrible thing, get away from here.'

'I do not know where it came from but it arrived at my door and it keeps reappearing as if it lives here,' Ursula admitted. She shrugged her shoulders. 'It does not seem to be doing any harm but it cannot come in my house.' Bending down she held her skirts out and wafted them up and down, ushering the bird back towards the door whilst behind her Katherine picked up an empty cooking pot and a wooden ladle and began to bang the two together. With a grumbling noise in its throat and a stretch of its wings at them both the bird walked back out. Ursula slammed the door shut and bolted it as if the bird were able to lift the latch. Looking out of the window she could see it had flown to the fence around her vegetable garden and was watching the house.

'That was most unpleasant,' Katherine said as she sat down in the living room. 'My legs are shaking. I have come to see you though because you were not at church again. Are you unwell?'

'I am in good health,' Ursula explained as she poured them both beakers of ale. 'But I am trying to keep myself inconspicuous because I have come to the unwanted attention of the physician who has moved to Great Mayling with his sister, having left his ailing wife and his two daughters in Cambridge. He wishes to bed me and although I told him I do not want anything to do with him, still he is sniffing around.' She relayed the events from when she'd visited the farm. 'And he's been here too, I am certain; someone was prowling at my back door. I also suspect he has someone watching me, hiding out there on the common. I can feel something, eyes trailing my every movement. I can no longer attend church because he is likely to be there and I do not wish to encounter him.'

'You must not be afraid,' Katherine exclaimed. 'Do not allow him to rule your life. You have fought hard for the right to live here on your own without fear, do not forsake that. I shall ask Paul to speak with him, to tell him to leave you be.'

'Please do not,' Ursula urged. 'I am not afraid, but I do not wish him to be riled with Paul or yourself.' She took a long draught of ale and could feel her hands trembling slightly at the thought of him. His behaviour had frightened her, despite her words to the contrary. 'Oliver Bruton is a different class of man and his intentions are not the same. The village men came calling to court me, to ask for my hand in marriage and I refused. You know why I rejected them.'

Her friend nodded. The two of them having been childhood friends; she'd witnessed the results of Ursula's father's fists.

'But Oliver does not care about that, he already has a wife. He wants to have my body for which he would give me his protection and pay me in gold. I do not need his shelter. I have looked after myself until now, and I shall continue to do so. And I do not want his coin either, I earn enough for what I need from my medications, my palm reading and my skills as a midwife.'

'I hope you are able to return to church soon,' Katherine said. 'Your soul needs to be at peace with the Lord.'

'As soon as I am certain that I can move freely about the village again then I shall attend once more,' Ursula assured her, 'but at the moment I am more concerned with my earthly body, than my eternal spirit.'

'And now also you have that strange bird hanging around,' Katherine said as she got up to leave, peering out of the scullery window. 'I must be away to serve dinner for my family. Sometimes I envy your solitary life with no one to attend to but yourself.'

'Except that, as at present, being on my own feels unsafe,' Ursula said as she too got to her feet. 'Although not as perilous as being with a man may be.'

After Katherine left, Ursula locked the door again. As she carried the cups back into the scullery she instinctively looked out for the gull, and whilst doing so a movement caught her eye. She thought she'd spotted a deer lifting its head from grazing, but then she realised it was a man partly bent over as he began running through the long grass. Everything she'd told Katherine she was frightened of, was unfolding in front of her.

Opening her back door she stepped out just at the moment

the man stood up and looked across at her, their eyes meeting. Immediately, as if he'd been shot, he fell to the ground and out of sight but not before she'd seen who it was. Daniel Hooke was a tinker who'd arrived in the area from the north of England the year before. Some people said he was a murderer on the run, although recently a wife and children had joined him and they lived in a ramshackle house, little more than a barn, close to Peddars Way. He travelled between villages selling ribbons and small household implements and was exactly the sort of person who would be happy to spy on a woman for a handful of groats from the local doctor.

Ursula stood and waited until eventually, as she knew she would be, she was rewarded for her silent patience. Tentatively Daniel re-emerged from the undergrowth again, a little way from the cottage. She'd guessed by the movement of the vegetation as it swayed from side to side that he'd been crawling along out of sight, but he hadn't known about her ability to stand quietly, watching and waiting, like the heron which spent hours on the rocks on the shoreline.

He looked at her as if he were a rabbit caught in her gaze. As though he were bewitched by her. He didn't seem to know where else to look and stepping forward a little she called out, 'I hope you are paid well for your spying, Daniel!' His mouth opened and closed and no noise came out, but she could see from his expression and the way his face coloured that she'd been correct in her assumption. He turned and ran across the common towards Great Mayling.

* * *

After she'd seen proof that her suspicions about being watched were correct, Ursula was wary each time she left her cottage but she didn't see Daniel or Oliver again, and slowly she began to relax a little.

The measles epidemic continued to scourge through the area, although thankfully the two children at the farm got better. The youngest lost her sense of hearing though, and Ursula had to inform Betty that regrettably she could offer no cure for that. Other children in the village did not fare so well and, despite her ministrations, one of Ruth and John's children at the smithy lay for a week without eating, becoming more and more listless, until she was like a sack of bones, laid beneath a coverlet on a truckle bed in the corner of the main living room. Her eyes looked huge in her gaunt face, her cheekbones casting shadows on her skin, which was scarlet with the rash.

Ursula visited the house frequently and she arrived one morning with a tincture of borage when a scream from another of the children alerted her to the sick girl, who was having a seizure – her body shaking, eyes rolled back in her head with blood dribbling from the corner of her mouth.

Kneeling on the floor, Ursula laid cloths infused with a rosemary lotion across her forehead. Where previously she'd been clammy and warm, now her skin was burning. The fit lasted several minutes while Ruth stood at the end of the bed crying quietly, rocking the new baby who was now back home from his stay with the wet nurse, in her arms. Eventually the child lay still, her breathing shallow. Ursula wrung out the cloths and told Ruth to rinse them in cold water so she could continue to swab the girl down and try and prevent another seizure.

'Let her sleep now,' Ursula said, 'but I cannot promise she will awaken. I believe the sickness has embedded itself in her head and she may not recover. Only time will tell. See here,' she took a small pottery bottle from her satchel, 'this medicine may help, just a sip every few hours. Do not give her too much though, it is very potent. I do not know if you will be able to get her to take any though unless she rouses a little. She slumbers too deeply at present.'

Leaving the house Ursula felt sad, her head and shoulders drooping. The prognosis for the child was poor, she'd seen it before. There was nowhere else for the other children to go either, nobody wanted to possibly welcome the disease into their home. John paused in his hammering of a horse shoe and looked across at her but she couldn't give him the news she knew he was hoping for. She turned the corners of her mouth down and shook her head. It could go either way and from his short nod she knew he understood her gesture.

When she arrived home the gull was stood on the end of her workbench.

'What are you doing in here? In fact, how did you get in?' Opening the front door, she waved her arms but this time, as if becoming more used to her efforts to get rid of it, the bird simply stood and watched her. Finally, in exasperation, she picked it up, its speckled, pale brown feathers soft beneath her fingers and its body warm and much lighter than she'd anticipated. Holding it out with straight arms in front with her hands around its wings to stop them flapping, like she did with the chickens, she opened the door further with her foot and threw it into the air, where it flew away slowly until it landed on her garden fence. She slammed the door shut before looking around, wondering how it had entered her house.

There were no doors or windows open downstairs and running up to her bedroom she felt a draught before she got there. Her bedroom window, which she was certain had been shut when she went out, was now wide open. She closed it again and placed a baton across the back of the shutters.

Downstairs she went into the scullery to inspect some

pansies she was distilling in a glass flask. A year ago, before Oliver had arrived and started using Daniel for his own devices, she'd asked the peddler to fetch it when he'd gone to King's Lynn where he bought the goods he hawked from the ships which arrived at the port.

He also collected the London pamphlets from which the villagers learned about what was going on outside their small world. There was a substantial increase in the number of leaflets now being printed and they were getting news of the war, which still continued with battles and skirmishes across the country, within a week of the fighting happening. It didn't make encouraging reading for the royalists, and the number of young men who'd been taken from the village to fight was a worry.

Taking out her journal she dipped her quill in the ink. The end was beginning to scratch where it was becoming worn and she hoped that she could find a suitable replacement feather. Perhaps her new gull friend could oblige.

23

1646

Sunday morning dawned bright with the warm, sweet scent of vegetation, tansy, meadowsweet and bay, drying in the summer sun. The sky, so wide that it stretched into the distance as if dipping down to touch the end of the world, was a pale blue with stripes of fine delicate cloud. It was a good day for the fishermen, Ursula thought, as she pulled on a clean head covering and added a linen square as a partlet to the top of her gown, covering her bare skin. If Oliver was in church, she didn't want to be showing what he was missing out on. She wondered about whether she could purchase a square lace-trimmed collar favoured by the Puritans, as Anne had worn. It wouldn't be cheap though and she could no longer ask Daniel to acquire anything for her, not when any requests would undoubtedly reach Oliver's ears.

Arriving just as the bells finished ringing, Ursula slipped into the back pew and dropped to her knees, before surreptitiously looking around at the other members of the congregation. Almost immediately she spotted the back of Oliver's square head with its thatch of pale blond hair at the front of the nave. Beside him sat Anne in a dark green gown and matching hood.

The long service stretched to almost two hours as the rector extolled the importance of innocence and virtue, which Ursula guessed Oliver wasn't listening to, and as the final blessing was being delivered, she scooted along the pew she was sitting in. Pulling the door open slightly she slipped through and ran around the side of the church to the graveyard at the back, weaving her way amongst the headstones. If Oliver had any idea she'd attended the service, then he may be looking out for her. She suspected at that moment he must still be following Lord Mayling down the aisle. If she'd left the church via the lychgate onto the village street she'd have been visible during the few minutes it took to reach her cottage. But this way she could hide beneath the yew tree in the corner of the churchyard, its ancient boughs creating a small green grotto suffused with an astringent, sharp scent of sap. Once everyone left, she'd return to her cottage.

She thought her idea was foolproof, however she hadn't envisaged that a group of the village boys would run to the tree to hide as part of a game they were playing. Before she could put her finger to her mouth to keep them from calling out, they were followed by Ruth who exclaimed loudly as she saw Ursula.

'What are you doing here?' she asked. 'Were you taken unwell during the service?'

The noise alerted the other parishioners who were still passing the time of day in the churchyard. The sabbath was the only day when they had slightly fewer chores to attend to, and chatting with their neighbours after communion was a pleasant occupation.

'Who is it?' The rector had heard the noise and was walking

down the path, his robes billowing out behind him as if he were a ship in full sail. Everyone else had also turned to look. With a red face, Ursula stepped out from her hiding place trying to think of an excuse as to why she was there. What had seemed like a perfect escape had now proved not to be so. She latched onto Ruth's concern for her health.

'I was feeling unwell at the end of the service,' she explained putting her hand against her stomach as if that may persuade the others to believe her and give her a wide berth, 'so I came here to sit in the shade until I felt recovered enough to walk home.' With a worried look on his face the rector stepped away, but from behind him Oliver came into view and his face said everything the rector's did not. His slightly greasy skin was slowly turning a deep red and his sparse, almost invisible brows were drawn over his eyes. Ursula noticed that he was alternately clenching his fists then stretching his fingers out. She glanced at Anne who seemingly had no idea what her brother was thinking as she smiled with her head on one side as if sympathetic to Ursula feeling unwell.

'Let me help you home,' Oliver said, his voice booming so loudly that nobody else, even if they had wished to, would choose to argue with him.

'An excellent idea, the physician can ensure you are not seriously unwell. I am sure that on our Lord's day, he will not charge you.' Having finished his speech, unknowingly committing Ursula to the very fate she was desperate to avoid, the rector smiled at Oliver and raised his eyebrows waiting for confirmation.

'Of course, let me help you, mistress.' Oliver almost knocked the other man off his feet as he swept past and gripped Ursula's upper arm to help her walk. Only the two of them knew that he was holding her so tightly she couldn't have pulled free even if she'd any thoughts of escaping. She lived next door, where else could she go?

Oliver was walking with long strides and Ursula's feet were barely able to keep up making her stumble a couple of times. Even Anne noticed that.

'Brother, you are going too fast,' she called out as she tried to hurry behind them. 'Remember, Ursula is unwell. She cannot walk as fast as you.' It appeared that Oliver wasn't interested in his sister's opinion.

'I just want to get her inside as soon as possible,' he said over his shoulder, not slowing down. 'It may be the hot day that has made her feel ill. After all she was beneath the shade of the tree, was she not? Let us help her inside her home where it will be cooler.'

His excuse seemed to have been accepted by Anne who didn't say another word but just followed silently as Oliver almost dragged Ursula to her back door.

'Key?' he growled.

'It is not locked.' Ursula's voice came out in a whisper. She may not have felt ill when she was first discovered hiding, but now she did. Her heart was racing and her legs hurt from the speed at which she'd been forced to walk. Oliver opened the back door and pushed her in. Immediately Ursula knew she had another visitor, she could see a pale feather floating to the floor. From the parlour she heard the now-familiar cackle of a gull.

'There's a bird in your house,' Oliver said, his surprise making his voice come out as a squeak. Behind them Anne made a sound of distress and she stepped back into the garden.

'It has perhaps come in through my bedroom window, I have been sleeping with it open during these hot nights.' Ursula managed to make herself sound as surprised as the other two, even though she wasn't. Oliver strode through the house to the front door from where the gull was ejected, hopping and flapping to get away from Oliver's boots made of thick, heavy leather.

Once through the scullery into the main room she sank onto her chair. If Oliver or Anne wanted to stay, they'd have to sit on her work stool.

'Let me get you some ale.' Anne had come back into the house now the bird had been evicted and was looking around for a jug and beaker.

'That is not necessary, sister.' Oliver put his hand on her shoulder. 'Until we know whether Ursula is suffering from anything dangerous, you must not remain here a moment longer. This woman visits the homes of the sick just as I do, risking our own health and it seems Ursula may not have been so lucky evading illness this time. She has been treating children in the locale who suffer with the measles. Leave now and return home. Take the stable lad with you, I can ride back later alone. I will return in time for dinner, tell Cook to delay it until one o'clock.'

At the mention of possible sickness, Anne had gone paler than her usual white countenance and she hurried back through the door to where their horses were now waiting outside on the street. Oliver watched her through the window, having to bend his knees slightly as the windows were low in the wall. In the silence they both heard hooves cantering into the distance.

'I was intending to visit you this morning after church, so it is fortuitous that our paths have crossed.' Oliver pulled the stool over and perched on it, his knees touching hers. 'I had a missive from Lady Mayling informing me that your potions saved Edward from his bout of the measles and that in future she will be requesting you to attend any ailments that the family may suffer from. This is a loss to my purse, and my reputation and it angers me.' He pushed his face, which had slowly been reddening, close to hers, making her attempt to stretch backwards away from him. Except there was nowhere to go. His loss was her gain as she thought about the gold which now lived beneath the floorboard just inches from his foot.

'I merely treated him with simple remedies that you yourself could have procured,' she replied. 'If that is all you have come to discuss, please leave now because, as you saw, I am feeling unwell.'

'That was not the foremost reason about which I wished to speak with you. Do you think I believe the pretence you enacted as you hid yourself beneath the tree? Maybe it was because you cursed Daniel Hooke and you do not want to be seen by those who suspect you. I do not know how you dare sully the Lord's house with your presence.'

His accusation broke her silence as he no doubt intended. 'What are you talking about Daniel being cursed? I saw him just last week and he was perfectly well. Enough to be out in the fields watching my movements and running back to you, he told me everything so there is no point denying it.'

'That is most unfortunate then,' Oliver replied, 'because Daniel suffered a paralysis of his body last week. He was found on the Peddars Way and has been unable to speak since, nor can he walk or use one of his arms. And indeed, he was seen by a labourer speaking with you just hours previously. It would seem like a curse to me. And I can assure you that, if I were asked, I would have to inform the constables I did not send Daniel – or anyone else for that matter – to watch you.'

'I have not cursed him, nor anyone else!' Ursula sprang to her feet holding her palms up in front of herself as if in protection. 'You talk in riddles Master Bruton. You are a physician, surely you can see he is ill?'

'Indeed, I am a medical man and that is how I can recognise when an illness is nothing natural, and Daniel's is thus so. I do not wish to put about talk that you may be responsible, you can see how being under my protection would save you from any such allegations.'

'There cannot be accusations without proof, I am simply a woman who makes herbal remedies and attends births. In this village and the surrounds, I am acknowledged and respected for my skills, nobody would believe I have brought about this illness.' Ursula's words came out in a stream as she tried to take in what he was insinuating. His pursuit of her had taken a frighteningly darker turn. 'I am no witch!' she shouted at him before pushing her hands against her open mouth, her eyes wide. Now she'd said the word, it hung between them, a quivering indictment.

'Ursula,' his voice had taken on an exaggerated patient tone, 'whatever you say in denial will not be believed against the words of a physician, a gentleman. Do you now see why you need me? And it comes at a very small cost as I have told you. Are you ready to change your mind?'

'No, I am not, nor will I ever do so. Nobody will agree with you,' Ursula spat. Although even as the words left her mouth she wasn't convinced of her position. Certainly, everyone in the village knew her but words whispered in ears had a habit of rolling like a ball of snow increasing and growing bigger the further it travelled. Her friends and neighbours may start to believe what they were hearing. Her fingers were pulsating.

She refused to be bullied by this man though, she had to stand her ground, or all would be lost. Let him throw around all the threats he liked. However frightened he made her feel, she wouldn't let him see it. An image of her mother, glassy eyes open, a pool of dark blood spreading around her head, flashed in front of her eyes. She looked momentarily to the stain on the hearth, as if its permanency was there to remind her. To warn her.

'I have told you before, I will come to no arrangement with you. I am not interested and nor shall I ever be so. I tell you again, please leave and do not return.' She knew how futile her words were. Empty. So far he'd shown no sign of backing down from his demands, and going to the back door, she threw it open.

'My patience erodes with each passing day,' he snarled as he walked past her, stopping to push his body against hers. He smelled of sweat and horse and faintly of incense from the thurible which swung at the front of the church. Some of the old church ways still clung on in villages where the winds of change blew slowly, and the rector was reluctant to give up all his popish traditions, despite what the missives from Norwich cathedral decreed. Ursula turned her head to one side and held her breath, not saying a word. 'I suggest you think about what I have just told you. Next time I visit I expect a more hospitable welcome. Or I will begin to spread tales. Before long I shall take what I wish, and you will have given me permission to do so.'

Slamming the door behind him, Ursula watched him stomp up and down the paths around her garden instead of simply leaving. What was he doing? He aimed his boot at a couple of her chickens but they soon strutted out of the way, and he kicked at the tops of her onions. She could see where he was heading and she remembered his comments about her dark bed where she grew the shadowy plants, those which were dangerous. Being a physician, Oliver had recognised what they were.

He stopped for a moment and looked as if he were going to turn around and walk back towards the house, but then he crouched down to examine them more closely. Wolfsbane, foxglove and hellebore, they all thrived there. Plants which any herbalist may require from time to time and not remotely suspicious, other than to those who were looking to make accusations of witchcraft. As he stood up again Oliver looked straight at her and she felt a hard lump in her throat as she tried to swallow, her face flushing. Suddenly she felt more threatened than ever before.

24

2024

Later the same day, Adrianna found herself wandering across to the pub in search of company. And a glass of wine. Being on her own all day, something that only a month ago had been what she wanted, now felt lonely and she looked forward to seeing a friendly face.

'Tell me everything, what have you discovered?' Jess said. 'I love the thought that there's a historical mystery attached to the cottage. I can't wait to go back to university, working behind a bar isn't a life goal, really. In fact, I've already been looking, there's a degree course in forensic archaeology at the UEA that I'd love to do.'

'I haven't found out as much as I had hoped,' Adrianna admitted. 'I definitely need some help if you have time?'

'I thought you'd never ask!' Jess clapped her hands together. 'I didn't want to intrude after you saying you are here to take some time out but I've been dying to help with the investigations. How about you come over early this evening and we can get our heads together? I'm up in the flat around seven o'clock usually, when I put Malachi to bed.'

'It's a date.' Adrianna grinned.

* * *

When she arrived back at the pub that evening with the few notes she had to discuss with Jess about what she could do next, Louise directed her upstairs to the flat.

In the corner of the living room were several plastic tubs piled up with brightly coloured toys but the rest of the room was sparsely decorated in shades of grey with occasional yellow cushions and hand thrown pottery pieces. 'Malachi is asleep, so hopefully we won't get interrupted,' Jess said.

'It must be difficult being a single parent,' Adrianna said.

'Best thing, being on my own with him really,' Jess replied. 'His dad was not a nice piece of work. He was lovely when we first met but then he was forever messaging me, wanting to know what I was doing. Every hour of every day, even though I was mostly in the university library if I wasn't with him. It became uncomfortable, then oppressive and then it felt more than that. Dangerous. So I came back home; it's not so hard with Mum helping. And now I know that his dad's no longer at uni, I can return when Malachi goes to school. Anyway, that's enough of my life history, show me what you've discovered so far.'

Adrianna got out her notebook and explained everything she'd found, happy to have someone so much more enthusiastic than Rick was.

'Do you think there was a rumour a witch lived there?' she asked Jess. 'The journal, and the witch marks, there must be a link.' She stopped herself from mentioning the strange things which had been happening since she arrived at the cottage, even though she was certain they were even more of a connection.

'And where can I go from here? I don't know what else I can do to investigate further.'

'I would put money on there being a witch as more than a rumour. The bricked-up cat, herbal remedy recipes and did you say she was also a midwife? And the witch marks at the church in a straight line with where the stone is,' Jess remembered. 'That can't just be a coincidence. Have you tried the local archives? There's a big Norfolk one at County Hall in Norwich. You can make an appointment and see if they have anything useful. If it's a morning while Malachi is at nursery, I may be able to arrange for one of the other mums to collect him and then I could come with you, if you don't mind me tagging along?'

'That would be brilliant, thank you.' Adrianna instinctively gave her new friend a hug.

Jess looked out of the window. 'We've got about thirty minutes before it starts getting dark, shall we go over and see if we can find any other marks or clues in the churchyard?'

She didn't need to be asked twice, and grabbing her jacket, Adrianna followed Jess out of the back door. She heard raised voices when Jess told Louise they were going out and asking her to listen out for Malachi. It was her own enthusiasm encouraging Jess to get involved and she felt guilty, but she said nothing, keen to use her friend's expertise.

Walking around a graveyard at dusk wasn't the top of Adrianna's list of activities she most wanted to try, but she was excited to see if they could find anything else which indicated there had once been a witch living in her cottage. Or rather, a woman who was thought of as one.

They stood beside the hexafoils carved in the church porch and turned towards the cottage garden.

'Given what we know about the line from one set of marks to the next,' Jess said, 'I wonder if there are any pertinent graves along it.' They began to make their way across the grass, once again grateful to Tom for keeping it short and easy to walk on. But the stones were just those of local people and mostly from the eighteenth and nineteenth centuries.

Reaching the dry-stone wall, Adrianna looked at the flat stones along the top. How long had they been here? They were covered in moss with bindweed and ivy climbing up through the stones but she began to pull the foliage away with her fingers, scraping the ends on the stone, filling her nails with mud. Jess started to join in despite Adrianna telling her not to because of the mess she was already making of her own hands. Before long they'd cleared a stretch of the wall adjacent to where they could see the stone in her garden.

As she brushed the last of the bits away, Adrianna said 'bingo' under her breath, stepping to one side so Jess could see what she'd found. Jess was more exuberant and squealed, throwing her arms around Adrianna. Before them, on the top of the wall, in the same line as the church and the stone, was carved a series of interlinked circles and stars similar to those on the one she'd found.

'I'm wondering,' Adrianna turned to Jess, 'whether the stone I uncovered has something buried underneath.'

'I know it seems a bit odd it just being there, but it was probably just placed there as a warning.' Jess said. 'You could do some digging though, it won't do any harm and if you don't find anything you can just fill the hole in again.'

Adrianna wasn't sure whether she'd further antagonise what she'd already disturbed, the presence she felt both inside the house and out, but she didn't mention that. 'It's possibly been hidden under the brambles and vegetation I cut back for decades, maybe even centuries. I read online that witches wouldn't have been buried in consecrated ground, but next to the church wall was possible. The symbols on here,' she rubbed her fingers over them, 'together with those on the church make me think they're pointing towards my stone. I'll start by digging in the archives in Norwich, and if I uncover anything, then I'll start digging for real.'

What she didn't admit was that she was beginning to become obsessed and she didn't know why. She was now certain she'd been meant to find the stone, it had been waiting for her, as though she was possessed by something or someone who wanted their story to be told. She caught her lower lip between her teeth at the thought.

As she entered through the back door of the cottage, she could instantly sense there was something different, although she couldn't work out for a moment what it was. Walking through to the living room she realised it was the same smell she'd noticed when she'd opened the cupboard the first time. Spices? No, that wasn't it. Herbs, the room had a pungent earthy smell. The sharp sting of mint and rosemary, together with something softer like sage, reminding her of the garden centre when she'd sniffed all the pots deciding which to buy. It was bizarre, and she looked around the room and in the kitchen to check if there was a herb she'd forgotten to plant, but there was nothing. What she could smell had a slight burned scent too.

Opening the cupboard door, the fragrance was stronger, just as she knew it would be. Quickly, she washed her hands and lifted out the journal laying it on the table. She untied the straps and opened the leather covers and waited to see if anything would happen, if she'd be visited again by a manifestation of some sort, but there was nothing. The corners of the room held no unnatural drifting shadows or darkness, she couldn't feel a chill creeping across the floor and the hairs along her neck were at ease.

As if being led to do so, she began to decipher the next passage, her heart beating faster. This entry held a sharp tangible fear that the previous ones had not. If she'd doubted it before, now she knew. She was being made to continue with this, she no longer had a choice. To put right a wrong from centuries before.

A plague of measles has reached the village, I hope my remedies will save the children afflicted but I fear that one of farmer's children may not survive as she once was. A child at the smithy is succumbing to the fever from which they will not return, but Lord Mayling's son has now recovered, praise be to God.

I am troubled still with the attention of the new physician, Oliver Bruton, who will not take my refusal of a carnal acquaintance. He and the power he wields frightens me though I do not show him. I believe he has now sent the peddler Daniel Hooke to watch me. A spy in our midst. He should be working for Cromwell's army where he would doubtless earn more silver than Doctor Bruton pays him.

Written this day the fifteenth day of June in the year of our Lord 1646.

She went online to see if she could find any records of Daniel Hooke, but as she suspected, there was nothing. It was unlikely, a seventeenth-century peddler. Whilst on her phone she noticed a WhatsApp message from Rick at half past eleven the night before, replying to her final goodnight message. They seemed to be ships passing in the night at present, with her being outside from first light and him up until all hours at night.

Quickly checking her emails, she immediately saw one from her workplace. Even the company name made her feel wobbly and she wiped her sweaty palms down her pyjamas. And it was from the department boss, James Sewell, one of the company partners, which made her feel even more sick. Someone must have drawn his attention to just what a mess she'd been making of her job for the past six months. In fact, it was closer to a year since things had started to fall apart. She slammed the lid of her laptop down without opening it and ran upstairs to the bathroom to throw up her cup of tea.

How was she ever going to return to work when even an email filled her with dread? She just couldn't face it. Once she'd thought she was one of the big players but now she knew differently. Rick had been right when he'd told her she was fighting too hard to prove she could do something which deep inside she knew she couldn't. Every day was a battle to keep the anxiety under control. Stress, which had started like a little worm, was now a giant octopus, its tendrils reaching out and filling her entire body, suffocating her.

25

1646

A series of events followed Oliver's visit which greatly increased Ursula's fears.

The first thing to occur was Rebecca arriving on her doorstep a second time, not eight weeks after her previous visit. Her face was flushed as if she'd been running, wisps of hair escaping the tight confines of the kerchief covering her hair. She was leaning on the door frame bending over as Ursula opened the door. Behind her, Ursula noticed the now-familiar herring gull stepping carefully around her garden, watching what was going on.

'Rebecca?' she said. 'Come in and sit down and catch your breath. Are you in need of help?' She suspected the girl hadn't run through the village to tell her that she was now with child.

'Tis my Sam,' Rebecca gasped as she tried to catch her breath. 'He was getting ready to leave for work, he said his belly was hurting him and then he fell to the floor writhing and howling like a kicked dog. Please, you must come quickly.' She turned and despite her breathlessness she began to run back towards her cottage which lay at the other end of the village. Snatching her satchel from the workbench Ursula followed, hurrying to keep up. With every thud as her feet hit the floor she remembered what she'd seen on Rebecca's hand. She hadn't thought it might come to pass quite so soon and hoped whatever had struck Samuel down was something she could easily cure.

He was laid on the stone floor of their scullery moaning quietly, his head in the lap of an old woman Ursula recognised as his mother. Curled up in a ball, his arms were wrapped across his stomach and beside him on the floor was a pool of vomit flecked with red blood. Ursula could see his face was pale and clammy.

'Sam, can you hear me?' she asked as she knelt down beside him. 'Can you tell me where you feel the pain?' The only response she got was another moan.

'Has he had any other symptoms these past few days?' she asked Rebecca. 'Has he complained of sickness or pain?'

'Yes,' she nodded, 'he was sick twice and said his stomach was hurting but then he seemed to become well again, I thought it was just something he had eaten. He is often inclined to help himself to anything he sees on the fire even if it isn't fully cooked.'

'So, what ails him?' Samuel's mother snapped, seeming displeased with this less than kind observation of her son. 'He needs a cure and quickly, you can see how much pain he is in.'

'Can you get him onto his bed if I help you?' Ursula asked. In truth she didn't know at that moment what sickened him, she needed some thinking time and also somewhere it would be easier to examine him. Besides, her legs were hurting where she was knelt on the cold, hard floor.

It wasn't easy for the three women to carry him to the truckle bed in the corner where his mother usually slept, but it would have been impossible to take him up the ladder to his and Rebecca's room. Immediately Ursula recognised the bed from her vision and her stomach lurched. He was not helping them in any way and groaning he allowed his feet to drag across the floor behind him as they half carried and half pulled him to the mattress where he lay down, still curled up. There was a smell of stale vomit on his shirt. Ursula tried to press on his stomach to determine where the pain was, but he began to shriek and then wouldn't let her near him, batting her away with his arms. She had no easy diagnosis for them.

'I do not yet know what troubles him,' she admitted. 'I can give him something for the pain, perhaps once he has rested he will be able to tell us more. It is strange that his previous symptoms went away and then he suddenly became like this.' She indicated where he lay in front of them. 'Might he have eaten mushrooms from the fields?' She knew that by adulthood the villagers all knew which fungus could be eaten and which should be left well alone, but she wondered if he'd somehow made an error.

'Like I say, he would forage from anywhere,' Rebecca replied, 'but he knows what he can have and what should be left untouched.'

'Try and get him to sip some ale,' she said, 'and give him this.' She removed a flask containing a syrup from her bag. 'It is a purge,' she explained, 'I believe he may have eaten something that is not kind to his stomach.' She knew better than to mention the word poison even though she suspected what he had consumed was exactly that. And what she'd just handed over could also possibly take him close to death, but whatever he was suffering from appeared to be doing that anyway.

The second event which happened was even more concerning than Samuel's illness. And it was brought about by Oliver Bruton. Even thinking about him now made Ursula feel nauseous, her palms damp and cold.

Her hopes that he'd leave her alone were now just in vain, he meant to have her, or do her harm if he could not. His first wish was never going to come to fruition without a fight and she was now worried of what he may do next. Yet at the same time she could feel her resolve grow, a power which had laid buried, building a strength in her breast. She'd chosen a life so she wouldn't live in fear, and whilst her waking hours were now stained around the edges with a tarnish of apprehension, she knew she was rising up to be equal to the man. She would not let him triumph.

One of Daniel Hooke's children came knocking at her door asking if she'd visit his father, who was still indisposed with the condition Oliver had described. She asked why she was being requested when they already had the doctor treating him. The child wouldn't meet her eye as he explained the doctor had only visited once and hadn't been seen since and his mother had no idea when his father would be healthy enough to work again. They needed him recovered before they all starved.

Ursula wasn't sure what she could do if the doctor couldn't provide a medication, but without a second thought she agreed and the child scampered away leaving Ursula to make her way alone to the shack where the family lived.

Inside the wooden house it was dim with a blue-grey haze from the smoking fire which didn't have a chimney, simply a hole in the roof for the smoke to leave by. It didn't appear much was leaving that way and almost immediately Ursula began to cough, holding her arm against her mouth. The room also smelt sour and she could feel herself gagging.

Daniel was laid on the floor beneath a grubby blanket which had been chewed by an animal, or vermin, in one corner. There was a tallow candle lit beside him, the black smoke and the smell of burning animal fat adding to the miasma in the hut and making Ursula's eyes run. Although Daniel was watching her, she could see that only one side of his face was mobile, the other side sloping downwards as if the skin was falling away from his skull.

'Can he speak?' she asked his wife but the woman shook her head.

'Nor can he walk,' she added. 'We have to drag him to the pot. He can still use his other hand so he is able to feed himself, but often his food just drops from his mouth.' She indicated Daniel's jerkin marked with dried food stains. 'Please tell me that you can help him.' She gripped Ursula's hands. 'The children are not old enough to go out working and earn what Daniel did.'

Getting to her feet, Ursula went to the open door to escape the smell in the room and breathe in some fresh air for a moment. She knew there was no cure for this, only time would help him improve and sometimes that didn't happen. Nobody knew what caused it, it was similar to the falling sickness, a palsy which often left a person permanently lame. No wonder Oliver had walked away and left the poor man to lie and rot in his miserable home.

As if by thinking about him would bring Oliver forth, like the devil he was, he stepped out from behind an oak tree in the clearing beside the shack. She chided herself for not paying more attention to the sounds and smells outside the cottage instead of just trying to clear her lungs of the contagion from inside.

'Have you come to look at your handiwork?' he asked. She noticed he was talking through a barely open mouth as if he knew what would hit him if he breathed in any of the stench emanating through the open door.

'I have no idea what you are talking about,' Ursula retorted.

'Daniel's son came asking me to visit. But, as you well know, there is nothing that can be done for this man.'

'Boy, come out here.' Oliver opened his mouth wide enough to bark out a command. The child who'd called for Ursula slipped around the edge of the door, although Ursula noticed he stayed as far away from Oliver as he could.

'Did you go and ask the remedy woman to visit your father? Did your mother send you?' As he barked out his questions Ursula felt her stomach drop. She began to realise she'd been lured there under false pretences which explained why Oliver had suddenly appeared. He knew she was coming and had doubtless been watching the cottage waiting for her to reappear.

'No sir, I did not,' the child replied. His voice wavered and he looked at Ursula quickly before looking away. The boy was lying, but his fear of Oliver was palpable. She'd never prove it.

'Why did you call me here?' she asked Oliver, raising her eyebrows and putting her hands on her hips. 'You know I cannot do anything for this man.'

'I did nothing,' Oliver said with a sly smile. 'It is obvious that having cursed Hooke you'd return to inspect your handiwork. Did you direct the devil to do this work for you? Do you have a familiar to do your evil bidding? Because we both know that you do, for I have seen it in your home.'

'You speak in riddles,' Ursula snapped. 'You have seen no such thing, I have no familiar.' As the words left her mouth though she realised to what Oliver was alluding. She watched as a smile spread across his face.

'A gull, as big as a swan, living in your house with you.' He spat the words out. She still had no idea why the bird kept appearing, but what he was saying was ridiculous.

'It must have simply come in by accident through an open window and then could not escape. I have neither seen it before, nor since.' In her pockets Ursula crossed her fingers against evil spirits as she lied. The gull had followed her part of the way here but thankfully the lad who'd been sent to fetch her hadn't noticed. She could hear Daniel's wife breathing behind her, listening to everything she said.

'You cursed my husband?' Her voice was hoarse, a result of all the smoke she was breathing in day in, day out.

'Of course I did not!' Ursula said as she turned to face the woman. 'What happened to Daniel was nothing more than a sad occurrence. It has happened to others who suddenly fall ill with the one-sided lameness. He may get better but I cannot predict that. I am sorry. I do not know why the doctor engineered for me to be here, but your husband's ailment is nothing to do with me and regretfully I cannot help him.' She went to put her hand on the other woman's arm but she stepped backwards, out of reach.

'Do not come near me,' she hissed. 'Witch!'

The word hung in the air between them, a terrible accusation. Shocked, Ursula turned to Oliver to see he was wearing a satisfied smirk. Slowly it sank in that precisely what he'd wanted to happen had played out. He'd warned her he would start to unravel her life if she didn't succumb to his pressure, and now he was doing exactly that. This would be a battle as she'd never encountered before and one she was unprepared for. But fight him she would.

Without a further word she walked away from the hut and back towards the village, her breath coming in shaky gasps. Her world was beginning to close in around her, as imagined whispers and murmuring came from the trees beneath which she passed.

26

2024

After Jess's suggestion of Norfolk archive office as a useful place to begin researching, Adrianna filled in the required forms and a week later they made their way to an appointment there. They had a short wait before a young lady, who introduced herself as Hayley, took them through to a private room in which there were a couple of archive boxes placed on the desk.

'These are all the parochial records for the diocese around King's Lynn for the seventeenth century that we have,' she explained, 'although there isn't a lot there. I did also find some news pamphlets about the civil war from the same era so, just in case, I've brought those for you.' She pointed to another smaller box on a side table, on which was also a laptop. 'I'm sorry but I have to stay in here with you, I've brought my work with me though, I won't disturb you.'

'Of course, no problem.' Adrianna smiled at her as she got her notebook and pencil out of her bag. If she were in charge of such valuable documents, she also wouldn't be leaving them with anyone who'd walked in off the street, even though they'd taken proof of identity.

She and Jess opened a box and took out the files, bound with faded red ribbon and began to unfold them. At first Adrianna avidly read about every christening and burial and the comments added by priests and occasionally other interested parties. These were from the eighteenth century, and although they made fascinating reading, they weren't relevant to what she was looking for so reluctantly she put them to one side. Having already been warned the appointment was only for two hours, she needed to be more methodical. She looked over to Jess.

'Found anything helpful yet?' she asked, but Jess shook her head.

'These are early twentieth century,' she said, replacing the files into the archive box. 'Very interesting but no help to you.'

Continuing to sift through the pieces of parchment looking for dates, eventually Adrianna came to the eldest and most fragile ones dating from the early seventeenth century. There were only three sheets from Finchingham, entries in the marriage register and a list of baptisms. The writing was almost impossible to read and it took her thirty minutes to translate the marriages but the dates were forty years later than she needed, and she turned instead to the baptisms. It took a while to decipher each name, until finally she found entries for the blacksmith's children. After her work on the journal it was as if she knew these people, even though they'd lived centuries before. Then on the final one she came across an entry for a baby born at Church Cottage.

It was for a little girl, Ursula Beal, born 1620. After reading the other entries she also discovered a record for a Peter Beal, then another for Richard. She couldn't work out one of the names but she then realised that next to the entry was also one for a burial days later so it seemed to be a baby which hadn't survived the birth. A sad but frequent occurrence in that era.

She could feel her heart racing with excitement and only Hayley being in the room stopped her from squealing out loud. Someone born in 1620 would have been twenty-six at the time her journal was written. Was it possible that Ursula was the author of the papers she'd discovered? An unmarried woman earning her own living and being of an age to be attractive to a doctor who was used to having his own way when it came to women? Excitedly she explained to Jess what she'd discovered.

She also wanted to study the news sheets in the other box and a glance at her watch told her she only had forty-five minutes left. Beside her on the desk her phone began to buzz with an incoming call from Rick but she cancelled it. She'd call him later, then she could update him with the results of her research. Despite his previous apathy, she hoped that now with more conclusive information it may pique his interest.

'Are these going to be helpful?' she asked Jess, who nodded.

'By the seventeenth century printing was a commonplace way of getting knowledge out to many people. Well, those who could read, at least. These will tell us what was happening in the country at the time. There will be quite a lot about the civil war of course, but hopefully there may be something about witch trials at the time.'

The words were not easy to understand and Adrianna was pleased she'd already been transcribing at home because it did make it a little easier. She picked up the first bound sheets and studied them for a minute before whispering 'yes' under her breath. Jess looked across and raised her eyebrows. 'These also look promising,' she said, pointing to what she was looking at. She couldn't stop a wide grin spreading across her face.

There was a lot of information about Margaret Read and her trial and subsequent burning in King's Lynn but that was a few decades earlier to the one Adrianna was searching for, and she kept scanning for names or dates that might help. She noticed the name Matthew Hopkins appeared in several accounts, a man she'd already come across, the Witchfinder General, as he'd apparently proclaimed himself. His name was synonymous with the persecution of innocent women during the civil war, especially in Essex and also in Suffolk, but had he also found his way into Norfolk? She made a note on her pad to investigate that.

By the time their two hours was up they'd collated some useful, though potentially dark, information about witch trials and Adrianna was desperate to know more. Was it Ursula who was drifting through the cottage still, unable to rest? And if so, why? The thought made her feel sick.

When they got back to the village they agreed that they'd reconvene in the pub after lunch. It was mid-afternoon by the time Adrianna arrived and they sat down at a table so Jess could jump up and serve behind the bar if needed, and both went through and compared their notes from that morning. 'I don't know for certain if Ursula is the connection I'm looking for, but now we know she was born in my cottage and baptised in the church, and she may have been living in the village at the time of the East Anglia witch trials. Those marks on the stone which look like initials, I've just been to check and they do look like a U and a B. I've decided I'm going to start digging and see if there's anything under the stone.'

'What if it's that dead cat they found? Supposing that's what's buried there? I wouldn't want to find it!' Jess pulled a face at the thought.

'You're the one who wants to be an archaeologist,' Adrianna pointed out. 'You'll come across bones doing that. I don't know if I'll discover anything, but Jason has already given me permission to dig the garden and really this is just an extension of that. I have a brand-new spade so why not? It's not like I have much else to do with my time.' Saying it out loud gave her a feeling of confidence she hadn't felt for a very long time. This was something she *could* do. Nobody would be checking her work or finding fault or questioning her ability. She was going to dig a hole, there was nothing that could go wrong. And afterwards if she didn't find anything, she'd simply fill it back in again.

27

2024

It was just seven o'clock in the morning but already Adrianna was wearing her oldest pair of jeans and walking boots. She collected her spade and made her way across the garden.

She'd wondered if she was completely mad deciding to dig a hole by the witch stone, but she was convinced there was something connecting the marks and the paperwork she was steadily deciphering. They were telling a story, one that someone wanted her to understand and she was determined to uncover its secrets.

Besides, if she was digging in the garden she wasn't in the house where her laptop was mocking her for her resistance in opening the email from work and reading its contents. If they'd decided to sack her would they do it by email? No, she told herself, they'd have to at least invite her to a meeting. Perhaps that was what it was about.

When she'd finally spoken to Rick the previous night, she'd tentatively admitted that she was going to do some digging, having to hold her phone away from her ear as he'd laughed uproariously.

'I know,' she giggled, 'I know nothing about it but I don't think I can mess *this* up.'

'It wouldn't surprise me,' Rick answered. 'Don't you need some kind of permission? I told you that all this research was a stupid idea but now maybe it's getting beyond a joke.' His previous joviality had disappeared. 'You'll end up doing something stupid.'

'It's fine,' she reassured him. 'I don't need permission other than from my landlord and he's said I can do whatever I want. I'm not wrecking the place.'

'I'm sorry but I think it sounds mad. And you know how you've been, I'm just worried this is an unhealthy obsession.' His voice dropped an octave and became gentler. 'Please don't go back to that dark place, darling,' he said.

'I promise, this is not the same at all,' she said. Although she could feel her previous excitement seeping away. Agreeing to give it some more thought, she said goodnight, wishing in hindsight she hadn't told him her plans.

Despite what she'd told him, she knew nothing would stop her now, and the physical act of digging gave her a boost. Soon she was stripping off her hoodie, the hair around her face beginning to stick to her skin with sweat as she tied it up in an untidy bun. She was starting to enjoy herself, this was something which she couldn't fail at, there was no right or wrong to digging a hole. No one looking over her shoulder or sending her emails and copying in the whole department about something she'd made a mess of. No one questioning her ability to uphold her position. If only her job was creating holes, she'd never need to worry again.

The gull, now a frequent visitor, was once again in attendance, this time sitting on the edge of the undergrowth behind her. She hadn't seen him arrive but she knew before she turned around that he'd be there. Watching her. Instead of making her feel uneasy as he first had, now she found herself looking out for him, a soothing presence. An ally. A familiar.

After an hour of digging, she'd made a hole four feet square and about eighteen inches deep in the stony soil but hadn't found anything other than an old piece of broken pottery which she put to one side. Her arms felt as though they were on fire and her shoulders were hurting. She couldn't deny she was disappointed. If someone had buried a cat, surely they wouldn't make a bigger grave than this? Maybe she was digging in the wrong place and she should be closer to the stone. Her stomach growled reminding her she hadn't yet had breakfast and she decided to pause for a while.

Moving around the kitchen making some toast and a mug of tea, Adrianna was all too conscious of her laptop, still taunting her. She knew she needed to grit her teeth and read the email, so reluctantly opening her inbox, she double clicked on it. Her heart was thumping so hard she could feel it pulsing in her neck and she tried to scan the contents quickly as if that may make it more palatable.

Dear Adrianna,

First of all I apologise for contacting you whilst you're on sabbatical which I appreciate is not company policy. Unfortunately though, the department finds itself in a situation which we hope you can help us with. As the questions have been asked by external auditors, I feel that I must contact you to clear the matter up.

The email went on to detail a project she'd overseen and which it transpired the client had potentially been overcharged for. There was a discrepancy in the original contract, what had subsequently been delivered, and an excess on an invoice of over two hundred thousand pounds which they seemed to think she would know about. There was also a sentence at the end about the possibility of the police being brought in.

Adrianna knew she shouldn't have read it. From juggling several high-profile projects successfully and with dexterity, she'd got out of rhythm and dropped them all. From one tiny mental question about her own ability which had slipped into her subconscious, a supposed mistake and it had all come tumbling down, brick by brick. Project by project. She hadn't been as competent at her job as she'd believed and now there was a financial inconsistency and they thought she was responsible. Heck, she probably was. Everything at the office was like a muffled, grey, suffocating fog in her head, she was having trouble remembering the project at all even though she could remember the client and their smart West End offices. Unless she could look at the initial specifications, and her subsequent reports, she wouldn't be able to help. Quickly she replied asking what they needed of her. This couldn't be ignored.

Picking up her phone she messaged Rick and asked him when he'd next be visiting. She didn't want to tell him what was going on, she couldn't even admit it to herself. What she really wanted was for him to come and give her a hug but she knew that was completely impractical mid-week, and she didn't want to be anywhere near London, not with work visible from her panoramic living room windows. When she'd bought the flat it had been marketed on the amazing views but right now that was the last thing she wanted to see.

Rick replied almost at once promising he'd be there on Saturday afternoon. He'd been invited to a party on Friday night and he expected to be the worse for wear first thing on Saturday morning. He followed that with various drunk and laughing and vomiting emojis but for once Adrianna couldn't raise a smile.

Going back out to the garden her excitement at the hole she'd dug had waned, in fact she wondered why she'd ever thought it was a good idea. Perhaps the connection she'd felt was all in her unstable mind, maybe she'd imagined it because she wanted it to be so. Jess would want an update though so she may as well carry on. Her thoughts were in overdrive now and she hoped the emotionally undemanding excavation would be calming.

Slowly, the pile of glossy freshly cut clods continued to grow as the void deepened. The smell of damp earth filled her lungs and her hands stopped shaking, the calm she needed resting like a mantle on her. Above, dark clouds were beginning to gather, reflecting those which had crowded her head and as the first spots of rain began she decided to finish for the day. As she pulled her spade from the earth she spotted something pale that she'd just uncovered. Thinking it was another piece of pottery she leant on the spade handle and bent down to pick it up before dropping it again quickly. Not only was it not a piece of broken pot, but it looked suspiciously like a bone. One that looked too large to belong to a cat. She peered at it again wondering if she was imagining things, but it was about eight inches long, a straight piece of bone with no ends to it.

'It's probably a sheep,' she said out loud. 'This was once common grazing land.' Behind her the gull squawked loudly as it ran across the churned-up ground towards her, its outstretched wings flapping.

Going into the kitchen she collected a plastic bag and turning it inside out she put her hand inside before picking up the bone without having to touch it. The gull was still out there, squawking and agitated, hopping from the church wall to the pile of earth she'd dug up, and back again.

She left the bag beside the back door, deciding to take it to show Jess later. With the weather now having put paid to any further digging she decided to continue with her transcription of the parchments. The mystery of what happened at the cottage centuries before was dragging her in further and now she couldn't let it go. Or it wouldn't let her go, she wasn't sure any more.

Today I was visited once again by Oliver Bruton who pressures me further into entering a relationship with him and warns me of dire consequences if I continue to refuse. He tells me that Daniel Hooke has suffered from a palsy and is very ill. Oliver wishes to lay the source of this affliction at my door but I am guilty of nothing.

Written this day the nineteenth day of June in the year of our Lord 1646.

28

1646

Despite Ursula's best efforts, within the week, Samuel was dead. The purge she'd given Rebecca had done nothing and the water distilled with blackthorn flowers she'd brought just ran through him. His face became grey and gaunt and over the course of three days his body shrunk into itself until he was simply a pool of shadowed skin stretched by his bones, covered with patches of violent discolouration. His breathing became shallow and rapid and the bowls of dried lavender around the room couldn't disguise the harsh stench of rotting flesh. On the fifth day Rebecca drew back the blanket he lay under and showed her a dark mottled rash on his torso that had begun to turn black as it spread across his body. One leg and foot were weeping and starting to smell rancid, the scent of decay. And death. Ursula knew it and she was certain that the other woman knew it too.

'I have prepared a tisane of blackthorn and wood sorrel,' Ursula handed Rebecca a flask, 'but in all honesty I do not know if it will help him now. You need to encourage him to drink it but is he still able to swallow?'

'Not since yesterday morning,' Rebecca replied, shaking her

head. 'Do you still not have any idea what ails him? When I visited your home, you told me I would have several babies and yet now I do not know if I will have a husband.' Her voice wobbled and her eyes filled with tears.

Ursula had witnessed a lot of death over the years but this terrible demise wracking Samuel's body was dreadful to see and she felt desperately sorry for the young girl, only weeks previously hopeful of having a big family. And yet she'd watched this very scenario in Rebecca's hand. Could it comfort the girl to know that she would have the chance of happiness once more?

'I did see babies,' she reassured her, putting her arm around Rebecca's shoulder, drawing her away from the bedside. She didn't want the man overhearing about a future which didn't include him. 'But I also saw that Samuel would die young. I did not want to tell you for I could not see when this would happen, but it seems that it was to be sooner than I had hoped. I am sorry I cannot tell you what you want to hear, I do not think Sam will live beyond sundown.' With an anguished wail, Rebecca's face folded up until her eyes had all but disappeared in the rolls of skin.

'Have you done this?' she whispered, her eyes narrowed as she stepped away from Ursula. She rummaged in the top of her shift until she produced a soggy looking rag which she wiped around her face before blowing her nose on it. 'You are killing my husband because you saw it unfold in my future and you wanted your profane omen to come true?'

'No, Rebecca, I would never do such a terrible thing! All I saw were the four babies who will come to you, not who would father them. I know how much you love Sam, but I cannot change what I see when I look for a life path for someone, I can only choose not to reveal that which will upset or frighten.' She wished at that moment she hadn't told Rebecca what she knew.

She'd divulged it as an act of kindness, but now she could see it hadn't been the right decision.

'Please leave,' Rebecca said as she walked to the door onto the street and flung it open. 'We do not need you here, we will nurse my Sam ourselves, as we should have done from the beginning. You have brought bad luck and malevolence to our home.'

Astonished at the way the scene had unfolded in front of her, silently Ursula gathered up her satchel and left, feeling a gust of air as the door was slammed behind her. She walked slowly along the village street wondering how Rebecca could think she herself had somehow brought on Samuel's death because she'd seen it happen. A cold feeling of unease cloaked her. For the first time her gifts no longer felt like a talent, a joy, but instead something to be afraid of. At her gate, unsurprisingly, the gull was waiting.

* * *

Three days later Ursula watched from her window as a solemn black-clad trail of villagers followed Samuel's coffin into the church. She could see Rebecca almost bent double in grief, being helped along by her sisters who both lived in King's Lynn and must have made the journey to pay their last respects. Ursula's heart ached for the young woman. She wanted to join them and recite the prayers which would send his soul to heaven. But the way she'd been expelled from his home as he lay dying made her doubtful of a kind reception and she didn't want to upset his young widow any further. Perhaps if she visited the house in a few weeks, Rebecca would have realised her accusations were simply those of a distraught young wife watching her husband fade away in front of her.

With no hope of attending the funeral, Ursula decided to clear her head by walking down to the sea. The hot weather continued its onslaught with the harsh sun baking the ground solid. She'd been drawing extra water from the well to pour over her vegetable plants and valuable herbs so they wouldn't wither and die.

The path to the sea led from between two cottages on the main street but with many of the villagers attending the funeral, she considered she was safe to walk there without encountering her neighbours. There was no knowing what rumours Rebecca had been spreading.

It was blissfully cool in the gloom beneath the boughs of the oak and beech trees whose leaves met together above her head in an arch of branches reaching towards each other and creating a living roof. Ursula slowed her footsteps to enjoy the respite from the sun, pulling the linen from her head and lifting her skein of waist-length hair to allow the fresh air to cool her neck for a few minutes. As she approached the dunes the track and trees petered out, and picking up her skirts to stop them dragging on the fine, loose sand, she clambered up the sandy bank, avoiding the sharp marram grass and yellow wort flowers.

She was rewarded with what she'd come to see, the wide sparkling expanse of sea stretching away until it became a soft blur blending with the far reaches of the blue sky as it fell away at the horizon. The tide was on its way out and she had to walk a long way across the flat, damp sand until she reached it. Behind her, her footsteps left imprints before slowly dissipating once more. At the sea's edge her toes gripped the sand beneath them ineffectually as it shifted and churned. She quickened her pace so she didn't fall as she splashed along the water's edge trying but failing to keep the hem of her skirt out of the waves. Above her came the calls of seagulls, and a slight breeze cooled her face. Her face felt hot and tight across her cheek bones and she knew she'd need some lanolin to spread across the dry skin later.

Just at the moment she decided to start to return home so she'd arrive back before the mourners left the graveyard, Ursula felt the now-familiar sense of not being alone. Immediately she was still, the waves continuing to roll over her feet, which were beginning to sink again. Her eyes scanned the dunes looking for the sign that someone was there, searching for the outline of Oliver Bruton. He no longer had Daniel to do his bidding so who was doing it now? Then a movement much closer to her shifted her attention. Just a few yards from her, standing on the beach was the gull that kept appearing at her cottage.

'Go away!' she shouted, relieved her uninvited companion was just the bird. Her words were pulled away by the wind, 'I don't know why you won't leave me alone, but go, please go and don't come back!' The bird took a couple of steps towards her then took to the air, flying so close to her head that instinctively she ducked, feeling a warm rush of air beneath its wings. The comfort the calm sea had given her leaked away into the water she was standing in and with a shiver, despite the blazing sun now directly overhead, she walked up the beach to retrieve her kerchief and boots. Fixing her headwear, she carried her boots and began to walk home.

In the cottage she drank two beakers of ale, one after the other. Peeping through the shutters at her window she watched the villagers walking back to their homes and workplaces, followed, she was surprised to see, by Oliver Bruton. Why had he gone to the funeral? When she heard a voice shout out *'hiding from your wicked deeds'* though, she knew why. Rebecca hadn't wasted any time speaking of what she believed Ursula had done and someone had fed the gossip back to the doctor. It had been the right decision to not attend the service. Opening the cupboard, she removed her journal and recorded the remedies she'd used that hadn't worked, hoping it may help her in the future.

Ursula's previously calm and quiet life, the one she'd carved out for herself, suddenly felt more precarious than it had ever done before. As if she were back standing on the dunes, the way the sand shifted beneath one's feet and could make you fall if you weren't perfectly balanced.

29

2024

Adrianna headed over to the pub, the piece of bone tucked in a bag in the inside of her jacket. Although she was sure her imagination had gone into overdrive, it felt as though there was an icy cold emanating from it sinking into her skin to chill her own bones. She almost went home and put it back where she'd found it, but now she knew she was starting to uncover a truth, a story waiting to be told. With a deep breath she greeted Tom, Roger and Jess and after buying a round of drinks she reached into her pocket and pulled out what she'd dug up, placing it on the bar.

'As you know I've been digging where the witch stone is in my garden,' she began, 'and this is what I've just found. I'm hoping it's simply an animal bone, please tell me that it isn't anything more sinister?'

The other three crowded round and passed it between them. They didn't seem to feel the cold radiating from it that she could.

'I'm no expert,' Roger said, 'and I know this isn't what you want to hear, but that looks a bit human to me.'

'Only a bit human?' Adrianna raised one eyebrow, 'I'll settle for human or not human, and to be honest I'd prefer the latter.'

'Personally, I think it's almost certainly from a person, probably part of an arm,' Jess said as she put the bone back on the bar. 'But what else were you expecting, excavating beside a strategically placed stone covered in witch marks?'

'I don't know. The cat? I was kind of hoping when I started digging that I was wrong and there'd be nothing there. What do I do now?'

'You call the police,' Roger told her, 'because right now you've potentially uncovered a dead body which may have been buried there centuries ago or may have been buried five years ago and be part of an ongoing missing persons or murder enquiry. Let them do their investigations first.'

Adrianna hadn't even thought of the police, but realised at once Roger was right and that she'd probably be reprimanded for taking a piece of potential evidence around the village. Carefully she placed the bone back in its bag and agreed to call them the next morning. After she'd had the glass of wine sitting on the bar, and maybe a second one too.

* * *

As Roger had warned, within thirty minutes of her call, Adrianna's garden was full of people, some uniformed and some dressed in white, papery overalls. A blue tarpaulin shelter had been erected over the hole she'd dug, and blue and white tape criss-crossed the front of her property preventing any of the locals or the press, who'd inevitably turned up, from entering.

'Hello.' The plain-clothed officer who'd been amongst the first to arrive was standing on the doorstep and Adrianna stepped aside to let him in.

'Are you all done now?' she asked as she filled the kettle and switched it on. She needed to go and restock on milk and teabags, she'd never made so many hot drinks in one morning, not even when she was an intern.

'Nope, not yet. But as you suspected we have uncovered a body. We're going to exhume it and take it away for further examination. I wondered if you'd like to come and look, it's just a skeleton so not shocking. Don't tell the boss though. We're pretty sure this isn't a recent death, so probably nothing to do with us. Although we'll get forensics to do their thing first, and once they've confirmed it, then we can let you know for sure. It's not what we're used to finding however, that's why I thought you may like to see.'

Adrianna wasn't sure she did want to, but she'd been the one digging and if the skeleton had anything to do with the witch stone, then she needed to know. It had merely served to fuel her interest further. She couldn't help thinking about how angry Rick would be when she told him she'd stirred up a whole lot of trouble. Following the police officer to the tent, she quickly put on a white paper all-in-one and blue covers for her shoes so as not to contaminate the area before ducking under the opening and going inside.

The men who'd been digging all morning had removed a sizeable pile of earth which would have taken her a week to excavate, and for that she was thankful. Moving carefully to the edge of the hole she peered in, almost falling in as well as her head swam and she swayed for a moment. As her eyes took in what she was seeing her hand flew to her mouth. The skeleton she'd been expecting, but where the upper arms and thighs lay, thick iron shafts were pushed through them.

'What the hell are those?' she said, her voice sounding abnormally high.

'We don't know,' the police officer admitted, 'we'll take them with us and examine them. None of us have seen anything like this and it looks as if it may be murder, even though it's possibly too old to even be a cold case. No one dies and is buried with their relatives deciding to bolt them to the bottom of the coffin, do they? Although, talking of which, we haven't found any remains of wood. Of course, most of a very old coffin could have rotted away but we'd have expected to find some shards of it. Can I ask please why you were digging here? I assume this is your cottage?' The officer steered Adrianna out of the tent and she was pleased to be back in the fresh air. She gulped in several lungfuls.

'It's not actually mine,' Adrianna explained as they returned to the kitchen that she was renting it for six months and what she'd discovered as she was gardening.

'So why *were* you digging there? Did you expect to find a body?' he asked. 'I mean, you described the stone with odd markings on, but not why you decided to dig beneath it.'

'I didn't think I'd find anything to be honest,' she said, before retelling the anecdote about a cat that'd supposedly been bricked up in the cottage. 'I thought that at most I might dig it up.' She went on to explain about her discovery of the journal and her interest in the witch marks. 'And also, look at this.' She led him to the living room hearth and pointed to the crimson stain. 'Does this look like blood to you? I've tried scrubbing it but it never disappears.'

'We can take a sample and send it to forensics too. But if it were blood, you'd be able to bleach it. Most crime scenes we go to look as if nothing happened but there are always clues if you know what to look for. Nobody would leave a murder looking like this unless they didn't care if they were found,' the officer replied as she stood up to leave. 'Can you give me your number and I'll let you know when our team have finished in the lab. If our suppositions are correct, then we can release the remains.'

'Of course,' Adrianna recited her number. 'What do I do with them when you've finished? I've never found a body in my back garden before.'

'If you chat with the local vicar, he'll probably re-bury them in the churchyard, or organise a cremation, that's most usual. Or you can return them to where they are now, there's no law against it, but you'll have to register it as a burial plot with the council. You may want to do further investigations to date the bones, but then you'll need to contact a specialist. The coroner will have to be involved and they can probably point you in the right direction.'

Adrianna thanked him and let the officer go back and help with the rest of the exhumation. When she'd started digging, she'd hoped there wouldn't be a body even though that had been naive of her. The sight of those heavy bolts with damp earth clinging to them were still making her stomach turn.

After making herself a cup of coffee she quickly emailed Jason with the barest of details of what she'd found and then messaged Jess and Tom to give them an update before sending a photo of the tarpaulin in the garden to Rick. Within thirty seconds her phone began to ring and his name appeared.

'For God's sake Addie, what have you done?' His voice sounded as furious as she was expecting and for a moment, she didn't know what to say. He seemed to take her silence as having no answer because he continued in a softer tone. 'Why on earth did you go ahead? I told you it was best left alone, didn't I? I can't imagine how angry the police are, not to mention your neighbours, now you've landed them with all this commotion. I thought you'd be able to keep out of trouble in quiet Norfolk. But trust you Addie, everything you get involved with turns into a drama.'

'I couldn't just leave it,' she said. 'I was certain there was something there, and I was right. Whoever was put in there deserves justice. I've got plenty of time on my hands, I'll see what else I can discover locally. It's good having something to do, I love doing the gardening, but this is using my brain.' She didn't add that stretching herself mentally and starting to achieve things were giving her a boost she couldn't have imagined when she'd started. She wasn't completely washed up, at least not yet.

'Honestly, darling, I don't think it's a good idea, just leave it all be now,' Rick said. 'Your brain was frazzled when you stopped working and you don't want to start something you can't finish again. Anyway,' he added, 'I must get on with work, I'm about to go into a meeting. I'll call you this evening, there's something I need to discuss with you.' Without a 'goodbye', or an 'I love you', the call was terminated.

Adrianna laid her phone on the table and stared at it for a moment. Perhaps Rick was right, she'd started something she wasn't capable of finishing. This was her all over, thinking she was something she wasn't, and then ending up in a mess which someone else would have to sort out. With a plummeting heart she remembered the email from work and wondered if there was a reply. It would have to wait; she'd had more than enough stress for one day and she didn't know what Rick wanted to chat about later. She hoped it wasn't something else to worry about.

30

2024

The back door of the cottage opened without a knock and in walked Jess and Tom, both carrying a bottle of wine. Adrianna looked at the pizza she'd cooked and wondered if it would feed three, she hadn't been expecting Tom as well.

'Sorry.' As if he had read her mind, he apologised. 'Jess told me she was coming over for a powwow about the skeleton and I invited myself along, I hope that's okay. I've eaten so I don't need pizza and I have wine.' He held up the bottle with a grin and waggled his eyebrows. 'Can I stay?'

'Of course,' Adrianna said, taking the bottle from him and collecting some glasses from the cupboard.

'Come on then, give us all the gory details,' Tom said.

'As I explained to Jess in my numerous messages, the body was in quite a shallow grave. I never thought I'd be uncovering that when I came to stay, I thought I'd just enjoy some rest and recuperation. It's actually quite disturbing.' She went on and explained about how the body appeared to have been shackled to the ground.

'How horrific,' Jess said. 'I wonder if the person was alive when they were buried? Pinned down so they couldn't escape? To think it's been there all these years, who knows how old it is.'

'I don't have any answers,' Adrianna apologised. 'The police have taken it away so they can ascertain its age. If it's ancient then it's of no interest to them and I'll need to find an expert with a laboratory who can do some investigations, because now I'm more invested in the mystery than ever. I can't find a body in the garden and then not research it further. Especially given the initials on the stone and whose I think they are.'

'How long before you hear back from the police?' Jess asked.

'I don't know for sure, but the officer who spoke to me intimated it won't take long. I was hoping that you, Jess, may know a way of getting the bones dated.'

'They'll need to be examined by an osteoarchaeologist,' Jess said. 'There's a lecturer at my uni, my *old* uni,' she said. 'I can email the head of my course and see if he can help? He might be able to give us some contact details.' She opened her phone and began to search. 'No time like the present,' she added. 'I'm as fascinated as you are now. Have you got any other leads to go on?'

'Not yet, I thought I might go and speak with Jack Miller over at Mayling Farm. The chap that Roger told me about, hopefully he can organise an introduction. See if he has any old tales of local witch trials, especially anything related to Finchingham. And I can try the archives in King's Lynn.'

'Let me know if you discover anything new,' Jess said. 'I think you're right that all this is something to do with witchcraft. You just need to uncover the truth.'

Adrianna nodded. Whoever it was in that grave, Ursula or someone else, she owed it to them to tell their story.

Once the other two had left, Adrianna went into the living room, which felt marginally warmer than it usually did, and took out the journal. She was now hoping even more that this held the secret to what had happened in the cottage all those years ago, and why there was a body buried beside the church wall.

As I foresaw in her hand, Samuel Thorpe, husband of Rebecca at Oak Tree Cottage died and he was buried this morn. Despite my ministrations nothing could save him, with severe pain in his belly. Over the space of seven days his body turned black and putrefied. My neighbours do now believe I brought about his death and I am certain these thoughts are placed in their minds by Oliver who continues to persecute me. Still I am followed by the gull who appears both within my house and without at all times, despite my bidding that he leave me.

Written this day the twenty second day of June in the year of our Lord 1646.

The death which had been foreseen earlier in the diary, and the finger of suspicion pointed at the author. Adrianna could feel the fear emanating from the pages and seeping into her own body, the creeping dread of something terrible approaching. From the description it sounded like the man had had sepsis, nothing in those days could have stopped his demise. Silently she replaced the papers in the cupboard.

Rick didn't call back as he'd promised, and eventually at eleven o'clock Adrianna rang him. Immediately she could hear that, once again, he was out somewhere, the sounds of a packed pub making it difficult to hear what he was saying. She heard a female say, 'There you are, darling,' and Rick grunted. Was it him being called darling?

'I'll call you in the morning,' he told her. 'I'm at a works event, I can't talk now. Love you.' Abruptly the call ended and Adrianna looked at the blank screen for a moment. She'd been feeling on a high that she was starting to make progress with her investigations into what she'd found when she was clearing the garden, that she was achieving something but all that adrenalin had, in that moment, slid through her to pool on the floor.

In her bedroom she went to pull the curtains and before doing so she looked across at the tent which was still erected despite the police, and the body, having now gone. What would they be able to tell her about the poor departed soul and would she be able to discover why the corpse had been left like that?

31

1646

A hammering at her door downstairs woke Ursula and she sat up, rubbing her hands down her face. Outside it was dawn, the sun now rising as early as it would all year with midsummer's eve only two days away. Even at night now there was a bright streak of daylight over the sea on the horizon as if it couldn't bear to be parted from land even during nightfall.

Scrambling down the steps to her parlour, Ursula peeped through her window to check who it was trying to waken the dead before she opened the door to admit Katherine. With an indignant cluck the gull slipped in behind Katherine who jumped out of its way.

'I swear, that bird was not to be seen when I walked to your door,' she exclaimed.

'It probably flew down, waiting for it to be opened.' Ursula was beginning to grow accustomed to her feathery visitor even though it was still unwelcome. Her plea for it to leave her alone had done nothing and she admitted to herself that as the bird couldn't understand her, she'd been wasting her breath. She had no idea why it refused to go, but picking it up, she threw it outside and shut the door.

'My friend, to what do I owe this pleasure?' Ursula asked as she poured ale and cut some slices of a honey cake she'd made, placing them on a wooden charger.

'I have brought you this.' Katherine pulled a pamphlet from where she'd secreted it in the top of her bodice. 'This is not the only copy I have seen around the village. It is a tract recently arrived from London and talks of witch trials in Essex and beyond in other parts of East Anglia.'

Ursula swallowed hard, her piece of cake sticking in her throat and threatening to choke her. Quickly she gulped her drink.

'Why would you think me interested in this?' she questioned, taking it from Katherine's outstretched hand.

'Look at the last paragraph. I believe this has been penned as a warning to you, my friend.' Katherine flipped the pamphlet over and pointed to the part she was referring to. The print was small and Ursula had to hold it close to her face to read it.

The pursuit and convictions of those who perform witchcraft continues. Lately Susan Manners, Jane Rivet, Mary Skipper from Copdock in the county of Suffolk, all convicted and hung at the Bury St Edmonds assizes. Every person must be vigilant. Watch out for the signs that those amongst you are harbouring the devil. Word comes from Norfolk of a man struck down by the palsy and then just weeks later of a healthy young man dying, his body congealing as his soul slipped away. We must all be aware of those who creep amongst us, and who consort with the Prince of Darkness. Look for familiars who undertake their work for them, carrying curses and stealing into other homes to lay them at their hearths. Evil cavorts around the good folk of England and Master Matthew Hopkins, the Witchfinder General, is helping to rid our land of this malevolence.

Ursula let the paper drop to the floor where it lay tormenting her. Those two incidents were surely those of Daniel and Samuel. Both deeds which she'd been accused of creating. Someone had travelled to London to ensure they appeared in the pamphlet, so the flames of trouble which were smouldering would be further fanned. There was only one person who had the time and money to do such a thing. Oliver knew as well as she did that neither of the two deaths were brought about by her. It suited him though to insinuate that they had been, he was still as intent on her succumbing to his desires.

For one awful moment she found herself considering agreeing to his demands. How far would these accusations of witchcraft go? Her eyes strayed to the hearth, to the stain – a permanent reminder of what she'd seen all those years ago. If she agreed to Oliver's demands then who knew what he'd do to her. She had no intention of being assaulted by a man who chose to take out his bad mood on a woman who was no more than a punch bag. Some of the village wives whose faces were rarely without a bruise were testament to how easily it was done.

No, she'd made the right choice and she would stand by her decision. She wouldn't allow herself to be fearful of a leaflet he'd doubtless had to pay to be printed and distributed. The man had too much money and too much spare time, he rarely seemed to practice any medicine. The devil did indeed make work for idle hands, not for those of hardworking innocent women who made their living with simple cures for their neighbours. She'd protected herself all these years and she would continue to do so.

'May I keep this?' she asked Katherine, holding the pamphlet up. 'We both know who is behind the accusations and I might have need of this as proof in the future.'

'Of course you can.' Katherine got to her feet. 'I must go home. I have been told I must not visit you any more. Doctor Bruton is spreading rumours through the village and some of the men are scared they too will die a terrible death like Samuel did. Or fall down with the palsy. I know these incidents were nothing to do with you, most of the goodwives hereabouts rely on you for your works. We know you do not dance with the devil as is being said, but we must obey our menfolk. I think it is best if you remain at home for the time being, I shall tell my neighbours to visit your back door if they need a remedy, so they cannot be seen from the street.'

'Thank you.' Ursula put her arms around Katherine and held her tight. She hoped her friend couldn't feel the trembling that was quivering through her body.

Katherine left via the back door, first getting Ursula to step outside for a moment and check that the bird had gone, before she hurried away.

Once her friend had left Ursula poured herself some milk, kept on the cold slab in her larder. Despite the cool she could taste it was beginning to turn. Would she be able to go to the farm for more when she ran out? Betty had been pleased that the children recovered from their measles, and hopefully the rumours hadn't yet reached her.

Going into her parlour she closed the shutters casting the room into a dim shadow. Better that nobody could look in. She lifted the board and placed the pamphlet Katherine had brought with her other papers. She wanted to add the conversation she'd just had, her fears, to the diary she was keeping, but she was too afraid to do so, as if writing it down would make it happen. Despite the fierce sun outside, dark was closing in.

32

2024

Finally, two days after he'd promised to call, Rick rang Adrianna back. She'd barely been able to sleep worrying about his comment about them needing to talk, and although she'd left voice notes and sent him DMs, he hadn't replied.

'Hey,' she whispered. It was gone midnight and she'd taken to sleeping with her phone on her pillow so she didn't miss his call. The late hour made her feel as though she shouldn't be talking at a normal volume. 'I've missed you so much,' she said before blurting out 'who was the woman calling you darling when I called the other day?' Her heart was beating fast. She'd told herself not to mention it, and yet immediately the words bounced out.

'What? When?' Rick asked and she could hear the surprise in his voice as it rose an octave.

'When I called you, I heard a woman's voice say something like "here you are darling", I was just wondering who it was.' She tried to make her voice sound more casual.

'Not me, you're imagining things, you must've heard something in the background. What are you saying, that you don't trust me?' Rick's voice became sharper.

'No, of course not,' Adrianna blustered. Of course she trusted him, she hadn't intended her words to come across that way, and now he was angry with her. 'I'm sorry,' she added.

'Anyway,' he said, changing the subject, 'life's been busy and I've only just found a couple of minutes to myself.' It did occur to her that surely he could have found some time to talk to her before the middle of the night, but she chastised herself at her lack of empathy. She'd had to work late into the night when there was a deadline looming and he often had to do evening viewings for houses. Not everyone worked nine to five.

'You said there was something you needed to talk about?' she reminded him.

'Yes, well, um,' Rick cleared his throat, 'I'm afraid I can't pay you my rent this month. Some of it,' he added quickly, 'just not all of it.' She waited for him to add an apology, but it didn't come.

'Seriously?' she asked. 'How come, have you lost your job? We agreed on what you could afford and I need that money to cover my bills here, given that I'm also paying the mortgage for my flat where you're currently living. What about your place, is that still rented out?'

'Of course I still have my tenants.' Now he'd broken the bad news Rick seemed to have recovered his usual coolness. 'But my commission was down this month and I've had some extra expenses. You know how it is. So right now, I can't pay you what I usually do.'

Adrianna didn't 'know how it was' though, she always made sure her bills were covered. There was a stony silence at the other end of the phone and for a moment she thought he'd hung up. Eventually she said, 'How much less are you paying?'

'I'm not sure yet. Whatever I can afford, I'll transfer on

payday. Anyway, it's very late,' he yawned loudly as if she didn't know what time it was, 'so I must get off to bed. No lie-in for me in the mornings. Night night, Addie.' He blew her a kiss.

'I love you,' she replied, but realised she was talking into the ether. Rick had hung up. She was getting tired of his constant comments about her lazing around in bed. No doubt he was now settling down for a good night's sleep whilst she was wide awake, laid on her back and staring up at the dark ceiling. How was she going to afford everything without his rent coming in? She'd have to dig into her savings.

* * *

The following morning, her head still troubled over Rick's lack of money, she was pleased to receive a phone call from the officer in charge of the investigations confirming the bones were indeed very old and of no interest to the police. She could liaise with the coroner to organise where she wanted them moving to. Making a note of the phone number she needed to call she hung up, relieved by the confirmation it wasn't a recent grave she'd uncovered. Hopefully now she could find out when exactly the skeleton dated from. Keeping her fingers crossed she sent a message to Jess to ask if she'd been able to get a name and number for an osteoarchaeologist who could do them a favour. She knew it was a big ask.

Whilst she waited for a response, she called James at work to find out how she could help him. She needed to face the problem and not hide from it.

'Adrianna, thanks for calling. I'm so sorry I had to email whilst you're taking time away but you know what auditors are like, everything must be present and correct before they can sign the accounts off. And this is a sizeable amount of money that we appear to have overcharged a client.' He went on to outline the project in question. 'Do you remember it?'

'I do, but it was a year ago so the details are sketchy.' She didn't want to remind him that she'd completely fallen to pieces in the interim, although very few people had known why she'd gone on sabbatical. Or tell him that, in fact far from just being sketchy, the details were completely lost to her. 'I'd need to go through the documentation. I could come down to London on Friday, and have a look? I no longer have a login so someone would need to organise that for me.'

'Really? That would be very helpful. I'll sort everything out and if you buzz me from reception I'll come down and collect you,' James replied.

Having made the arrangements Adrianna felt a weight lift from her shoulders. She reminded herself she may feel different when she had to walk through the entrance doors, but she'd taken the first step. Now she could push it back into the box in her head which contained all the things she didn't want to face.

She could stay in London with Rick for the weekend and maybe even have dinner at their favourite restaurant. It was an expense because he enjoyed fine dining, and she was still angry that he wasn't paying her the rent they had agreed on, but they hadn't been out together for a proper date night for a long time. Long before she'd escaped to Norfolk. As she thought it, she realised that was how she was now viewing her stay at Church Cottage, she'd fled her London life and escaped somewhere she felt safer. And now she wasn't sure she'd ever want to return permanently. The thought unsettled her.

33

1646

Ursula woke in the night, a sudden jerk bringing her back from sleep to being wide awake. Immediately she sat up and put her head on one side, listening. A noise somewhere, not the usual night-time animals, had woken her.

After a minute she was content there was nobody in the house below her, but then she heard it again. The crack of a twig, the grumble of a hen disturbed. Something, or someone, was prowling around the outside of her home. There was always the danger of a fox investigating her hen house.

Climbing off her bed she crawled on hands and knees to the small window which was close to the floor. She hadn't bothered closing its shutters the previous night as it looked out across her garden and the land beyond to the sea, so she could peep out without the noise of creaking wood alerting anyone who may be below.

She spotted the silhouette of a lone man just visible despite the night, moving about her garden. The full moon lit up the trees and plants in stark relief to the shadowy hollows of darkness and she could see her visitor's shape as he flitted back and forth. She couldn't see what he was doing, but at one point he stopped moving for several minutes before he stood up and she watched him climb the wall which separated her garden from Lord Mayling's land as he disappeared into the undergrowth there.

By the time it was light enough to go and investigate Ursula was dressed, her boots on. She'd broken her fast and ushered the gull away from her door. For whatever reason it wasn't going to leave her alone so she'd chosen him a name, Wicker, as his speckled plumage matched the colour of the baskets she used.

Walking along the path through her neat beds of vegetables she paused at the chicken coop to let them out, relieved not to find a bloodbath and her valuable hens gone. So that was one suspicion written off, whoever her visitor had been he wasn't after her livestock. She continued, her eyes constantly flicking from side to side, wondering what her nocturnal guest had been looking for.

Eventually at the point where she began to wonder if she'd imagined seeing someone, she found evidence that she wasn't mistaken. At the end of her garden in the small patch of poisonous plants she could see some had been trampled on, the leaves and stalks still glistening with leaking liquid. Many shoots and branches had been trodden into the ground whilst others were completely snapped off.

This didn't appear to be a wholesale destroying of the patch though, more that someone had been looking for something and had walked where they wished. She shook her head. If a villager had need of these remedies, they could come to her. And few people knew that she grew these plants, they were well hidden by the tall vegetables and plum trees which partly obscured them. Apart from one person who'd made it his business to discover her secrets. She was certain it wasn't Oliver in her garden during the night but she would bet a groat that he was behind whatever was going on. Her world closed in on her a tiny bit more.

By now she had a headache and she sat at her work bench inside, crushing some feverfew in her mortar to brew into a tisane. A hammering at her front door made her drop the pot she was holding and it rolled across the trestle table top, the herb inside slowly falling out as it turned.

'God-a-mercy,' she muttered under her breath, going to the door and unbolting it. No longer did she leave her house open, her trust in those around her had waned. It was a long time since she'd felt so wary.

'Thank goodness you are here.' Katherine almost fell in through the doorway as it opened. Frowning, Ursula closed the door and looked at her friend who was already sitting on the chair beside the fire which was lit with only a small flame emanating from a block of peat. Despite the heat outside she still needed the fire to cook dinner and boil water.

'My friend, what is so urgent? You look as though you have run here.' Ursula couldn't help noticing how flushed Katherine was, her chest heaving as she placed her hand on it breathing in and out deeply.

'At the well this morning, I was waiting my turn,' Katherine spoke between gulps of air, 'and something was found. One of the smith's children was collecting water and it came up in the bucket.'

'What was it?' The villagers sometimes found bits of vegetation or dead rodents in the water. Ursula couldn't imagine what could have been found which had shocked her friend so much.

'A poppet. A wooden doll crudely fashioned as a person, with three pieces of wolfsbane tied with a strip of reed to its chest. And stabbed with thorns from the blackthorn.' As she named the plants Ursula began to understand what was unfolding before her. Whoever had been in her garden had been taking cuttings from her poisonous plants to then insinuate she'd thrown a poppet, the favoured instrument of witches who wished to curse someone, into the well.

She'd used blackthorn juice to try and cure Samuel. There was no doubting who was behind the doll's discovery and she swallowed hard, trying to dislodge a hard lump of fear caught in her throat. Oliver was beginning to unwind his plot, like threads from a spool. And it was far more sinister than she'd credited him for. He might be clever, she reminded herself, but she could be shrewder than he. She'd have to be. Now she would have to use everything at her disposal to protect her way of life and her ability to earn money.

34

1646

Ursula's concerns about the poppet being pulled from the well were soon justified. The following day she walked to the mill for flour but the reception wasn't as she expected, the mill owner's wife handing over the flour with barely a word of greeting, keeping her head down.

'Goodwife Miller, have I done something to upset you?' Ursula asked. She'd been called to act as midwife at the woman's two births and frequently provided medications for the children growing up. She'd also once dressed a bad hand injury one of the apprentices at the mill had sustained. Her swift work and knowledge saved the young lad from losing his limb and he'd been able to carry on with his work a few months later. She knew she was respected and well-liked in this establishment.

'No, Ursula.' The miller's wife pocketed the coins she'd handed over but still wouldn't look her in the eye.

'Then why do you dip your head and examine the floor?' Ursula demanded, walking to where the woman stood to look at the stone flags beneath her feet. The mill was old and made of huge slabs of ancient, solid stone, the floor always covered in a fine pale brown film of flour and husks of grain. 'Is there a mouse worrying you?' Even as she said it Ursula knew that no mouse would concern a miller. Despite a plethora of cats, there was always a vermin problem where so much barley and wheat were stored.

'I heard what happened to Samuel, mistress,' the woman dropped her voice to a whisper, 'and that a wooden image of him was discovered in the well. It is said he was poisoned.'

'And you think that was something to do with me?' Despite her fears Ursula's voice rose as she took in the shock that her friends would believe the rumours Oliver was trying to spread. After Katherine's visit she'd examined her wolfsbane plant and could see where three small cuttings had been removed cleanly, with a knife. Whoever had been prowling around her garden the night she'd awoken was the culprit behind this, but who would speak out for her? How quickly would friendships falter and fade away when whispers of witchcraft leached through the village? And she'd told Rebecca she'd foreseen a second marriage. She had made a grave error, if only she'd kept her counsel and said nothing.

'I promise you, I had nothing to do with it. Why would I wish to harm my friends? This is the work of the new doctor who lives at Great Mayling. He has asked me for womanly favours, and I have refused. He is trying to sully my name hoping it will make me consent. But I shall not, I can never be beholden to any man.'

Ursula placed the sack of flour measured out for her into her basket and left the mill, flicking her skirt from side to side trying to dislodge the inevitable coating of dried grain. Small clouds of white and brown fell away to coat the nettles she pushed through as she walked the path back to her cottage. It was two miles inland to the mill which sat on the flat land where winds blew hard and fast across the fields, whipping leaves from trees and oft-times flattening crops, but providing enough power to turn the big sails.

As she walked, Ursula's mind turned over what she had come to realise was to be Oliver's decisive method of bending her to his will. If he were to denounce that she was practising witchcraft, then she'd have difficulty defending herself. Everyone in the village knew her, and knew of her innocence, but a few words spoken in the ears of those who were afraid, who couldn't understand her desire to live a solitary life, could have a terrible consequence. There were men in the village who didn't trust her, who saw she was shrewder and cleverer than they, and for that reason alone she was in grave danger. Now she no longer knew if she was able to continue refusing the doctor.

Arriving home she left the flour in her scullery and went straight out again. She was followed along the lane by Wicker, and trying to discourage him, she kicked out before he hopped up onto a wall and continued to walk a few feet behind her. Arriving at Rebecca's cottage she rapped on the door, catching her knuckle on a splinter which stuck out of the worn oak. The salt which carried across the fields on the sea air destroyed any exposed wood over time, whitening it to the pale, rough planks she was now standing in front of. The door suddenly opened, and Rebecca looked at her, her eyes narrowing as she saw who was visiting.

'Do not cross my threshold!' She spat the words one by one. Silently Ursula reached up and wiped the spittle from her face. 'You are not welcome here. I know now what you chose to do, to prove your skills in the seeing of the future you poisoned my husband.'

'Friend, I did no such thing, please let me come in and speak with you. What was found in the well was nothing to do with me, I promise. And whatever caused the demise of Sam, was not my doing. He did not show symptoms of being poisoned.' At this juncture she paused for a moment. The dark mottled rash in his last days were not she considered a sign of being poisoned, but his ill stomach for the days and weeks preceding were indicative of a body trying to expel something which disagreed with it.

'The poppet proves what I say is true. You are a cruel woman, Ursula, to have done this to my husband, just to demonstrate your fortune telling was exact. Who knows what other illnesses and deaths you have caused in these parts? I have heard tell that you had an altercation with the peddler Daniel Hooke and he is now laid up with a palsy which he cannot recover from. People are beginning to question your behaviours and you are not welcome at my door again.'

It slammed in her face, causing Ursula to quickly take a step backwards onto the street. She looked around but given that it was midday, thankfully the other villagers were eating dinner and hadn't witnessed what had just happened. Hurrying home, her heart thumping so hard she was finding it difficult to breathe, she half expected Oliver to be waiting, as if her fear could invoke him to appear, but the street and her garden were mercifully empty, other than the now-familiar Wicker. Going inside, she battened the doors closed and pushed the shutters together. It meant she had to light a candle to see what she was doing, but the stench of burning animal fat from the tallow and dark wispy strands of smoke dropping flecks of black soot were worth enduring to gain some privacy.

Pulling out her parchments she recorded everything which had just happened, leaving blots of ink as her hand shook, droplets dripping off before she could put the quill to the paper. For the first time since her father left she was terrified by what lay ahead, a fight which may cost her everything she had. Including her life.

After making some bread dough and leaving it to rise in the warmth of the scullery, Ursula slowly cracked open the shutters at the back of the house to see if she could see anything amiss in her garden. There was no sign of anyone and needing to see if any of her chickens had laid that morning she went to check, rewarded with three eggs, still warm, which she placed in the voluminous pockets of her apron.

Her eyes strayed towards the patch of dangerous plants. Never had she regretted more her decision to grow them, even though a lot more people in the village would have died without her expertise and the potions she'd concocted. And people would have perished in more pain with a prolonged death without her knowledge to help them into the next life a little sooner than they otherwise would have arrived. That was information she'd always keep to herself, medicines her mother had shown her how to make with recipes brought from her homeland, some of the plants in the garden which had arrived as saplings and now thrived. Not known to others, and not to be shared.

A rustle behind her elderberry tree alerted Ursula to the arrival of a visitor and before she could call out to ask who was there, Katherine appeared once again. Despite the warmth of the day, she was wearing a dun brown cloak with the hood pulled over her head and most of her face, making it difficult for a moment for Ursula to see who it was.

'Why are you dressed like that?' she asked.

'I did not wish to be seen, but 'tis very warm beneath here,' Katherine explained, hurrying along the path beside the cottage and in through the back door, throwing off the cloak. Ursula stepped backwards from her herb bed and followed her, her heart sinking at the sight of her old friend having to disguise herself to visit.

'Tell me everything, please,' Ursula said as she put the pot on to boil and kneaded the dough back into shape before throwing it into the bread oven in the wall by the fireplace alcove. 'I went to visit Rebecca and I received a sour reception, before being turned away. The miller's wife was only slightly less unfriendly.'

'Then I think you have already realised what is being said in the village. I told you about the doll found in the well, and that has lit an angry fire beneath the rumours,' Katherine said.

'You know I would never have fashioned such a thing. And I did not harm Sam. Whatever ailed him was already violating his body when I visited, it was nothing to do with me. I tried my hardest to save him and yet I am now accused of causing his demise. Others have died after I have tried to cure them, but never have I been blamed thus.'

'If you did not make that poppet, who did?' Katherine asked. 'They are saying it was your wolfsbane tied to it.'

'I believe that is correct,' Ursula admitted, she explained what she had witnessed. 'Pieces of my plant have been cut off with a knife. Someone wishes to sour my name in the village and have me for a witch.'

'People around here have always relied on you for your cures,' Katherine said. 'Why would they choose to turn on you?'

'Because of the physician, of course.' Ursula's voice came out so harshly it caught in her throat and made her cough. Her head was starting to hurt across the back of her neck she was holding it so tensely. 'I have told you previously of his "offer". Despite his blatant threats I have refused him every time he calls, and this is how he will now play it. I cannot acquiesce and if there is to be a battle may he draw the lines, for I shall fight him. He has abused his position and wealth to pay people to do his misdeeds and wrong me, I am certain. I doubt that he himself was fashioning a piece of wood into a poppet, and I'm sure he paid someone to steal those pieces of wolfsbane. His money will slip from his purse to someone's hand and they will carry out his foul wishes. Or speak the ills he has dripped like beeswax into their ears. There is always someone poor enough to need the coins. And young Rebecca is too grief-stricken to realise what she says.'

'The man is evil,' Katherine said. 'That he would insinuate you are in league with the devil in order to bend your will to his own.'

'He does it because he is a man and does not expect a woman to contest him. We see what occurs within a marriage when that happens. You are the only person in the village who knows the truth of my mother's death. And I have had Jane at my door twice now in as many months with her face bruised and broken.' Her mind drifted towards her own parents' marriage before she dragged it back to the present. She needed to concentrate on how she was going to prevent the rumours from spreading. 'In some way I need to stop him, without agreeing to what he wants.'

'How will you do that? It seems that so far you have not succeeded,' Katherine said.

In silence Ursula poured the now boiling water into two beakers containing a scraping of ginger and some honey. Her hand was steady, belying the way her mind was turning like the paddles of her butter churn.

The truth was, she didn't have any idea how she was going to defeat Oliver if he continued with his charges of wrongdoing. If she didn't, before long she would find herself at the assizes pleading her innocence. She may not even get that far, if her neighbours and friends turned on her at his behest and strung her up from a tree.

'In all honesty, I have no idea,' Ursula admitted as she blew on her hot drink taking small sips. 'When he realises these witchcraft accusations shall not make me change my mind, doubtless he will have some other idea. He can force himself on me physically, although I would put up a fair fight. Not enough to stop him though, if that is what he chooses to do, but his sister Anne told me that he considers it is beneath him to do so. He believes himself more superior than that. Perhaps because he risks his reputation if I then speak out against him. He would deny it, but the accusation would damage his good standing and he has already run from a previous incident. No, I shall remain in hiding here in my cottage. If you can bring me flour, hops and milk when you are able, I will have enough to sustain me. If there are any villagers who still wish me to treat them, they will have to knock at my door after dark for medications. I no longer feel safe with it unlocked. Can you tell the goodwives this please? Although, in God's truth, after what Rebecca has been saying, I do not know if anyone will want to buy from me.'

She considered her small purse of coins hidden beneath the floorboard in the cupboard with her journal. They would not last forever if she was unable to earn more. If that happened, then she'd have to leave the village and find work elsewhere. But she owned her cottage, and she had a roof over her head whilst she remained there.

Katherine left by the back door and Ursula shut it behind her. The future was looking very bleak, and lonely. She'd have to visit the well to collect water under the cover of darkness in future. And, with no likelihood of a share of the killing of any animal in the village, she'd have to rely on poaching rabbits or pigeons, something that always held a large element of danger. She'd be strung up if she were caught doing that too. She put her hands to her neck, stroking the soft skin. It felt as though the hangman's noose was starting to tighten.

35

2024

The more of the paperwork Adrianna transcribed, the more involved she became. This journal of a woman's life, Ursula's life, she was certain, was both fascinating, and frightening, and she felt a kindred spirit with her. When she transcribed an entry which described a poppet found in the village well Adrianna felt a cold chill creep down her spine. She knew about the connection between witches and poppets.

A wooden doll, a poppet, was found in the well, impaled with blackthorn spines and tied with wolfsbane harvested from my own garden. I fear my name will be brought into this deception. Last night my garden was visited and my plant has been cut and now those pieces are found tied to the poppet. This bodes badly for me. Written this day the first day of July in the year of our Lord 1646.

Laying the sheet down on the coffee table, Adrianna picked up the piece with the warning on and read it again. There was no doubt Ursula knew something evil was coming for her. Adrianna felt the hairs along her arms stand up. Outside, the gull rapped on the window, making her jump.

* * *

Following a quick call to Roger, she was able to organise a visit to see Jack Miller and, clutching a Victoria sponge and a bottle of wine, she arrived at a modern bungalow behind a large old farmhouse. She was greeted by a swarm of black and white collies who crowded around her barking.

'Hello, can I help?' A woman had appeared at the back door of the farmhouse and Adrianna explained the reason for her visit. 'Oh yes, Dad said you were coming. I see you've brought him cake; he will be chatting for hours! Go on over, I'll come and make some tea in a moment.' She disappeared again and Adrianna went to knock at the bungalow door.

Jack was exactly as she had imagined. His face was ruddy and lined, the sort of skin which had spent its working life outside and despite being in his nineties he was still sprightly. As his daughter said, he was delighted to accept her cake offering.

'Thank you for letting me come and see you,' Adrianna said. 'Roger told me that you may know about local history. I'm staying in Church Cottage at Finchingham and I think there may be a connection to a witch hunt there. I'm just trying to find out whatever I can and I wondered if you knew anything.'

'Indeed, I saw on the local news that a dead body had been found at the cottage,' he said.

'Yes, I was digging in the garden. The skeleton is possibly centuries old, I'm arranging to have it properly examined. There's a stone where I found it with witch marks on, and there are similar ones on the church as well as the wall dividing the graveyard and the ground where the body was.'

Jack nodded. 'I should say that this is all a surprise, but it's not. There have always been tales of witch trials that happened around these parts. I heard them when I was a child and it was my grandfather who told me, and his grandfather who told him. A witch living beside Finchingham church who poisoned a man and plagued another with the palsy. And old Mrs Murray who lived in your cottage knew more than she ever let on.'

By this point his daughter had arrived bringing in a tray of tea with the cake already cut into thick slices. 'I've heard some of these stories,' she said. 'They're complete rubbish. Some poor woman living on her own so being blamed for any misfortunes. And I bet it was a man who was pointing the finger, it always is.'

It certainly was in Ursula's case. A man trying to determine how she lived her life. Coercing her to believe what he told her was the truth, even when he was lying to her.

'What do you mean that Mrs Murray knew something?' Adrianna asked Jack.

'She lived there all her life and if anyone mentioned the rumours about a witch she would just smile and nod. She once told me that the cottage held secrets that would only show themselves to someone who could uncover the truth. Now, did you get my book?' Jack turned to his daughter.

She tutted but went and collected an enormous book from the sideboard.

'These are the records from the mill which my forefathers owned before we bought this farm. They go back hundreds of years. Prices of grain, good years, bad years, it's all in here. When the vicar explained why you wanted to come for a chat, I remembered that there were some entries in here you may be interested in.' He opened the book where a scrap of paper was marking the page, and turned it towards Adrianna. 'See here at the top of this page. Are you able to read it out?'

After her weeks of deciphering the journal Adrianna no longer found it as difficult to read the old words although this was a different hand and it took her a few minutes to begin to understand what it said.

"'July 1646. My sister has wed and a fulsome and happy celebration it was. The sun is harsh every day, the grain does not grow well in the fields and we shall have little to mill this winter. They say it is the work of the witch at Finchingham, she who has poisoned and cursed with the palsy. The Witchfinder General makes his way north, we must be rid of her before we are all penniless, or dead.'" Adrianna stopped reading and looked at the other two. It was just as the journal at the cottage. And was what Mrs Murray had said true? That the cottage had been waiting for someone who believed the truth? That it had been waiting for her?

Adrianna looked outside at the sky, an expanse of blue. The country was experiencing another heatwave and she'd seen warnings of hosepipe bans. What must it have been like to have almost no water and how the oppressive heat could have contributed to stirring up an angry mood amongst the villagers of Finchingham. It was as if she was reliving that fateful summer, the only way to find out what happened to Ursula.

'Go to the Guildhall in King's Lynn,' Jack told her. 'They've got records for the witch trials there, then you can see it's not all rubbish.'

* * *

Friday finally arrived and Adrianna got a cab to King's Lynn station early in the morning. It would take almost two hours to get to London and she'd arranged to be at the office at ten o'clock. She was becoming increasingly worried that, when the time arrived, she wouldn't be able to walk into the building. Her weekend case was packed and she intended leaving it at the flat, then after she'd finished at work she'd go to a gallery or a museum, or maybe just sit in a park and watch the world go by. Being outside now was so much more important than it used to be.

The train journey was uneventful and as they approached London, others began to board in droves until there was standing room only, and not a lot of that. Then she was on a tube train, hemmed in by other people, and she began to feel light-headed, the enormity of what she was about to do threatening to overwhelm her.

At Canary Wharf she followed everyone up the escalator before heading to her flat. Her insides were liquid and she walked quickly, waving her hand to the concierge at his desk and tapping her foot as the lift rose silently to the eighteenth floor. With her hand shaking it took several attempts to fit her key in the lock and turn it before hurrying inside, picking up the post from the floor and slamming the door behind her.

This place had always been her place of safety, but today it didn't feel right. For a start it was the most untidy and dirty she'd ever seen it. A pile of unwashed crockery was stacked on the worktop above the dishwasher, which was clean but only partly emptied. She guessed that Rick was using the washed items straight from the machine and then just reloading it all. The recycling bin was full of empty bottles, some beer but mostly wine. And, she noticed, two bottles of scotch.

The living room wasn't quite as bad, dusty with several copies of the *Metro* slung on chairs. Her beautiful teal coloured velvet sofas with their cerise piping looked untidy and she found a pair of Rick's socks balled up in one corner. The matching cushions were piled up at one end with an indent where his head had squashed them, opposite his precious seventy-inch television. On the coffee table stood three empty beer bottles, and when she picked them up they left rings in the dust.

Looking at her phone she realised she only had thirty minutes before meeting James, and she took her suitcase through to the bedroom. Here the mess was even worse, clothes on the floor, the bed unmade, and it didn't look as if the toilet and shower had been cleaned since she'd left.

After tidying herself up, putting her hair into a neat ponytail and reapplying her lipstick, she felt as ready as she'd ever be to go and face the music. At the last moment she decided to swap her normal handbag for a designer one she'd treated herself to when she'd been promoted. It would give her some added confidence. Going to her wardrobe she stood on tip toe to reach the box – it had never lived anywhere other than in an especially bought box – but her hands only met a space where it should have been. Confused, and wondering if she'd put it away somewhere else the last time she'd used it, she quickly went through the rest of the wardrobe but it wasn't there. There was no time to have a closer look because she needed to leave, but she'd examine all the storage in the flat properly when she got back, it had to be somewhere.

Once she was outside the building it was only a fifteen-minute walk to the office. She'd done it thousands of times before without even thinking about it, but this time she was conscious of the other people going about their day, a busy, frenetic life moving on without her.

She found herself comparing it to the quiet of Finchingham with its wide expanses of sky which touched the horizon, not just glimpses of it between towering buildings. A pigeon strutted across in front of her, two of its toes missing. Her friendly gull still possessed every part of his feet. There was no sound of skylarks here, or the drumming of a woodpecker. And all she could smell were fumes, not the fragrant lavender and herbs now flourishing outside her back door.

Walking up to the office building she kept her head down hoping she wouldn't see any of her former colleagues. They'd all been lovely when she'd announced she was taking time away from work, but she could imagine the gossip which had flowed once she'd gone. Anyone who had half an ear to the ground would know she hadn't been up to her job.

At reception a young man she'd never seen before took her name and gave her a visitor badge on a lanyard, inviting her to sit on one of the sofas nearby while he called up to her office. The last thing she wanted to do was be in full view of everyone as if she were waiting outside the headteacher's office, so she stood with her back to reception examining the random works of art she'd walked past without interest for years.

'Adrianna, how lovely to see you, thank you so much for coming in. How's your sojourn in Norfolk going?' James greeted her warmly, giving her a hug. Although he was her senior they knew each other from work away days well enough to forego any protocol and, smiling, she assured him it was no bother. Even though it was, she reminded herself, her sweating palms were testament to that.

'I'm doing some research,' she explained as she followed him through the turnstiles to go and wait for the lift. She went on to tell him briefly about her historical investigations, and the skeleton she'd uncovered.

'Wow, that's fascinating,' James replied. 'This is like something on the telly, trust you to find something exciting to use your brain for whilst you are supposed to be taking it easy. You've always been a human whirlwind, that's why I've always fought to keep you on my team, even though the other directors are forever trying to poach you.' Were they? Adrianna had no idea and despite her worries being there, hearing that considerably lifted her spirits.

Thankfully he'd booked a meeting room and Adrianna's fears that she'd have to walk through the big open plan office didn't materialise. One of the reasons she'd decided to come on a Friday was because a lot of her colleagues chose to work from home that day. There was a laptop already waiting and, after refusing a coffee, keen to get the job over and done with, Adrianna sat down and took a deep breath. Her heart was racing, but now she was here she had to do what was needed and she started searching the file system. She'd only been gone a few months but it took her a couple of minutes to start to recall where things were archived.

She could feel the nausea rising and a prickle of sweat across her forehead. It felt as though the oxygen was being drained from the room. Gradually she started to open documents until she had everything she needed and heaving a big sigh of relief she turned to James and said, 'They haven't been overcharged. Everything is correct.' She couldn't help a confident note creeping into her voice as she leant back in her chair and smiled.

It took ten minutes to go through the document trail, including the emails she'd also filed in the project folders to show where the client had requested a substantial change to the code, after they'd bought a subsidiary company. It hadn't been added to the original blueprint but she pointed to her final report where it was detailed including the exact amount of money on a purchase order on the system.

'Adrianna, you are a star,' James exclaimed. 'I don't know why nobody else could find this, but you've saved me a big headache. Can I take you for a coffee? Or tea and cake?'

'Thank you, but no. I'm just pleased I was able to clear things up.'

'We're missing you here,' James admitted. 'You're quick to find issues and even faster at suggesting solutions. We really need your expertise on these big projects.' He held his hands up. 'I'm not asking you to cut your sabbatical short, that time is yours, but I hope you realise that when you're ready to come back, we'll welcome you with open arms. And a night at the pub on expenses.' They both laughed, his expense account was legendary.

Walking away from the building and heading to the underground to take her into the city, Adrianna had a hundred thoughts jostling in her head. Suddenly the thought of returning to work in the autumn wasn't the roiling mass of dark dread sitting malevolently on the edge of her consciousness that it had been. Wherever the anxiety about her ability to do her job had first been germinated, she realised that it was built on lies and falsehoods. She was capable, in fact more than capable of carrying out her work, and she deserved the position in the company that she held. She was a high achiever, proficient at her job.

And yet knowing that didn't make her want to go back any more than she had previously done. Now she'd seen another way to live, one where the quality and pace of life beneath the wide-open spaces of her adopted county was more important and it was enticing, teasing her with the possibility of a whole new world.

36

1646

Ursula was constantly on edge, waiting to see what happened next. Her body trembled, nausea washing over her every time she imagined she could smell Oliver's distinctive odour. A week after the doll was found in the well and gossip about witchcraft began to circulate, he arrived outside her door.

The sound of a horse stamping outside reverberated through her home, making the floor beat in time with her thumping heart. Even without peering through the small gap she left in the closed shutters, just enough to see to work and cook, she knew it was him. Wicker was hopping along the wall at the front of her cottage shrieking loudly as if she needed a warning and she watched as the bird opened his impressive wingspan and flapped towards Oliver who shouted and waved his hands at it. The noise disturbed his horse which began to dance and snort. Annoying as the bird was, Ursula couldn't help smiling at its antics.

The moment Oliver had calmed the horse he threw the reins and a coin to a young lad who'd appeared almost immediately, before banging on her front door.

'Open up Ursula,' he growled, his head close to the door as the words pushed their angry way through the planks, 'or I will break this door down.' Ursula didn't want any more attention from her neighbours, especially as she could no longer rely on someone to do repairs, if needed. Reluctantly she unbolted the door, just as Oliver was in the process of shouldering it to try and gain access. He almost fell into the room, and if Ursula hadn't been so frightened, she would have laughed at the sight of him staggering across the floor as he tried to right himself. She left the door open in case she needed to shout for help, although who knew if anyone would come to her assistance. Leaning around her, Oliver slammed it shut and replaced the bar locking it into place. Fear and hot bile rose in Ursula's throat and she swallowed hard, feeling it burn into her gullet.

'Once again you arrive without invitation,' she said, putting shaking hands on her hips to try and still them, placing her feet slightly apart. If he were to take a swing at her she had more chance of not being knocked down. She was sure he could hear the tremor in her voice but she needed to appear unafraid, even if it was a ruse.

'I do not need to be asked to enter a poor person's home.' Oliver showed his teeth in a tight grin, but it didn't reach his eyes, as pale and insipid as hers were dark and fiery. 'I hear from village gossip you have been accused of witchcraft. That is a dangerous position to be in, you must be greatly afeared.'

'I am not,' she retorted. 'I know you did not hear it first in the village, for these malicious rumours have been put about by yourself to slander my reputation. My friends know me for who I am. And I have no doubt it was at your behest that cuttings from my wolfsbane were taken and tied to the poppet found in the well. The one stabbed with blackthorn spines. You are a physician and you know as well as I that Samuel did not die from being poisoned. Something else produced the symptoms he had, the bleeding from inside, the dark rash which spread across his body as if consuming him. You whispered in Rebecca's ear it was poison and encouraged her to believe I had dosed him with it.'

'And how do you explain Daniel's palsy? He does not improve, his wife is having to do everything for him as if he were once again a babe. And she has a houseful of children to feed with no income and only charity to rely on. People are believing what I tell them, I could make all this go away if you would only agree to my request.' Oliver stretched his mouth into a grin which didn't reach his eyes.

'A person can fall ill with the palsy at any time. When I was a child, Goody Welton lived with her daughter thus inflicted for many years. I saw Daniel watching me from across Lord Mayling's field and I know it was you who sent him. He admitted as much. Why would I have cursed him? Even if I could, which I cannot. I am no more a witch than you are, but you already know that.' Ursula wrapped her arms around her body and stared at him. Her fingertips were burning and twitching and she was sure he would be able to see.

'It matters not one half-groat whether I believe it or not,' Oliver pointed out. 'The fact is that your friends and neighbours understand it to be true and unless you finally now agree to my wishes, then you will find yourself in the sort of trouble from which you cannot extradite yourself. Now, only my protection can help you. And I shall not offer it forever, my patience wears thin.' His smile widened and he put his hand out to touch her. She stepped quickly back. 'You are even prettier when you are riled,' he added.

'I have said I will never agree to your proposal, nor be beholden to a man under any guise, not a husband or a… night visitor. I have told you this, and yet still you persist.' Ursula was afraid, but she tried to sound bored as if she were tired of the continued pursuit.

'So, you do not fear the rough edge of the rope around your neck? The drop and the tightening as you dance and gasp as your last breath leaves your body. Can you tell me that does not make the contents of your stomach turn to liquid? I do not believe you are as brave as you wish me to believe, mistress.' His face was pressed close to hers, his breath stinking of beer and onions. He was right, she was terrified of what may happen, but she needed to keep up with her boldness even though it was now parchment thin. If he knew how frightened she was, her fight was lost.

'Your words are empty,' she sneered. 'If you have no more to say then take your threats, your accusations, and leave my house forever.' Her voice rose at the end and pushing his face so close his greasy nose grazed against hers, he laughed loudly.

'You have drawn the battle lines, mistress,' he spat in her face. She was getting used to wiping away people's spittle. 'I have played with you long enough and now you will see how wrong you are to cross me. You shall let me have you, or nobody else will. I am not a man to force myself on you, but heed my words, you will come begging to me before the month is out.' Unbolting the door, he walked out and snatched his horse's reins from out of the small boy's hands so fast the leather must have burnt his skin as he whipped them away and he looked at his palms, his mouth turning down.

'Come here, I can give you salve for that,' Ursula called, but it seemed even the smallest of villagers had been warned to stay away from her because, with his eyes wide, he shook his head and turned and ran down the street towards home, dirt flying up from his bare feet.

Slowly she closed the door and pushed the wooden bar back

down. She walked through to the scullery and poured herself a small cup of the potent mead she kept for occasions such as this. When she was as frightened as she'd ever been, as fearful as when her father had still been at home. She drank the contents of the cup straight down and without thinking twice she poured a second, carrying it through to sit beside the fire. Raking the embers and throwing another log onto the fire she watched as the flames began to lick against it, sending dancing sparks up the chimney, bright against the soot blackened bricks.

Was what the doctor was asking for really worse than what may come next? Most women would acquiesce to such demands and Ursula could not blame them for doing so, considering what the alternative was. And yet, she could not. She yearned to live her own solitary life as she had been. As her own mother was unable to.

Her knees were still shaking as she sipped the second cup of drink more slowly and its warmth began to relax her taut muscles. Without a doubt she was now facing a battle she had to win. One for her life. Oliver had an arsenal of weapons, and she had none. Certainly not the Prince of Darkness on her side, as he was telling all who would listen. Sitting on her own beside the fire she felt the dark clouds gathering and the walls around her closing in. Never before had her confidence been thus challenged and in her heart, she knew that she was going to have to find reserves she wasn't sure she possessed. Terrible days lay ahead, the tight strands of worry sang in the air.

37

2024

Arriving at the flat, Adrianna let herself in, her hands no longer shaking when she turned the key, as they had been earlier. Immediately she could smell the bitter aroma of Rick's strong coffee as the steam from the machine floated through the apartment. It made her feel a little nauseous.

'Hey, it's just me,' she called, 'I thought I'd surprise you with a weekend visit.'

As she wandered into the kitchen she found him leaning up against the worktop, his cup in his hand. She gave him a hug and a kiss but she noticed that he kept his arm with the cup across his chest as if barring her from getting close. She also spotted that the pile of dirty dishes had gone, although there were still crumbs and a hand of brown, weeping bananas on the worktop.

'You really shouldn't have come down,' Rick snapped at her and immediately she felt her previous ebullience deflate like a week-old balloon. 'Why didn't you ask first? I could have told you it was a bad idea.'

'Ask? To come home?' she questioned. 'I thought you'd be pleased to see me. A weekend together in London.'

'Of course, I would normally.' He put his spare arm around her shoulder and grateful, she snuggled into him. She had so much to tell him, but his reaction to her being home had stalled her momentarily. 'But I've been so busy, the flat's a complete mess.'

'It's fine I can soon give the place a quick clean. I'm only here for two days, I'll go back to Norfolk on Sunday.' As she said the words, she realised that she couldn't wait to be back there. London no longer held the thrall it once did. 'I came down because I had to go into the office, one of the bosses emailed me about some cock-up with fees a customer was charged on one of my projects.'

Before she could explain any further, Rick interrupted her. 'What the heck Addie,' he said. 'How could you have been so stupid? If it's your fault, then you've really messed up this time. You'll be sacked before you've even completed your sabbatical and then what will you do? You certainly won't be able to keep this flashy apartment.'

'It was all fine.' She held her hand up to stop him talking. Her jaw tightened as she clenched her teeth and she waggled it from side to side. 'I went into the office when I arrived this morning, it wasn't an error on my part and James was very grateful I was able to sort it out. In fact, he said how they're missing me and asked when I could return.'

'Until you end up in a state again,' Rick said.

'To be honest as time goes on, I'm not sure a job, or a life, in London is what I want any more.' It was the first time she'd voiced her thoughts and she realised with a start that what she'd said was correct. The road her old life had travelled no longer felt like one she wanted to rejoin.

'Nonsense.' His voice came out sharply. 'Surely you don't want to leave this lovely apartment. Perhaps you just need a less stressful job, something not so high-powered. Look, don't worry about it now.' Rick's voice was back to its usual soothing cadence. 'Why don't we go out for dinner? There's a new steak restaurant down by the docks.'

'Good idea,' she said, 'and whilst we eat, I can tell you about my investigations.' She looked up at him just in time to catch him rolling his eyes before he plastered a smile on his face.

'Great,' he said, pouring himself another coffee. 'Let me get showered and changed so we can get a table at the restaurant, I'm starving. Then maybe we can go to a bar for a couple of drinks.' He disappeared to the bedroom and Adrianna flopped on the sofa. The cushions were still in the same place but at least the beer bottles were gone, even if their sticky residue remained.

She stared out of the window at the view across the Thames, but her eyes saw nothing. Her head was full of the realisation that whatever Rick had told her – when she'd had her break-down as he'd chosen to call it – she had in fact been doing her job correctly. The recognition that she hadn't been on a precipice, as her head had persuaded her at the time, swept over her in a sense of searing relief, bringing tears to her eyes. Why had she thought she was washed up, not up to the job? Once she'd had a couple of wobbly thoughts, it had all snowballed and every little worry became immense. Yet these figures on the screen that morning showed her that her fears were groundless. She was as strong and capable as every other member of her department.

Dinner wasn't as Adrianna had imagined or hoped for. The restaurant seemed to be popular amongst Rick's friends and he spent half of the meal jumping up to greet others with a lot of clapping people on the back and then giving them a thumbs up across the room. He didn't introduce Adrianna to any of them but would announce who they were when he resumed eating.

There was no one familiar, mostly they seemed to be other estate agents or people he met and drank with in the evenings. As they had left the flat, she'd spotted a chunky shining Rolex on his wrist, but as he was in a good mood again, she decided she'd mention it later. They had plenty of time and she didn't want the evening to begin with him in a sour mood.

'You seem to know lots of people,' she joked. 'Do you come here often?'

'Not much else to do,' he replied. 'Now that I'm on my own every night.' Adrianna ignored the barb. He'd been the one who'd encouraged her to go away and take a break, and yet now she felt guilty.

'I could come back to London sooner if you want,' she said.

As she made the suggestion the thought filled her with more dismay than she'd envisaged. She'd become accustomed to living in the countryside. The flat horizon, the apple trees bending to every whim of the salt-scented wind which blew across from the sea. But she'd give it all up in a heartbeat to make Rick happy, he was her world.

'No, no.' Rick held his left hand up waving his fork about and dripping peppercorn sauce on the white tablecloth where it sat in little globules. 'You said you needed to be away from London for six months, and I fully support you on that.'

Adrianna couldn't stop the laugh that came from her. 'I didn't say I needed to be away for six months,' she exclaimed. 'I took that time off work, intending to stay somewhere for a month and have a rest. It was you who insisted I went for the whole six months. And after my meeting with James today, I've realised that I'm not the confused mess I thought I was.'

'Addie, Addie, you were in such a state you can't even remember what you said. You looked at a month's Airbnb and decided it would be no more expensive to rent somewhere for six months and then found that decrepit little place you're currently living in,' Rick said, putting his hand over hers. 'Honestly you were so out of it, with all those pills your doctor gave you, I'm not surprised you can't remember it properly.'

She couldn't deny that the medication she was on at the time had made her feel disconnected from normal life, so Rick was probably right. 'I've stopped taking the pills,' she told him. 'I'm feeling so much better. And James said he'd be happy if I wanted to come back to work now. Delighted, in fact.'

'And then when you've been there a couple of weeks and been shouted at for not completing the work properly, you'll be back to square one.' Rick raised his eyebrows and pushed a big forkful of meat into his mouth, saying, 'You know I'm right.' A fine spray of food spread across the table. Adrianna laid her fork down, no longer hungry, even though she'd only taken three bites of her risotto.

Perhaps he was speaking sense, it was one thing to go into a single meeting and be able to clear up an issue but it was completely different to find herself in charge of a multi-million budget and a large team of staff. And having to meet with clients and tell them their project wasn't going to be delivered on time. Maybe she was telling herself what she wanted to hear.

'You're right, I know you are.' She smiled at him even though she could feel tears welling up. Embarrassed, she searched in her bag for a tissue.

'For Christ's sake,' Rick muttered under his breath, 'don't make a scene.' Adrianna shook her head and gave him a watery smile. 'Anyway, if you aren't going to eat that...' Abruptly changing the subject, Rick stretched across the table and lifted her plate before tipping her dinner onto his own, now empty, one. Adrianna was pleased the subject of her returning to London appeared to be closed.

After dinner they went to a bar which appeared to be filled with workers who hadn't yet made it home. There was very little room even to stand but despite Adrianna's suggestion that they took their drinks outside where the evening was still warm, Rick insisted they stood close to the bar. It didn't take long for her to realise he'd set himself up in a place where he could see everyone entering and leaving and after an hour during which she'd nursed a glass of prosecco and he'd downed three pints of ale, he shouted across to a group of men and women who'd just arrived. Grabbing Adrianna's hand, he pulled her through the crowds whilst she kept apologising as she cannoned into people holding drinks, until he reached the others. She didn't recognise any of them.

Rick introduced her to everyone but she couldn't remember all the names other than the woman standing to her left, Stacey.

'So how do you know Rick?' Stacey asked. 'I don't think I've seen you out with him before, have I?'

'I'm his girlfriend,' Adrianna explained. 'We live together, but I took a sabbatical from work so I'm currently renting a cottage in Norfolk and taking a break from city life.'

She'd noticed the look of perplexity on Stacey's face when she'd said they lived together but the other woman chose not to mention her confusion.

'Rick said he lives in one of the dockside apartments. You must have an amazing view, they're in a lovely location. My husband,' she indicated a man on the other side of the group who, as if he knew she was talking about him looked up and smiled at her, 'he's an estate agent too, but he can't be making as much commission as Rick, because we're living in a studio apartment in Stratford. You're very lucky.'

'Oh no, that isn't Rick's apartment, it's mine,' Adrianna corrected her. 'I work in Canary Wharf. It's easier for him to share my flat.' How easy it was now as apparently Rick couldn't afford to pay her his contribution, she wasn't sure. And judging by the number of people who greeted him enthusiastically she could tell he spent many evenings in bars downing pints and shots as he currently was. Whilst, it seemed, telling everyone that the flat with her name on the deeds and which she was paying the mortgage for, was his. It dawned on her that the reason Stacey had looked surprised when they were introduced was possibly because Rick had omitted to mention that he had a girlfriend, let alone that he was effectively now squatting in her home.

Putting her still-half-full glass on a nearby table, she sidled her way through the group until she was beside Rick. Smiling, he slung his arm across her shoulder and kissed the top of her head whilst he carried on good naturedly arguing with another man about the likelihood of Arsenal winning some football cup. She tapped him on the hand to draw his attention. Eventually he looked down at her.

'I've got a headache,' she said. It was the first excuse that came to mind because she knew that his response to her telling him she was sick of the crowd and the heat and the noise would be dismissive, 'I'm going to head home. It's already eleven o'clock, isn't it last orders anyway?'

'We're not out in the wilds now,' he laughed. 'You really have turned into a country mouse. This bar will be open until one in the morning and there are others which stay open later. Are you okay to get home? Shall I call you an Uber?'

'Oh, um, no it's fine I can do it, thank you.' Adrianna had hoped he'd finish his drink and leave with her, but it seemed he wasn't ready to call it a night. Slipping out through the crowd of people thronged outside she called a cab and was home twenty minutes later.

Letting herself into the flat she put the lamps on and stood in front of the sliding doors which opened onto the balcony. Stacey was right, the view was superb up here. In fact, it was what had sold the apartment to her.

Nothing had changed in London. The vista was still amazing. The flat was still gorgeous, even with the mess that Rick had let it get into. But she didn't fit in any more, it was she who'd changed. This shiny home, which went with her high-flying career, felt lacking, as if London had moved on without her. The lustre had tarnished.

'Don't be a fool,' she muttered under her breath. She'd simply got used to the slower moving pace of life in Norfolk but she needed to remember *this* was home, and work. Her job paid the bills and had allowed her to pause her life for six months. She needed to be thankful she was in a position to step off the hamster wheel and take a break.

Instinctively she walked around the flat tidying surfaces and rearranging the photo frames of her and Rick. The post which she'd picked up when she'd first arrived was still on the side table where she'd left it, and picking it up she shuffled through, but it was mostly for Rick. Everything she needed to deal with had been moved online before she'd left for Norfolk. The final envelope however had her name on and she opened it, glancing at the letter inside. It was from a credit card company, a circular confirming that she'd been approved for a card, which she tore up before throwing it into the recycling bin.

38

2024

When Adrianna awoke at nine o'clock the following morning, Rick's side of the bed was empty and hadn't been slept in. He did sometimes sleep on the sofa when he got in late, so getting up and finding an old night shirt she wandered through to the living room where the morning sun was streaming in and lighting up the room with its gold rays. She checked her phone to see if he'd messaged her, whilst looking around the kitchen to see if there was a note. Perhaps he'd gone to the gym or for a run first thing, but there was nothing. She called him and it went straight to voicemail.

'Out of battery I suppose.' She was trying to convince herself as her voice echoed around the empty flat, but she knew it was unlikely. Where the hell was he? It wasn't the first time he'd ended up at someone else's home and spent the night there, but this was her first visit to London in almost three months and she'd thought he'd be more pleased to see her. Her previous day's happiness seeped away. She'd been looking forward to a wander around Borough Market together to buy something delicious for dinner, maybe a look around the National Portrait

Gallery, as she hadn't been since it reopened. Just normal enjoyable weekend activities for a couple. Now she had no idea when Rick would return, but if it wasn't soon, the day would be over.

Making the decision not to sit around waiting for him to come home, doubtless hungover as well, Adrianna showered and dressed before heading out.

She tried Rick's phone several times but still there was no reply. Eventually she returned home with the ingredients for a curry, and a guidebook from the gallery. As she walked into the flat she could smell cigarette smoke and stale beer and she wrinkled her nose in disgust.

Rick was sitting on a chair on the balcony, a cigarette dangling over the edge of the top of the glass balustrade but he was doing nothing to stop the smoke from wafting back in where it hung, floating in a blue haze against the ceiling.

'Hello,' Adrianna called out deliberately keeping her voice cheerful as she picked up a cushion and wafted it up and down to try and get some of the smoke back outside.

'Where have you been?' Rick got to his feet, scowling. He looked as if he was about to walk back into the apartment with his cigarette but at the last moment he flicked it to the floor and ground it under his foot before stepping back into the room, leaving the butt on the balcony and sliding the door shut. *A bit late for that,* Adrianna thought as she put down the cushion she was flapping about.

'I went out for some food so I can cook us curry tonight, seeing as it's your favourite.' She held up her shopping bag. 'I did leave a couple of messages for you. And I went for a wander around the National Portrait Gallery, have you been yet?'

'Of course not, why would I want to go there?' he scoffed. 'Anyway, I thought we could go out to eat tonight.'

'Out again?' Adrianna said. She could hear a pathetic note in her voice. 'I thought it would be nice to spend some time just the two of us together. Like we used to.'

'We used to be out all the time when you were down here,' Rick replied, his face darkening into an all-too-familiar pout. 'You've just got too used to being a stay-at-home country bumpkin. What would we do here all evening?'

'We could find something on Netflix? I've missed being able to snuggle down with you and watch a film. I have to go back tomorrow and I've barely seen you.'

'Well, you shouldn't have turned up unannounced, babes. I'd already made plans for the weekend. I'm going to grab a shower and maybe if you cook now, we can go and meet some of the guys for a couple of drinks later?'

Despite it being one of his favourite meals, Rick pushed his curry around his plate before declaring himself not hungry. He tipped three quarters of it into the bin and told her his friends were all meeting up at nine o'clock. The time on her phone told her that it was eight thirty, but luckily she'd already showered and, leaving the dishes on the kitchen worktop, she hurried through to the bedroom to change into clean jeans and a T-shirt which didn't smell of spices and garlic. She only had a couple of minutes to apply some make up.

'Good, are we ready then?' he asked in a cheerful voice. It was a shame his voice wasn't reflected in his countenance. 'We're wasting valuable drinking time. Oh, and can you buy the drinks tonight please. I'm a bit skint, remember?'

'Of course. I thought I'd take my orange handbag tonight, the posh one I keep in a box in my wardrobe, but it's not there. Can you remember where I put it?' Adrianna asked.

'The big one? The one you said was too heavy? You sold it, don't you remember?'

Adrianna didn't, but now he'd mentioned it, the leather was

thick and it had hurt her shoulder; she could remember saying something about it.

'No problem, I wasn't getting a lot of use out of it anyway. Come on, let's get going.' She was rewarded by a bright smile and a hug, and heaving a sigh of relief at his improved mood, she followed him out to the lift.

The evening at the bar followed much the same pattern as the previous one and by eleven thirty Adrianna had had enough and told Rick she wanted to go home.

'But the evening's barely begun,' he replied. 'I'm not ready to call it a night yet.'

'It's fine,' she assured him. 'You stay here, I'll see you later.' She gave him a quick peck on the cheek and turned to go, but his hand grabbed hold of her wrist stopping her. He was holding her so tightly it was burning her skin and she tried to pull her arm away.

'Lend me your bank card, can you?' he said. 'I might need to buy a couple of rounds.'

'Rick you're hurting me, let go.' She tried again to pull her arm away, but his grip tightened.

'I won't go mad, just so I can get one more drink after this one and then I'll be home I promise.' He eased his hand a little and drew her closer, kissing the top of her head. Did he really have so little money, she wondered? Reluctantly she took out her purse and gave him her card.

'Don't lose it,' she said, but made sure she was smiling as she did so.

'Of course not,' he laughed, his mood suddenly a lot brighter. 'You can trust me, darling.'

Adrianna hurried to her flat rubbing her arm as she went. She was sure Rick hadn't realised how tightly he was holding her but she was feeling uneasy. When she got back, she packed her belongings into her case ready for her journey home. She was looking forward to being back in the cottage. Perhaps Rick was right and she'd turned into a country mouse. There was nothing in London, other than him, that made her want to return.

* * *

The following morning she was up as soon as it was daylight, having got used to doing so in Norfolk. Once again Rick wasn't in the bed beside her, but this time he was stretched out on the sofa, snoring loudly, with one side of his hair sticking up. The dishes from the previous night's dinner were still on the worktop and had been joined by a frying pan coated in congealed fat and smelling of bacon. It didn't cover the stench of cigarette smoke though and sure enough she found two butts in a saucer. His previous attempts to disguise his habit seemed to have been abandoned.

Screwing up her nose, she put everything in the dishwasher and switched it on, enjoying the loud whooshing of water as she also filled and flicked on the kettle. There was no movement from the sofa so she told the smart speaker on top of the fridge to play her loudest playlist. Sure enough, that roused him and he pushed himself upright scratching his head and looking around bleary eyed.

'Ouch Addie, can you turn that down please? I'm hanging here,' he groaned. She instructed the speaker to lower its volume and carried on making herself a cup of tea.

'Any chance of a coffee?' he asked. Adrianna looked at the coffee machine and then took the jar of instant powder she used to have from the cupboard. Once the kettle had boiled she made them both drinks and took his over, perching on the edge of the chair opposite.

'I'm going back to Norfolk today,' she reminded him. 'I had thought we could do something nice together first, but you don't seem in a state to go out for a Sunday walk and brunch.'

'I'm so sorry darling, I'm really not,' Rick said. 'Next time you're coming down, can you give me some notice so we can plan to do some things together? I'm not very good with surprises, you know that. I feel rotten we haven't done much.'

It hadn't been the weekend she'd been looking forward to either, Adrianna thought. But she'd had been a much better meeting at work than she'd envisaged. There was a lot to think about now she knew she'd be welcomed back with open arms. She'd done most of what she'd intended to in London, visiting the gallery and shops, it was just the spending time with her boyfriend on his own which hadn't gone to plan. She did know he didn't like surprises though, so really it was her own fault he hadn't been able to spend so much time with her.

Once she was showered it was still only eight o'clock but a quick check of her train app showed her there was one leaving in an hour so she booked a ticket and picked up her bag and jacket. Rick didn't suggest she left later.

'How about I come and see you next weekend?' he said. 'We can have a lovely time, just the two of us. Get some food in and we can spend the weekend in bed.' He raised his eyebrows at her and she laughed.

'That sounds like a plan,' she agreed, feeling her despondency about the past two days lift a little.

'Do you want me to throw some clothes on and come to the station?' he asked before adding 'please say no, I don't think my head can take it.'

'It's fine,' she laughed at his turned-down mouth. 'Now give me a kiss and a cuddle because I need to be on my way.'

Rick prised himself off the sofa and gave her a hug before

kissing her for so long she thought she'd pass out from lack of oxygen. She could taste the cigarettes but she didn't care. This was the Rick she loved.

'I'll see you next Friday evening,' he promised. 'Two days just to ourselves.'

'That sounds perfect.' She blew him one last kiss goodbye and left, transferring her bag to the other arm as she did so. Her right arm was still aching and she'd noticed a bruise starting to come up in the shape of five fingertips. She was sure Rick would be mortified if he'd realised how hard he'd been holding her, and she pulled her sleeve down to cover it.

39

1646

The unremitting summer heat continued. The balmy late spring had now segued into a violently hot summer. The thatched roof of the inn opposite Ursula's cottage caught fire and almost razed the building to the ground. Fire and its ability to spread across rooftops was a danger everyone feared, and soon buckets of water from the well were being passed hand to hand down the village street to douse the flames.

The following day Katherine arrived at Ursula's back door, tapping at the wood until she was let in.

'Did you see the fire last night?' she asked as she sat down in the scullery accepting the cup of ale Ursula proffered. Katherine was once again with child and her ankles were swollen, even though she was not yet seven months gone. Her belly was still high, but huge. She'd asked Ursula to look at her palm and see if there were twins predicted there, but Ursula could only see a line of seven single babies. 'I heard voices claiming they had seen you at your door mouthing an incantation and you were the cause of it. I am sorry to have to bring this to you.'

'It is a falsehood, you know that, do you not? I opened my

door, it is true, but just to see what all the noise was about. A stray spark from their chimney would have started that fire, everyone knows that. It has happened many times before.' Ursula could hear the weariness in her own voice. She was growing increasingly tired of the continuous accusations.

'I said that to Paul, but he told me to not speak out. Any danger you may encounter could find its way to our door as quickly as the fire spread last night. Rumour and ill feeling dances from house to house at present, as fast as the galloping flames across the rooftops,' Katherine answered.

'He is right.' Ursula pulled a face as she took hold of Katherine's hand. 'You have more important things to concern you. And soon you shall be lying in, you must concentrate on your health and that of your baby.'

'That is the other reason I am visiting,' Katherine admitted. 'I have been forbidden from having you as my midwife this time, I must use Mary Smith from Great Mayling. I said that you are no witch and reminded him you safely delivered our other children and those of our neighbours, but he will not heed my words. I am so sorry.'

'It is no surprise to me,' Ursula admitted. 'I overheard two goodwives on the street saying that a baby had been born in Great Mayling three days ago. I would usually be asked to attend that house, but this time I was not. They chose Mary Smith too, even though she is not as experienced as I. And as I did for yourself, I previously delivered their other babes. I can only hope the claims against me will soon be forgotten. But let us talk of happier things! Tell me how everyone in the village fares.'

'They are mostly all well. One of the ploughmen wed the miller's sister yesterday and a great deal of beer was drunk,' Katherine said. 'I suspect there will be several babies born next spring.'

Ursula laughed. 'Tis the same after every wedding when the weather is good and the carousing carries on long into the night. With the nights so warm and sticky at present I am sure people were still enjoying the festivities as the sun rose. It is far too hot this year, I cannot remember a summer like this, we are living in a bread oven and there has been no rain for weeks. The harvest will fail if the weather does not turn soon.'

'Let us hope the rain arrives shortly, because I do not want that to be another thing the villagers can blame on you,' Katherine said as she stood up to leave. Ursula held her arms out at her sides, her palms up.

'How can anyone believe that I can control the weather? It can only be orchestrated by God and to think otherwise is simply foolishness, and blasphemy,' she said.

Katherine nodded in agreement. 'This heat brings a fever of madness, which is starting to stir in the village,' she warned. 'A dark animal is awakening. Do not tell yourself that your friends will disbelieve the lies they are told. These are being passed around the village.' Her voice dropped to barely more than a whisper. 'I have been shown more than one this morning.' She passed a pamphlet similar to the previous one to Ursula, who lit a candle so she could read the tiny writing printed on it. There was also a woodcut image of a man with an oversized head like a bull with horns. She knew immediately it was a crude imagining of the devil.

It described the arrival in King's Lynn of a man called Matthew Hopkins, known in the East as the Witchfinder General and apparently so named by the king himself. He'd been invited by the mayor because of a case of suspected witchcraft. Hopkin's biography was alarming, telling of the inordinate number of witches he'd found in Essex and subsequently sent to their death.

Ursula felt a chill crawl up her body taking her breath away. Was it coincidence he was in the area just when rumours were circulating that she was a witch? Or had someone brought him here? King's Lynn was but half a day's ride from Finchingham. It felt like a pivotal moment; she could stay and fight, or she could run. But time was short and she'd have to decide very soon. She'd done nothing wrong, whatever rumours Oliver chose to spread. He knew the truth. If Hopkins was coming for her, she'd show him he was mistaken. She was strong enough to do this, and she would do it not just for herself but for every woman in the country who had no charge over their lives, forced to marry men they did not love and then abused at the hands of those husbands. Or lay with men because they were always more powerful than women. And she'd do it for her mother, who'd lost her life to such a bully.

After they said their goodbyes and Katherine slipped once more out of the back of the cottage, Adrianna picked up her pestle and laid it back down. What was the point of making medications for her neighbours if no one was coming to purchase them? Katherine was right, there was a dark madness crawling on its belly like a snake through the village.

40

2024

Adrianna was halfway between Downham Market and King's Lynn when she remembered she'd given Rick her bank card. Pulling out her phone she quickly sent him a WhatsApp asking him to bring it with him the following Friday. She could use her phone for most purchases but occasionally she still needed her card. Looking at her banking app to see how much he'd spent the previous evening, her mouth fell open as she saw the numerous amounts spent at the bar she'd left him in. Quickly she ran her eyes down the entries, none of which were less than forty pounds and often more. She estimated a rough total of at least four hundred pounds. She sent another message to Rick telling him that under no circumstances was he to use the card again.

Finchingham was basked in sunshine when she arrived back at the cottage, a heat haze shimmering over the fields behind her making the trees and hedgerows dance. It made her think of the fierce summer recorded centuries before. Dropping her bag inside she immediately changed into T-shirt, shorts and sandals and set off to the footpath which led from the Post Office to the beach.

A few families were sitting on the sand, but she walked in the opposite direction towards the rocks at one end enclosing the small piece of the beach in its own secluded bay. How wonderful to own a house within walking distance of this secret place.

Perching on a boulder which was already warm from the sun she took some photos and sent them to Rick with a 'bet you wish you were here!' message. She noticed that he hadn't replied to her message about her bank card, but remembering how he was after a night out, she didn't doubt that once she'd left, he'd crawled into bed and was still there asleep. Such a waste of a day. Beside her the now-familiar herring gull flew down and alighted, but she barely took any notice of it these days. Why it was always following her, if indeed it was the same one and not just a coincidence, she had no idea. She turned back to the sea and closed her eyes, enjoying the warmth on her eyelids.

Being in London with all that had happened there, had unsettled her. She could feel the tension beginning to seep away and the muscles in her shoulders loosen a little as she slipped back into her calm Norfolk life. She was two different people, the person she was with Rick, and the more relaxed one she was on her own. The thought perturbed her.

Eventually she felt the skin on her face growing tight where it was beginning to burn, and reluctantly she decided she'd better return home, it would be cooler in the cottage. Hearing a shout, she looked across the beach where she spotted Roger and Tom with Apollo. Or rather, the two men on the beach while Apollo ran in and out of the waves, pausing each time he was on the beach to shake himself over them. Adrianna was laughing so hard she didn't notice when the dog suddenly changed direction and bounded up to her, ensuring that she too was covered in droplets of salty water.

'Sorry!' Roger ran across to her waving his arms in apology. 'He loves the sea but he doesn't usually go this mad when he gets wet. Are you totally soaking?' He looked her up and down as she ran her hands over her face rubbing away the water. She was about to confirm that she was fine when she noticed that Roger was staring at her wrist. Looking down at it she cursed herself. She'd forgotten about the bruises from the night before and they were now a deep livid purple like an amethyst bracelet.

'What on earth have you done to yourself?' he asked, holding her fingertips so he could see properly.

'Oh, it's nothing.' Adrianna gave a little laugh although she was sure that she didn't sound very convincing. 'I managed to trap it in a train door when I was on the tube,' she said.

'You may need to go and see a doctor,' Roger suggested. She looked away from his prying eyes, certain he knew she was lying.

'Honestly it looks worse than it is,' she reassured him even though in fact it was aching badly and she couldn't remember if she had any paracetamol in the house. 'Anyway, I've been sitting in the sun too long and I need to get back. I was in London for a couple of days, I haven't even unpacked yet.'

By this point Tom had also joined them, Apollo slumped on the sand at their feet panting, his tongue hanging out of the side of his mouth.

'Any news about the dead body?' Tom asked.

'Nothing yet,' Adrianna shook her head, 'but I've had confirmation it's now at the lab which Jess kindly arranged, so it's just a matter of waiting now.'

Saying her goodbyes, with Roger suggesting again she should seek medical advice, she walked back over the dunes, holding her sore arm across her body with the other one. It was throbbing now and for some inexplicable reason, Adrianna could feel tears welling up.

'You're just tired,' she muttered to herself. 'A cup of tea, some toast and a doze and you'll be fine.'

* * *

After several hours of sleep Adrianna woke up to see long shadows stretching across her bedroom, the sun a deep orange orb resting on the horizon as it slowly slipped away.

Annoyed with herself for wasting half of the day in bed and knowing that she'd have trouble sleeping later, she ate some dinner before clearing the kitchen table and getting out the papers from where she'd tucked them away. There on top, the warning tormented her. Putting the pages that she'd already translated to one side, she turned to the next one and began to meticulously copy each letter down. These next two pages were more concerning than the others she'd read.

The danger to my life grows daily. My neighbours say that I cursed Samuel and killed him to fulfil the prophesy I saw in Rebecca's palm. I am certain Oliver dropped the poppet down the well, he is more intent than ever to bend me to his will and is turning my friends against me. He twists everything to become the tale he wishes to tell and I am fearful for my life. I believe that a charge of witchcraft is to be brought against me.

Written this day the fourth day of July in the year of our Lord 1646.

It confirmed what she'd read in the Millers' ledger: that Ursula was in grave danger and Oliver Bruton was at the root of the persecution. Because she'd spurned his advances. What a dreadful time for a woman to be alive, Adrianna thought, even their body wasn't their own. She read the entry through several times. There was something snagging at her brain, but she couldn't work out what it was. Then as if a cloud had moved from her vision she stared at the sentence about Oliver twisting what was said to suit his own agenda. It felt painfully, worryingly familiar and her face, already pink from the sun, flushed with shock.

Behind her a loud bang made her jump as the back door suddenly swung open hitting the wall behind it. Going over to close it, for a moment she looked outside and across the garden and surrounding land pulsating in the heat. There was no wind, not even a breeze. The air felt static and pensive, as if a fissure in time between her and the past had momentarily opened, letting Ursula's spirit through. Something was stirring. There was still an element missing in what she now knew, and it was the piece of the puzzle which would tell her the full story.

The more she discovered, the closer she felt to this woman who'd occupied the house long ago. She stared out of the window at the vista beyond. A pair of magpies shrieked at each other as they hopped from tree to ground and back again in some sort of elaborate mating dance. Adrianna realised that this had been absent from her life. She needed to be in the wilds, this was where she belonged. Here where she could feel the earth turning beneath her feet, the ancient vibrations of the cycle of nature throughout the centuries. Close to others who had felt the same.

41

1646

Ursula was now living in a constant state of fear. The weather matched her mood, shards of tension could be felt every time she breathed in the scorched, still air shimmering with anticipation. Just when it felt as though the weather couldn't get any hotter, it did. The land behind her cottage had the bleached look of a cornfield at harvest, except it was still a month before that time and now the crops had stopped growing and were beginning to die. She knew she was being blamed for the fact that, every morning, the sun rose over the sea into a cloudless pale blue sky, roasting those who worked the land. Katherine had visited briefly before she was confined to ready herself for the birth, and told her there were several cases of burned skin, but nobody would call on Ursula to purchase the balm they knew she could provide to ease their pain.

Ursula only ventured from her cottage to go out scavenging for meat and to collect water late at night when the sun was down, though the air was still warm and thick like honey as she breathed it in. The water in the well was now low and it took many turns of the handle to raise the bucket. With the ground so parched, there were few rabbits, but she managed to cull the occasional pigeon with her slingshot, a skill learned when she was young.

One night she walked to the sea and wandered in the cool waves as they rushed up the beach. She looked out at the darkness, the sky stretched above scattered with a dense aurora of stars watching her. Waiting, as she also waited, for whatever would inevitably come to pass. Her mother had spoken of the night sky when she'd travelled on the ship to England. That the darkness pressed down as if she could reach up and touch it, and she'd look at the moon and imagine it shining on the family they'd left behind. The same moonlight that now fell on Ursula. Perhaps now was the time for her to think about leaving to find where her ancestors came from if she could afford her passage.

When she awoke, the morning after her night visit to the sea, the sun had already risen and her cottage, despite its stone walls which usually kept it cool inside, already felt stiflingly hot. Her shift was stuck to her skin with the sweat running down her. A sharp wind had blown up and the shutters were banging against the window frame despite being barred from within.

Downstairs she could hear the doors also rattling and a squawk that was without doubt Wicker somewhere in the garden. He rarely seemed to leave the cottage and immediate area now. Standing up she wafted her shift away from her skin to try and cool herself. There was an unpleasant stale smell to her skin, but she didn't have enough water to spare any to wash herself. She'd tie some dried lavender muslin bags to her dress which was still damp from the sea, feeling cool against her bare legs. It was too hot for hose.

As she climbed down the ladder there was a brisk draught coming from beneath the front door brushing against her ankles, sweeping up dust and dirt from the road as it swirled and eddied across the flagstones beneath her feet. Opening the shutters in her scullery, Ursula could see the trees and hedgerows in the distance, bowed to one side in the violent wind. The heat hadn't abated and a storm was brewing on the horizon, a gathering of oppressive, heavy bruised clouds like crushed blackberries, piled up one on top of the other. Over the sea where she'd sat and looked at the stars the previous night, she could just make out a black line where the sea ended and the vicious sky began, a single strip of something suspended, something unearthly waiting to make its way inland. Taking out her journal she added a short entry describing the harsh, steamy heat, the feeling of expectation.

The day rolled by with every minute seeming to last an hour. Ursula could sense something terrible hovering in the air, a dreadful anticipation. She wished she could read her own future, but that wasn't possible, she could only see what others may meet in life. Or death. Perhaps it was better that she couldn't see what God meant for her.

Her musing was interrupted by a banging at the front door. She'd got so used to the lack of visitors, she gave a jump and without stopping to think about who it may be, lifted the wooden bar and opened it.

Immediately she wished she hadn't, but it was too late to slam it shut as the three men on the doorstep strode in. Oliver, of course, followed by two others, one of whom was clutching a tall black hat in his hands as if he'd snatched it off his head before the wind did the job for him. With his puritan black clothes, collar-length dark hair and narrow face with a sharp pointed beard, she instantly recognised him from the woodcut image on the pamphlet now stashed beneath the floorboards. Matthew Hopkins, Witchfinder General. She had no idea who the other gentleman was, but he was picking things up from her bench and sniffing at them. She clenched her teeth together and said nothing, instead turning to Oliver narrowing her eyes and waiting for him to speak. Behind them the door banged as Hopkins pushed it shut. He wasn't a tall man and he had to lean his shoulder against it battling into the wind.

'Mistress,' Oliver said looking at her. She stared back and continued to say nothing, breathing in and out with shallow breaths to try and slow her racing heart and not display on her face how scared she was. She pushed her fingers beneath her armpits, her arms across her chest. 'I have brought these two gentlemen to visit you because it is said both in the village and beyond, that you are a witch. They have the authority to question you and decide if you should stand trial.'

'Matthew Hopkins,' the man with the hat introduced himself, 'and this is my assistant John Stearne. We have been furnished with a list of people you are purported to have cursed and killed, together with other offences you have committed.' He held up an official looking document but as Ursula went to snatch it, he whipped it back out of reach. 'I will read it to you,' he said.

'I can read it myself.' Ursula finally found her voice and she was relieved it wasn't wavering despite how frightened she was. Oliver looked at her in surprise. He'd obviously not realised that she was literate. Ignoring her, Matthew held it up and began to intone.

'On the fifteenth day of the month of June, you did see Daniel Hooke going about his lawful business close to your home yet not within its environs. You shouted at him in a way that was unwomanly and told him to stay away or something terrible would befall him.'

'I said nothing of the sort,' Ursula burst out, but holding up his hand as if to ward off her interruptions, Hopkins continued.

'Thereafter Master Hooke did suffer a severe case of the palsy and is no longer able to speak or move the left side of his body.' Ursula opened her mouth again to point out that as Daniel couldn't talk how was he able to blame her, but she knew by that point she wasn't going to be listened to. These men had a plan to be fulfilled and they would not be silenced.

'Further, on the thirty-first day in the month of May, you were called upon by Rebecca of Oak Tree Cottage who wished to know if she would be able to bear children. She asked for you to see her future in her hand. You later informed her that her husband was to die, following which you poisoned Samuel by dropping a poppet stabbed with wolfsbane twigs and blackthorn from your own garden into the well. He subsequently fell ill and is now deceased.' During this Oliver kept his eyes down trained on his highly polished boots but at this point he looked up at her. His face gave nothing away but his eyes, shining with triumph, said everything. She opened her mouth to refute the accusations but glaring at her, Hopkins continued.

'It is also said that you have brought forth this burning weather, the flames of hell which scorched the crops in the field and caused the roof of the inn to catch fire.' Now Ursula had heard enough.

'Commanding the weather?' she scoffed. 'Only the good Lord above can do that, and everything you have said is simply hearsay and pitiful village gossip. I did see on Rebecca's hand that she is to be wed twice, but I could not foresee Samuel was to meet his maker so soon afterwards. I have never seen someone die in such a way, I do not know what caused it. Perhaps you should ask Master Bruton if he has any ideas given that, according to him, he is a physician.'

'Of course I could not identify it,' Oliver spat, 'because it was a cursed body the likes of which I have never before encountered.' His face was red, his fists clenched and with a small degree of satisfaction Ursula could see that her comment about his qualifications had riled him. She had nothing to lose now.

'And anyone can fall down with the palsy,' she continued. 'Daniel has always been of a high colour, which the doctor here will agree is oft-times indicative of suffering an attack such as this. If he is now struck dumb, how exactly was he able to tell you I had been shouting at him?' she pointed out.

'We have a written submission,' came the answer. Ursula knew that Daniel could neither read nor write but it felt futile arguing with them any longer. 'And finally, it has been noted that you have a familiar who is doing your evil bidding. Who was seen dropping the poppet in the well. A large gull which even now is flying outside in the street and trying to attack those who would approach your cottage.' Ursula imagined Wicker doing that, even though she knew he was just a bird and not really doing anything at her behest. She battled to keep her face straight and not laugh. It would only further inflame their wrath.

'That bird is just the same as any other which flies inland in search of food. Nothing you have said this morning has any base in the truth,' she said. 'Yet it seems that you have made your minds up. Undoubtedly prompted and abetted by Master Bruton, who has fabricated these allegations.' She narrowed her eyes as she studied him. He dropped his gaze so once again he was examining his boots. A large spider scuttled across the floor and lifting one foot, he stamped on it.

'You shall be taken to King's Lynn gaol for further questioning,' Hopkins told her, 'and when it has been proved you are indeed a witch you shall go before a judge at the county assizes, where they will hang you until you flail on the end of the rope.'

'Let me at least put on my boots,' Ursula said as she moved towards the back door where they'd been left. Across the fields, the leaden skies she'd observed earlier had rolled in closer and were now hung heavily above them, suspended in the stifling air and darkening the day, a threat of violent suffocation. There was a crackling, splinters of noise that not only could she hear but could also feel as they fractured and hissed around her. As she watched, the clouds were suddenly lit up from behind turning their melancholy grey momentarily radiant as if the sky were on fire, flames reaching down to raze them all to the ground. The air was almost too hot to breathe in, singeing her throat. The three men had moved from the other room so they were crowded into the scullery behind her, looking out at what she could see.

'A storm is coming,' Stearne announced from where he stood at the window. It was the first time Ursula had heard him speak and she was surprised at how high pitched and womanly his voice was. 'We cannot take the horses back in this, the weather will spook them.' He flinched as another vivid white flare of lightning flamed the sky.

'Indeed,' Oliver agreed. 'Take them to the inn across the road, they have stables where the animals can be kept. We will wait with the witch to ensure she does not magic her disappearance whilst the storm is upon us. It seems coincidental that just as we arrive to confront her with a list of offences, the hot weather breaks and the fury of Lucifer descends.' He picked up the ewer of ale which sat on the scullery table and poured out two beakers, draining the last drop so there was none left for Ursula even if she'd wanted some. Stearne left and the other two men drank in silence as they watched and waited.

The intense sky above them deepened further as if it were night and Ursula could hear her chickens clucking in their shed. She was relieved she hadn't let them out that morning. The birds in the trees were hushed though, as if they did indeed think nightfall had dropped again. Wicker flew onto the windowsill and banged sharply on the glass with his beak making the men jump. Hopkins swore and banged his fist on the window but the gull didn't move. Ursula cursed it silently. It was adding to the danger she now found herself in, even she was beginning to question its presence. Cracks of lightning came one after the other, illuminating the sky – a portent of what was to come.

A sudden loud clattering made them all jump as something began to fall to the ground. It was too loud to be rain and looking out at the ground Ursula could see large pieces of white stone landing. Round as if hailstones but nothing like the size she'd ever seen before, these were huge. Big enough to kill a person if they were struck. Stearne burst through the door from the street shouting as if he was being flayed alive and the other two men looked at her wordlessly. Wicker took to the air and flew away.

Ursula waited for the rain she was expecting after the hail, but it didn't come. The black clouds were now directly overhead and through the window she could hear the crash of thunder as it spread across the village, making the ground beneath them tremble. This was a storm unlike anything any of the occupants of the room had ever encountered. The lightning and thunder in a pattern, the scorches of white light and the subsequent cracks happening almost simultaneously. The dried grasses in the field and the remains of her vegetables were laid flat by the wind now whipping across the land. Ursula put her hands by her side and stretched her fingers out slowly until they were straight and rigid. It felt as if they were on fire. The land, her land, was waking up and coming alive.

She saw what was coming before the others did, her eyesight ever sharp. A dark pillar stretched from the clouds to the sea, growing in size as it raced inland.

'What is that?' Oliver's voice wavered and Ursula was pleased to hear the horror as he spoke. Finally, his boldness had deserted him.

'I do not know, but it is coming towards us,' Hopkins answered, his voice coming out as a squeak. He looked behind him as if there was somewhere to run, but there was nowhere. Nobody would risk going outside, it was as if the devil himself had sent a tempest. Ursula swallowed hard, knowing she'd also be blamed for whatever this was. The fury twisting its way around her body was so intense she wasn't convinced that she hadn't invoked it, that it wasn't flying from her fingers. She closed her eyes and prayed that they would all be killed instantly.

When she opened them again the pole was now a column, wider at the top and tapering to a narrower base, flying across the land towards the village. It appeared to be made of water as if the sea had reared up and become a terrible monster, the water one of Satan's horns. Whipping across the land it snatched up plants and bushes as it went before throwing them back out. Ursula saw a young red deer being spat out of its depths to lie on the ground. It just missed her cottage but whipped close enough to make the thick, rough glass in her windows shatter, flying inwards, catching her across the cheek and also stabbing into Oliver's hand. She let out a scream. All around the house raindrops flew and an unearthly howling, wailing sound filled their ears.

It felt like hours of terror but it was all over in less than a minute and they were left shaking and wet where the water had blown in through the broken window. Oliver was sitting on her stool wrapping his handkerchief around his hand and the other two had run to look out of the parlour window which had mercifully remained intact. Ursula put her hand to her cheek where a trickle of blood ran down.

'It has gone,' Hopkins said. 'Disappeared. Whatever you invoked, witch, has departed. There is a river of water flowing down the village street now. Despite the high winds I suggest we take our leave before she kills us all. Master Bruton, can you tie her to your saddle?'

'I can. I am sure someone in the village will have rope with which to assist me. After what we have just endured, nobody will want her here for a moment longer, they will be thankful we are taking her away.'

Hopkins and Stearne, both still looking shaken, hurried across to the inn, their boots crunching on the hail spread out on the street like a fall of snow, slowly being washed to one side by the now falling rain. Oliver slammed the door shut, capturing Ursula in the cottage with him.

'Now see where you find yourself,' he said, pushing her up against the wall, his thick stumpy fingers resting on her neck. His arms were short but muscular, and she knew there was no point in trying to escape his grasp. 'This could have been avoided if you had agreed to my demands. I did warn you that I would not be crossed. There is still time for you though, consent now and I will speak with Hopkins and ensure you are not kept in gaol or subjected to his methods for discovering witches. They are harsh, and often women do not survive the investigations.'

'He would have me ducked in the pond?' Ursula asked. She knew that had previously happened in the pond beside the well in Finchingham. The accused would have their thumbs and opposite toes tied together before they were thrown into the water. If they floated, they were a witch helped to the surface by the devil. If they sank, they were innocent, yet dead anyway.

'Nay, Hopkins has other methods. Ways that, if I may say so, are far more brutal.' Oliver looked out of the window. 'I see the stable hand at the inn bringing my horse and a length of rope, we shall be in King's Lynn before dusk.'

It didn't take long to lash her wrists together and attach them to the front of Oliver's saddle. She was able to sit up as long as she hunched over but it was preferable to being slung over the hind quarters for her head to bounce against the horse's flank and her body to be shaken like a piece of rag. Although she kept her head dipped, she sensed the villagers watching as they stood outside their homes discussing what had just swept through the village.

'Aye, take her away. Witch!' She recognised the voice of John Blacksmith and flinched as a sharp piece of flint bounced off her head. His son Henry still had deformed feet and although he was a beautiful child, as he was unable to walk he'd forever be a financial burden on the family. For years John had been happy for her to deliver his children safely into the world, and yet now he believed the rumours instigated by Oliver that she possessed unworldly, un-Christian powers. She chose not to respond and looking down at the horse's mane she felt blood trickling down from where she'd been scratched by the flying glass, mixing with the tears that were now starting to fall. They weren't for herself but were for her friends who believed these trumped-up charges fabricated by a powerful man who wouldn't be thwarted in his desires.

As Oliver turned the horse to ride away, from the corner of one eye Ursula caught sight of Wicker, flying and darting just above their heads as though he were about to dive as the hawks did. 'Goodbye friend,' she mouthed and with a lurch the horse beneath her began to move.

42

2024

'Are you free for a coffee this week?' Adrianna asked Jess. She'd made herself wait until she'd seen her friend arrive home from taking Malachi to nursery before she called. 'I want to tell you about my visit to Jack Miller.' Originally, she thought she'd have tales of a lovely weekend in London, but it wasn't so.

'I've got a better idea,' Jess said. 'Why don't we go into Norwich one evening? It's been a few years since I went dancing and nobody else in the village is interested in a decent night out. What do you think? We can talk over dinner and then go and cripple our feet in a nightclub.'

Adrianna was delighted at the suggestion and they agreed to go on Thursday, if Jess was able to organise a babysitter.

The good weather continued to hold and, after a lot of watering, the flowers she'd nurtured started to come into bloom. Buoyed up by her success Adrianna went back to the garden centre and bought more bedding plants and a further array of herbs. She knew she'd only be able to get the use of the herbs for a few months, but she'd dry some and take them back to London to make her own herbal teas.

The thought of no longer being in the cottage made her heart lurch. She'd begun to think of it as her home and the flat in London as somewhere in a life now detached from the one she was living. The way she and Rick had parted hadn't helped either. He had yet to call and apologise, nor had he replied to the two bright and breezy messages she'd sent. Was he unwell, or was he punishing her for not wanting to stay for the day on Sunday? Despite knowing she sounded needy, she sent him another message asking him to call her and let her know he was okay. He was due to visit her in a few days' time but she was beginning to wonder if he'd turn up.

Finally, Rick called her on Thursday just as she was getting ready to go out with Jess. She chatted away about what she'd been doing, how the garden was blooming, and how she was about to have an evening out with Jess. Her comment was met with silence at the other end of the phone.

'Are you still there?' she asked.

'Of course I am. Listening to your wonderful life in the country spending time in the sun while the rest of us are working our fingers to the bone in hot and sticky London.' Rick replied, a familiar sullen note creeping into his voice. Adrianna felt her own mood dip.

'You're coming up here for the weekend though?' she reminded him, keeping a positive tone to her voice. 'Why not come tomorrow evening instead of Saturday? And bring your swimming shorts then we can spend some time at the beach if you like. The good weather is set to continue.'

Rick grunted and she couldn't decide if he was agreeing or not. 'I'll let you know tomorrow what my plans are,' he said eventually. 'I assume you can pick me up from the station. If you aren't on another night out with your friends.'

'It's just one friend,' she said quietly. She wanted to point out that he wasn't being fair, given that he was out almost every evening, but she knew better than to say something that would upset him. Once again, he was twisting the narrative. As if to remind her, her wrist began to ache. 'Oh, and please don't forget my bank card,' she said.

'I won't,' he replied, after a pause.

'I must be getting on,' she said. 'Jess will be here in a minute and I'm not dressed yet.'

Rick made a growling sound like a lion, deep in his throat. 'Hmm, tell me what you're wearing now,' he said.

'Oi, cheeky,' Adrianna laughed. 'And I will be wearing my burgundy slip dress tonight. Remember the one I wore to that Christmas party in Hoxton when I was freezing? At least it's the right weather for something so slinky today.' There was another long pause at the other end and before Rick could say something disparaging about her choice of clothing as he often did when she'd got dressed up to go out, she decided it was a good point to end the call. 'Bye, love you, let me know when you're coming and I'll be there to meet you.'

She lay her phone down on the chest of drawers which she was also using as a dressing table and, picking up her mascara, she pulled it through her eyelashes slowly. Rick's reaction to her night out, despite his own busy nightlife in London hadn't really surprised her, but it had taken the shine off her excitement.

Downstairs there was a banging at the back door before Jess's voice called up the stairs. 'Are you ready, missus? I don't get a night off very often and I'm wasting valuable drinking time!'

'One minute,' Adrianna called back. She took a deep breath and told herself that she was just being silly about Rick's behaviour. He'd probably just had a bad day at work, he was always grumpy if a sale had fallen through and maybe he was missing her being there with some sympathy and a home-cooked dinner. She'd make a fuss of him at the weekend. They could take a picnic to the beach and perhaps finally she'd drag him into the pub to meet everyone. There was a lovely garden behind it where they could spend an afternoon enjoying the sun and drinking beer. He couldn't find anything to complain about with that. Slipping her dress over her head and enjoying the cool of the silk as it clung to her skin, she hurried downstairs.

* * *

Adrianna gave Jess a condensed update of what else she'd discovered. 'Her situation is definitely starting to become more dangerous. Despite what I learned from Jack Miller, I'm still missing a piece of evidence or information to tie Ursula to a witch trial or to the skeleton. Other than what I'm certain are her initials on the stone. I still haven't found anything to link the two threads together. I've got an appointment at the archives in King's Lynn next week to see what they have about the witch trials there.'

'Definitely keep me updated,' Jess said as she put her knife and fork down and finished her wine. 'But right now, I want to go dancing.' Laughing, Adrianna got out her phone to pay and waved her hand at a waitress to ask for the bill.

'My treat,' she insisted as Jess also took her purse out. The card machine appeared but despite putting her phone against it three times her payment was declined. 'This doesn't make sense,' she said as Jess quickly paid for the meal. Once they were outside, she opened her banking app. Her account was empty, and there were almost two thousand pounds worth of purchases against her bank card. Her eyes scrolled down the list of shops. The Apple store had taken over a thousand pounds, there was another payment to a designer clothes shop and several at bars and clubs around where she lived.

'I don't believe it,' she said in a small voice. 'There's no money in my account.'

'What? Have you been hacked?' Jess said. 'You need to call your bank, pronto.'

'No, there's no need,' she replied. 'It's Rick. He has my bank card – I left it behind accidentally and it appears he's been on a spending spree. I can move some from savings, it's instantaneous. But I'll be getting the card back from him the moment he arrives tomorrow.' With a sinking heart, she transferred some money.

They spent the following four hours in a club on Prince of Wales Road, but Adrianna wasn't in a partying mood and mostly sat at the bar looking after Jess's bag whilst she danced. Adrianna normally loved dancing but finding out that Rick had effectively stolen so much money from her, not including the amount he'd also spent the night that she'd lent him her card, made her feel sick. She should never have told him her pin.

Eventually Jess staggered over. 'My feet are burning,' she groaned, 'I can barely stand up on them. Why did I decide to wear heels?'

'Because, in your words, "I hardly ever go out and I am going to glam up and enjoy myself",' Adrianna said.

'I did say that, didn't I?' Jess pouted. 'Do you mind if we go home now? Before I fall on the floor and have to be dragged out by a bouncer?'

Adrianna was only too pleased to agree and, as she held Jess up with one arm, her friend hobbled along the cobbled streets to where they'd parked. She wound down the windows, hoping the cool air would revive Jess a bit, but by the time she'd turned onto the A140 there was loud snoring from beside her.

Having delivered Jess home, Adrianna quickly removed her make up and got into bed. She looked at her phone but there hadn't been a message from Rick all evening, not even asking if she was having a nice time or if she'd got home safely. As she drifted into sleep, her ears still ringing from the loud club music, she wondered if he'd had even considered that at some point, she'd check her bank balance and see what he'd spent.

* * *

After a fitful night when she woke every hour, Adrianna finally gave up on sleep and got up at six o'clock. Making a cup of tea she opened the back door to sit on the rickety garden chair and enjoy the warmth of the early morning sun before it got too hot and she'd have to retreat inside. She listened to the birds as a flock of chaffinches jostled for position in the rowan tree beside the shed. A loud squawk drew her attention to the herring gull perched on the witch stone, replaced on the disturbed ground by the police. Dotted through the garden the numerous wild foxgloves, previously just showing glimpses of their beauty to come, were now fully in flower, clumps of totem poles festooned with purple and pink trumpets shouting out for attention as they swayed in the breeze coming off the sea.

She'd already messaged Rick and asked him what time he was arriving so she could collect him but hadn't received a reply. And there was going to be a showdown when she mentioned the money, so she wanted to do it when he was in front of her. Every time she thought about it her heart began to race and her hands felt clammy. She was no longer any good at confrontation, the downward spiral of her working life having drained her confidence. When she'd first met Rick she'd been outgoing and self-assured, but she'd been knocked back and the poise she'd once had was gone. Thank goodness she'd had him to lean on for support.

After breakfast she checked her emails to see if there was a follow up from James, but there was nothing. 'No news is good news,' she told herself, battling to keep a wave of panic that what she'd shown him when she'd visited wasn't enough for the auditors. There was, however, an email from Jason. He'd been away and had just found the one where she'd informed him about what she'd found in the garden.

Hi Adrianna, thank you for letting me know the cottage is still standing! It sounds like you've had a busy couple of months, my grandmother certainly didn't clear the garden as far as you did, her vegetable patch and lawn were only cultivated directly behind the cottage. All the land to each side was left to its own devices, she always said it attracted the wildlife.

It certainly did that, Adrianna thought, remembering the birds that morning, as well as the kites which soared overhead, together with buzzards wheeling on the thermals high above the land. And the gull which wouldn't leave.

As for the skeleton, that's a turn up. Gran told me about the witches' marks on the church door and the wall but she didn't know there was a witch buried in her garden! I can't imagine she'd have cared though; she used a lot of herbal medications herself and I did once tell her that she was probably a witch in a former life. Do let me know if you find anything else out.

By the way I had an email from someone called Rick? He said he's your partner and he's interested in buying the cottage and land, I assume you passed my details on. I have decided that I probably do need to sell it, can you let him know that I'll think about it? Although, as you're currently the tenant you should get first refusal! You certainly seem to love the place as much as my grandmother did.

Adrianna was so stunned she sat in front of the open email for five minutes staring at it, yet not seeing it. Somehow Rick had got into her emails and found Jason's email address. The only reason he was interested in the cottage was to sell it to a developer and make a pile of money whilst a dozen houses were built on the beautiful wild garden. The house deserved so much more, someone who loved it as she now did, who understood its many moods.

43

2024

Finally, at five o'clock, Rick called. 'I've just finished work,' he was shouting and she could picture him striding along the pavement, his suit jacket flying behind him as he nipped around anyone he considered to be walking too slowly. She should know, she always seemed to be trotting to keep up with him. 'I'll get changed quickly and throw some things in a bag, I've booked a ticket on the six fifteen train.'

'Okay, I'll be there to pick you up,' she found herself shouting in return and lowering her voice she added, 'I'm looking forward to seeing you. Love you.'

'Yup, me too,' he yelled before the line went dead.

Adrianna went into the garden where clouds were gathering on the horizon as the land and clouds blurred into one, a grey smudged blur. She'd watched the clouds before, thinking that they would provide a respite from the continuous heat, but they always cleared again within hours, leaving the day as humid as before.

Walking over to the witch stone she ran her fingers against the marks on it, feeling for what she was now certain were Ursula's initials. She was now used to the tingling in her hands when she was close to it, the cool beneath her fingertips. There was an energy within it, just as there was in the house. A strength that she was sure had been accumulating over the months since she'd arrived. Out of the corner of her eye she saw a shadow move across the garden and as she turned her head, it hung in the air and for a moment she thought she could make out the hazy image of a person before it dissipated and drifted away. The fear she'd once had of what was trying to reach out to her had gone, now she just wanted to know what she could do, what was wanted of her.

Making her way to the wall, where the cow parsley, bracken and grasses were already claiming the ground back for themselves, she stretched up and ran her hand along the top of it. The stones were baked warm in the sun, but as she suspected, her hand moved against one that was as ice cold as the rock in her garden. In the churchyard standing on the top of a gravestone, the gull watched her before, with a shriek, he lifted up into the static, cautious air.

Despite leaving in plenty of time to collect Rick, her journey was hampered by a combine harvester moving its wide bulk slowly along the country lane that led to the village, and it was twenty past eight by the time she pulled up on the station forecourt. He was standing under the canopy, his face dark with an expression she'd seen before. One that didn't bode well for a harmonious weekend.

'Sorry,' she said as he opened the passenger door, 'I got stuck behind some farm vehicles, they're everywhere at the moment.'

'Yes, well it's no fun waiting around after a long week at work,' Rick grumbled, 'and it was like a furnace on the train.' He was wearing a white T-shirt tight against his muscular chest and flat stomach. Adrianna noticed the Rolex still on his wrist but said nothing. When she broached the subject about her bank card, she needed to do it when he was in a good mood, and that definitely wasn't right now.

'We could go and get a cold beer at the pub if you want?' she suggested. Rick didn't reply, instead getting out his phone and starting to send messages. Adrianna felt a stab at her heart, this wasn't the start to the weekend she'd hoped for.

When they arrived at the cottage, she opened all the windows and the front door whilst Rick dithered about because he couldn't find his phone, which he'd just spent half the journey on.

'It can't be far,' she said in a calm, reasonable tone. 'You had it in the car.' Snatching up the keys she'd left on the coffee table, he stalked outside, only to return two minutes later holding up his hand.

'It had fallen down beside my seat,' he said. 'Sorry, I've been a grump. I was just hot and grouchy.' Pulling her up to her feet, he kissed her and she relaxed against him, breathing out slowly. This was the Rick she needed, the one she loved.

Over dinner, which he helped her prepare, squeezing around her in the kitchen and making her laugh, Adrianna decided she couldn't delay it any longer, it was time to tackle the subject of her bank card. He'd already drunk most of a bottle of wine and a sizeable glass of whisky.

'Did you remember my bank card?' she asked, hoping it sounded like a throw away question. She kept her voice steady but she could feel her heart beginning to speed up, a pulse thumping in the base of her neck.

'Of course.' He pulled out his wallet and took the card out, handing it over. She waited for him to start an explanation about the amount of money spent on it, but he just carried on sipping his drink and cutting off slivers of cheese from the board between them on the table. She couldn't decide if he was trying to brazen it out, but his relaxed countenance decried that thought. She went and slipped the card back into her purse whilst her mind went over the various ways she could continue the discussion without it descending into shouting.

'I checked my bank balance,' she began, 'when I was out in Norwich with Jess. I couldn't pay for my meal because my current account was empty. It seems that there's quite a lot of money gone from it.' Despite her best intentions she could hear her voice crack slightly and she took a large gulp of her wine as she watched him, waiting for an answer.

'I'm not sure what you're getting at.' His hands stretched across the table and took hold of hers. 'Yes, I went shopping, because I really needed a few bits and I've been short of cash. You know that because I couldn't afford to pay all my rent. But when I moved in, you said on more than one occasion, that what's yours is mine and if I needed money to just pay out whatever I needed to and you'd sort it. I just thought that, rather than me going into overdraft and asking you to transfer the money across, I could use your card. I never thought for one minute that you might have changed your mind about the arrangement. Remember when I needed some running trainers, you gave me your card to pay for them? This isn't any different to that.'

Adrianna could remember giving him her card to go shopping for trainers; even then she'd been shocked at how expensive they'd been but as she didn't buy specialist active wear, she just took it at face value. She certainly couldn't remember saying that she'd cover *anything* he needed if he was short of money, but it had been a year ago and an awful lot had happened since then, so she probably had said it. At least she had her card back now so it couldn't continue. She just needed to keep an eye on her outgoings.

'I'm sure you're right, I just can't recall the conversation,' she agreed and Rick smiled and squeezed her fingers.

'Good girl,' he said. 'Now let's go and chill out. Leave the dishes,' he added as she stood up and began to gather them up in a pile. 'I'll sort them out later.' She followed him into the living room, which was feeling cooler, and snuggled down next to him but her mind was still turning over the conversation they'd just had.

The following morning, once again, the landscape was washed in a soft cloak of early morning sun, already burning away the night mists. Opening the back door, Adrianna could smell the dry earth as the dew evaporated. The vibrant red of poppies, the frayed edges of dusky blue cornflowers were a splash against the foil of prolific green vegetation. There would be nobody to tend the plants in a couple of months. Before she knew it summer would be over, the flowers would be gone and so would she. The thought of not being there to watch autumn blow through and wipe the verdant beauty from the landscape to leave it brown and dour made her well up, a lump growing in her throat. She remembered Jason's email and decided not to mention it to Rick. The next custodian of the cottage needed to be someone who would love it properly.

Walking down to the herb patch she gently tugged some stalks off the mint she'd planted, now preferring homemade herbal tea even more than her usual English breakfast. She'd add some to a cup of chamomile tea for Rick when he woke up, he'd almost certainly have a sore head and she had promised him lunch on the beach later. It wouldn't be much fun if he had a hangover.

Having assembled the picnic food, although the cheeses she'd bought were somewhat decimated after the previous evening, it was already mid-morning and she decided she'd had enough of the house reverberating in rhythm with Rick's snoring. Going upstairs she gave him a shake.

'Come on sleepyhead,' she chided. 'It's nearly eleven o'clock and we're supposed to be going to the beach. We don't want to miss the best of the day.' Rick groaned in response and pulled the duvet over his head.

'I'm not feeling so good,' he croaked. 'I think those prawns last night were off.'

'Rubbish, I ate them and I'm okay,' she pointed out. 'If anything was off, it was the amount of scotch you drank! Go and jump in the shower whilst I make you a drink to clear your head. And a full English breakfast, if you ask nicely.' At this, his head reappeared from the duvet, his hair sticking out at right angles.

'You are the very best girlfriend.' He gave her a lopsided smile, the one that always made her heart melt. 'I should make you my wife,' he added, 'so you don't get snapped up by some other lucky chap.'

'If that was a proposal, it was pretty lame,' she said, laughing. 'I hope whenever you ask me to marry you, it's because you can't imagine your life without me, not because you want to make sure I'm unavailable for anyone else. I'm not a second-hand car you know.' She tried to keep her voice light-hearted but she was surprised to hear a waspish tone creep in. 'Right, you've got fifteen minutes, so get a move on.' She kissed the top of his head to take some of the bite out of what she'd just said and left him to it.

Downstairs in the kitchen she heard the thump of his feet across the floor followed by the shower starting, and taking the frying pan out of the cupboard she put it on top of the stove and began to pile it up with eggs, bacon and sausages. She'd even remembered black pudding when she'd been at the supermarket, even though the sight of it turned her stomach. The sound of footsteps down the stairs alerted Adrianna to Rick's presence and she poured hot water on the herbs she'd crushed and left ready in the cups.

'Breakfast is almost ready,' she told him. He looked a lot better after his shower, his hair once again smooth and shining, his chin clear of bristles.

She put the laden plate on the table and immediately he began to grind copious amounts of salt and pepper over it, followed five seconds later with a mouthful of his herb tea sprayed over the top.

'What's this?' he snapped. 'I only drink coffee in the morning, you know that. Are you trying to poison me?' Adrianna didn't reply, silently picking up her own mug of the tea she'd made and taking it to sit outside whilst she drank it.

Eventually she went back into the kitchen. Rick's plate and two mugs, one with coffee dregs in it, had been left on the table, but at least the breakfast had been eaten. He was now talking loudly on his phone in the living room, and there was quite a lot of swearing going on. She loaded the crockery into the dishwasher and pottered around the kitchen, cleaning the worktops and tidying the cupboards until he reappeared. His hair was in a cockscomb on top of his head, looking as if he'd been repeatedly running his hands through it.

'Everything okay?' she asked.

'No, not remotely,' he said. 'Honestly you can't leave work for a single day without it all going to pot. One of my purchasers has withdrawn their offer because they've found something else and I need to go back to the office immediately and try and stop it all from falling apart. It's a Georgian town house near Sloane Square, they're rarer than hens' teeth these days. It's worth millions, I can't let this sale fall through my hands, I really need the commission. Why are people so unreliable?' He pushed his clenched fist into the palm of his other hand.

Adrianna stopped herself from pointing out that previously, when the shoe had been on the other foot, he'd crowed with delight about stealing a sale from another agency. No doubt someone was currently doing exactly the same. 'What can you do though?' she asked.

'I need to go and speak with the buyers,' he said. Getting to his feet he ran upstairs, calling back down over his shoulder to her. 'I'll just grab my stuff, can you run me to the station, babes? I'm really sorry to wreck our weekend, but work comes first.' Didn't she know it. She thought about the lovingly prepared picnic in the fridge.

'Of course,' she said quietly. 'I understand.' She knew his work was important to him, just as her own had been when she was in the middle of a big project, it just couldn't be helped. Within minutes Rick reappeared at the bottom of the stairs with his weekend bag and his shoes on. He gave her a hug, pulling her in close.

'A rubbish proposal and me scarpering off early, I'm sorry it's not been the weekend we'd planned. Next week, eh?' He put his finger under her chin and tilted her head back kissing her softly. 'I'll miss you,' he added.

'I'll miss you too,' she whispered as she leant against him enjoying the feeling of his warm body and the scent of his expensive aftershave enveloping her in a comforting embrace. Probably paid for by herself she thought, before pushing the idea out of her head. 'Come on then, let's get you to the station.' Picking up her car keys she locked the back door and followed Rick around to the car.

44

1646

The journey to King's Lynn took two hours, Oliver's horse being strong and able to gallop for a fair distance before they slowed down to a trot which bounced her up and down, the saddle now digging into her hips. The ropes around her wrists chafed until there were rough grazes. With the wound on her face also stinging, Ursula couldn't help thinking of the cooling burdock balm she had at home which would sooth her skin.

Oliver drew his horse up at the gaol in the marketplace, where Hopkins and Stearne were already waiting. He untied Ursula but left her hands lashed together.

'I shall leave the witch with you,' he said as he gave her a push in the back causing her to stagger forwards. 'And I will return shortly to ascertain what you have discovered. I must warn you she is both stubborn, and dangerous.'

Ursula could hear the mocking tone in his voice as he said his last sentence but she didn't give him the satisfaction of responding. Instead with her head down she was dragged over to the front door of the gaol. A wide brick gateway, towers either side, held a pair of tall oak gates with iron studs in them. A small door had been cut into one of them and it was through this that Ursula was taken.

Behind the gates was a courtyard with a flight of steps at the far side, leading to a series of rooms. From behind one she could hear a woman shrieking, a wild high-pitched noise which made her ears ring. Her stomach turned to liquid. A gaoler stepped out from the office.

'Master Hopkins, you have unearthed another witch?' the man growled. He was well into his middle years and whip thin, most of his hair gone and what remained was long and straggly down his back. He wore a worn leather jerkin, pale and cracked with age and breeches that were too short. It looked as if there was a bloodstain down one leg. Ursula turned away.

'I believe I have,' Hopkins answered. 'My questioning will soon bring forth a confession, of that, I am sure. Take her to the cells, I have other work to finish before I start my interrogation.' He pushed her towards the gaoler and strode away towards the room from where the dreadful screaming continued.

The gaoler picked up the end of the rope still attached to Ursula's wrists and tugged her, as if she were an animal, down a long flight of steps disappearing into the darkness, as if descending into hell itself. Maybe that was indeed where she was bound, and perhaps shortly, she would wish to be there instead of in this terrible place. By the light of his dimly lit lamp, she could see the walls were dripping with water and covered in places by strings of slimy algae. They were close to the port so were now probably below the level of the sea.

Once they reached the bottom of the stairs she followed him along a dark, narrow corridor, only the circle of light from the lamp keeping away the shadows which jostled against her. How many prisoners had died down here and haunted the darkness, forever searching for salvation?

The end of the passage opened out into a small space with cells around three walls. Metal upright bars filled part of the wall and each cell had a heavy wooden door, the thick planks nailed roughly together. The gaoler pulled a key from a selection attached to the large ring at his waist and opened one of the doors, giving it a yank as it snagged on the stone floor, pushing her inside.

'Will you not remove this rope?' Ursula called as the door closed once more, but without a word the gaoler took his lamp and walked away, his clanking keys receding into the distance as the light got smaller and smaller. Eventually she was plunged into complete darkness, a deep black fog, as if the haar had crawled in to suffocate her. Nothing was visible and it mattered not if her eyes were open or closed. The room smelled even worse than the passageway she'd just walked along, a tarnish of fear and betrayal buried beneath the stench of effluence and other bodily liquids. And the foetid reek of death, a corpse that had not yet began to rot.

As Ursula stood still, poised for what may come next, she became aware that she was not alone. She could hear the quick shallow breathing of someone else, and the hairs along her arms prickled. Was there someone in the cell with her, or in one of the others? The dead didn't breathe, so she was not in the company of ghosts. At least, not yet.

'Hello?' she said quietly. 'Who is here please?'

'Amy,' a young voice said. She sounded little more than a child. 'And my sister Esther is here too, but she sleeps. I have not been able to waken her for a long while but I can feel her breath on my neck, she lies close to me. There is another woman, Maud, she has not made a noise for a long while. I told the gaoler when he brought us food and ale many hours ago, but he said he did not care and he left again. I fear she has died. There was also our mother, she was taken away and has not returned.' Ursula thought about the screaming she'd heard when she arrived but said nothing. If that was Amy's mother, it was better she didn't know.

The lack of any sound from Maud explained the smell, Ursula suspected Amy was correct. Shuffling forward with small steps her bound hands held out in front of her she made her way towards Amy's voice until she felt the cold stone wall and turning around, she slowly slid down until she was sitting on the icy floor. The heat from outside would never permeate this far below ground. Her hips were still aching from the horse ride and as she sat down the pain increased. Beside her, she felt Amy shift a little so their shoulders were touching and the chill of the thin body against hers made Ursula's eyes well up. For so many years she'd prided herself on her ability to live without the help of anyone else and not miss the human contact others wanted. And yet this young girl's simple act, the touch of another person was a balm more powerful than any she could make and sell. Perhaps she'd been missing something, although Oliver certainly wasn't the answer. He wouldn't give her any solace.

'Why are you here, Amy?' she asked.

'They say we are witches. We live away from the village, in an old cottage and we have nothing. Our father disappeared one day. Mother has been selling potions and charms which can ward off bad omens, to earn money. One of the village lads tried to have his way with me and Mother attacked him and now his arm does not work. We were accused of witchcraft and brought here.'

So many women who had no voice, open to the desires of men and unable to refuse or they faced punishment. Amy's mother had meted out justice as it was deserved and she'd have done the same, confronting those who believed they could take whatever they wanted. Indeed, what she'd already done by standing up and saying no to Oliver. And now here they all were, probably soon to be hung on the end of a rope because refusing men what they desired was not an option for them. Women deserved to know they were not alone, that there would be justice for them and they could survive and heal. But they couldn't, for they had no voice, there was no truth.

'I am sure your mother will return soon,' she comforted Amy. Talking was difficult, her face swollen up from the wound she'd sustained from the flying glass, which had dried on her cheek stretching as she spoke. The cut cracked open and began to seep again. Her hand was throbbing and she tried to ease the ropes away from her wrists a little but they were tied too tightly. Biting her lip, she tried not to cry. She didn't want Amy, whose head was now lolling on her shoulder, to know how terrified and bleak she felt. Now she needed to harness every ounce of courage, of the powers she knew she possessed, to fight the biggest battle of her life.

They sat in the darkness for what felt like hours until finally Ursula's head fell forwards, her chin on her chest as she slept. She had no idea how long she'd been asleep when she was woken by the sound of the key turning in the door. Beside her she felt Amy grunt and sit up a bit. The door opened, the dull glow from the gaoler's lamp made Ursula screw her eyes up, now unused to any light. A trencher was slid in along the floor and the door slammed shut again, plunging them back into darkness.

Rolling onto her knees Ursula slowly crawled forwards still hampered by her hands being tied together. Feeling about eventually she made contact with the slab of wood and she pulled it towards herself. It held a piece of stale dry bread, hard as stone and holding it up to her nose Ursula could smell that it was rancid. She broke it in half and shuffled back passing the other piece to Amy, together with the flask of beer.

'Is Esther awake?' she asked. 'She can have some of my bread if she is.'

'Esther, Esther, wake up there's food.' Ursula could hear the tears in Amy's wavering voice but no answer from her sister. It seemed there was no hope for her now, she would likely quietly slip from one world to the next in the next day or so.

They ate the bread in silence, passing the flask of sour beer between them. Ursula could feel her stomach churning as it decided whether it was going to reject what she'd just consumed. She also needed to use the pot, but Amy confirmed her suspicion that there wasn't one in the cell. That explained some of the stench. Getting to her feet she staggered, her legs now stiff with the after-effects of the horse ride and having been sitting down for many hours and made her way towards the back of the cell to relieve herself. The smell from Maud was even worse here and she was frightened she'd accidentally trip over the corpse.

They settled down again in the darkness. Whilst they'd slept Amy had begun to cough and the still, cold air was punctuated every couple of minutes by the harsh wracking sound. Ursula knew that a syrup of thyme and honey might help, but either way Amy could develop a fever and possibly follow her sister into unconsciousness and then death.

The door reopened an hour after the food had been brought and Ursula heard a low guttural groaning as the door opened. The gaoler stepped in and threw someone on the floor and immediately Amy whispered 'Mamma?' before she crawled across to where her mother lay in the filth on the floor, not moving.

'You're next.' The gaoler grabbed Ursula's arm and hauled her out of the cell and into the corridor. Her still painful legs shook and she twisted her body to hold onto the wall and keep herself upright using both hands as the gaoler pulled her along. She wondered if Amy's mother would survive what had been done to her, and whether she herself would, if she was about to be subjected to the same treatment. As they climbed the stairs the light from above hurt her eyes. The gaoler finally untied the rope around her wrists and the relief from the rubbing of the coarse hemp was momentary before a heavy pair of shackles were clamped on, the cold metal pressing against the open skin making her draw her breath in sharply, her eyes watering.

Pushing her before him the gaoler took her up to the hall she'd arrived through and from there into a small back room where she was unsurprised to see Oliver together with Matthew Hopkins. She looked around for a chair to sit on, but there wasn't one. Her heart was beating so hard she was sure the two men could hear it, but she wasn't going to let them see how afraid she was feeling.

'Gentlemen,' she said, sneering as she battled to keep her voice from wavering. 'Although I do not believe that salutation is due to either of you. Why have you brought me here?'

'We are giving you the chance to confess your sins,' Hopkins answered. 'To welcome the Lord into your life and repent, so you will go to your death cleansed.'

Ursula looked from him to Oliver who bared his teeth in a false contorted smile, whilst his eyes remained cold and bitter. *See where your choices have brought you.* His mouth may have been smiling, but his face said everything he was thinking.

'I am a God-fearing woman and a Christian. My Lord will see that and when *I* meet him I shall be welcomed into his house.' Slowly she stared at each of the men in turn, watching as they digested what she had said. It was they who should be frightened.

'It's not too late,' he said. Whether he meant too late to accept his offer or too late to repent, she had no idea. It didn't matter either way, she'd rather go to the gallows than be a whore, a slave to a man. It may not be every woman's choice, but for her it was the only one.

'I cannot confess to something that is not true.' She moved as if to open her arms, wincing as any movement of her hands stretched the sore and now weeping skin around her wrists.

'We can draw a confession from you,' Hopkins stood up and took a step towards her. She could smell garlic and tobacco on his breath and she leant away from him. 'You will break, as others have before you. You cannot hide what you are and before long we shall hear you declare your guilt for all you have done.'

45

2024

'Two nights out in two weeks, are you sure?' Adrianna asked. She hadn't been expecting a call so soon from Jess after their previous late night.

'This isn't like before,' Jess pointed out. 'I really want to see this show and I've got two free tickets. I thought you'd like to join me.' Adrianna had never been to a musical but she was willing to give it a go.

'Okay, you're on,' she said. 'But only if you let me buy you a drink to say thank you.'

'Well, if you don't mind driving again then we'll call it quits, especially after you got me home in one piece last week. I thought I'd got away with rolling in so late, but Mum guessed immediately when I got up with Malachi. My head was pounding and I looked like a zombie. I hoped she'd take pity on me and let me go back to bed for a few hours before she went downstairs, but she didn't,' Jess laughed.

'I can't say I blame her. But at least we won't be late home this week,' Adrianna said.

'No, and I've got one of the nursery assistants who lives in the village to babysit, so that's all sorted.' They made arrangements and said goodbye. Adrianna was pleased to have something to look forward to after the deflating weekend. Although she'd left a voice note for Rick, she hadn't yet had a response. She imagined he was busy trying to stop his sale from falling through so she didn't like to keep bothering him.

* * *

The evening out at the theatre was a great success. Adrianna enjoyed it far more than she'd imagined and found herself humming along with Jess as she sang the songs on the drive home.

When she got home there was still no message from Rick, even though she'd now left him several voice notes and WhatsApp messages and she kept checking her phone. Despite the late hour Adrianna decided to transcribe another page of the journal, hoping a diversion to take her mind off him would be a good thing.

The summer strengthens, the heat is increasing daily bringing a sense of expectation which I cannot read, and yet I feel a creeping malevolence. I sense something wicked snapping and spitting in the air around me and I am much afeared of what will come to pass. Written this day the sixteenth day of July in the year of our Lord 1646.

The tone of the entries had changed considerably since the first ones she'd read. These were no longer concerning the ailments of her neighbours but increasingly about the impending doom of something terrible rolling in. But what made Adrianna swallow hard and wrap her arms tightly around herself was the date. The sixteenth of July, the same date as was currently displayed on the front screen of her phone. The same hot summer, the expectation and malice that Ursula wrote about was building once again. That which she'd been investigating was coming to a head.

Suddenly, the windows which had all been shut before Adrianna went out rattled loudly as if something was attempting to gain entry and a draught whipped across the room blowing the papers off the table. The high-pitched ringing she'd heard at the stone whistled down the chimney and she winced as she quickly snatched up the papers again and held them to her. A dark shadow on the floor slowly began to rotate and grow until it was suspended, the insubstantial outline of a person hanging in the air in the middle of the room.

'I don't know what you want,' Adrianna shouted. 'I can't help you unless you show me!' She hurriedly pushed the journal and papers into the cupboard slamming it shut. The wind subsided as quickly as it had appeared and the room lightened again. All was silent. Now she understood what Ursula had meant about evil snapping in the air, she could feel it herself.

* * *

With very little sleep she was still feeling tired when she got up the next morning. Putting the kettle on she picked up her phone from where it was charging. It was full of notifications from Rick. Immediately thinking he was ill or in trouble, she swore under her breath as she quickly unlocked it.

Out on the town again

The first one said, whilst the second continued with:

I thought you were in the country to rest and enjoy some peace, not get pissed all the time.

They were followed by another dozen, all in a similar vein although they became increasingly aggressive as he accused her of more and more outlandish things, including meeting another man with whom she was having a secret affair, calling her a slut and a whore.

'What the actual...?' she muttered, calling him. His phone was switched off and she left a bewildered voice mail. What had kicked that off? He must be under a lot of pressure at work to suddenly turn on her like that. Perhaps one of his friends had got hold of his phone and sent them as a joke, some of his circle of drinking buddies would think that was funny. No doubt he'd be horrified when he saw what they'd sent to her.

Her phone buzzed again and she opened it quickly, hoping it was a message from him, but instead it was Jess wishing her luck with that day's visit to the archives. She gave it a thumbs up, but then on impulse she called Jess and asked if she was busy.

'I'm cleaning out the pipes in the pub,' she replied. 'I get all the glamorous jobs. Have you made an exciting discovery?'

'No, not since I saw you last night. It's not that.' She wasn't yet ready to share what had happened in the cottage the previous evening. Instead, she explained about the messages she'd received from Rick. 'I'm sure it's just one of his friends thinking they're hilarious, they are quite an immature bunch but it's given me a bit of a shock. Some of the messages are really nasty.'

'What, wait a minute. Didn't you say last night that Rick had whizzed back to London on Saturday because of some house sale going down the drain and you hadn't heard from him since?' Jess asked.

'That's right,' Adrianna said, 'then I got all these this morning out of the blue.'

'Did you tell him you were going out again with me?'

'Yes. No.' Adrianna quickly scrolled back through her messages she'd sent. She remembered distinctly not telling him as he'd been displeased about her first foray into city nightlife, and although she was only going to the theatre, she'd decided not to mention it. 'I must have told him in a voice note, he's always saying how scatter brained I am.'

'Says the woman who's close to solving a centuries old mystery,' Jess pointed out, her voice sharp. 'Addie, I hate to ask this but are you... safe? I don't know Rick, we've never met but I'm worried about you. For you. Remember when I told you how Malachi's dad was? He started by messing with my head, then he became more controlling. Are you sure you're okay?'

'Yes, honestly it's nothing like that, it will all be a misunderstanding,' Adrianna reassured her. 'I'm sure he'll call later and there'll be a simple explanation.' She rubbed her hand across her forehead as a headache began to clamp the side of her head. 'Anyway, I must get on if I want to get to King's Lynn in time, I'll let you know later if I uncover anything new.'

Cancelling the call, she found some paracetamol in her handbag and took two before going upstairs to stand under the shower for ten minutes waiting for her head to clear a little. There was something going on, an undercurrent she couldn't work out. A similar sensation to when she'd stood in the shallows at the beach and the sea washed out, dragging the sand from beneath her feet and making her wobble. Something was pulling the ground from under her, waiting for her to fall. It was the same feeling as when she'd begun to falter at work, nothing made sense and the more she panicked, the worse it got. She was losing her grasp on reality again.

* * *

Arriving promptly for her appointment in town she waited in reception reading a leaflet about the history of the building and a particularly disturbing note about a bloodstain on the upstairs floor which couldn't be removed. It reminded her of the similar stain in the cottage.

Eventually, she was shown into a room which looked like a university library but on a much smaller scale. It was full of racking containing ledgers, and at two desks were microfiche readers. The lady who'd collected her from reception showed her quickly how to find what she was looking for and then left her to it. Adrianna could hear her moving about the shelves somewhere.

There were many town records, along with those from the assizes, and she realised it was going to take a long time to search through them all. She'd need to narrow it down somehow. She knew the dates in the journal and decided to begin with those and work forwards from there.

Within thirty minutes she spotted the word Finchingham and she stopped scrolling for a moment. It told of an episode on the seventeenth of July 1646 when a terrible storm and column of water had carved through the village destroying homes and killing livestock. Adrianna remembered the journal entry on the sixteenth of July which had mentioned the oppressive heat of an unending summer, and the Millers' book. Had the weather conditions created a tornado? Her knowledge of meteorological events was close to nil, but she did know that where she grew up in the southern states of America they sometimes had tornados. She made a note to investigate it further. It was hot enough for another one if the weather didn't break soon.

A further thirty minutes of scanning through the documents

on file, and she located what she was hoping, yet dreading, to find. Matthew Hopkins, Witchfinder General, bringing the cases of six witches in front of Judge Everard in King's Lynn.

The records were difficult to understand, just as the papers she'd found at home were. Finally though, her eyes snagged on the name she'd been dreading to find, and yet expecting. Ursula Beal, accused of witchcraft. The litany of so-called crimes, ones that she'd read about in the journal, had been brought to the attention of the court by Doctor Oliver Bruton. Ursula, the inhabitant of Church Cottage. As she still was, waiting for her truth to be told.

Adrianna leant back in her chair and pulled her hands down her face. Oliver Bruton had clearly done what he threatened to and had Ursula accused of witchcraft, indeed the paper she was reading said 'being possessed.' Because she wouldn't bow down and let him possess her himself.

Gathering up her bag she called out goodbye before making her way back to her car. She still suspected the body she'd found was Ursula's, although what it was doing there, she had no idea. The story she was unfolding was crawling inescapably towards a potentially terrifying end.

46

1646

Ursula couldn't see any point in denying the accusations laid in front of her or arguing with the men. Oliver had threatened her with what would happen if she refused him, and now that time had come. She looked the two men in the eyes and said nothing. Let her silence speak for her.

Behind her the door opened and Stearne entered.

'Take her,' Hopkins snapped. 'Take her next door and walk her.' Turning to Ursula he pushed his face up to hers so his long nose was squashed against hers. 'See how you feel after you've walked without food or rest for hours. Days, if needs be.'

Ursula had heard about this punishment, a way to make witches admit their pact with the devil. Let them try their worst, she wouldn't tell them what they wanted to hear. She'd die, either because of their tortures to prove her a witch, as had happened to Maud, or dancing on the end of a rope.

Stearne grabbed her upper arm, his hand forming a tight vice around it as if she may try and escape. She had considered it but already discounted the idea, she wouldn't get very far with her hands clamped together. He dragged her from the room, her feet tripping on the uneven floorboards.

The second room was larger than the first, long and narrow, almost like a gallery. One wall had windows with small panes of glass in leaded frames, the top panes in coloured glass. There was no other decoration around the almost empty space, the other walls bare stone. Two women sat on chairs sewing, one of whom she recognised as her fellow midwife, Mary Smith. Ursula tried to smile at her but received nothing in return. They had sometimes attended births together and shared news, and yet now someone she believed was a friend was working for the Witchfinder.

'Walk her, and do not stop,' he barked. 'I will fetch others to take over from you in due course.' He flung himself into one of the chairs the women had vacated as they put their sewing into a wooden trunk on the floor and came over to Ursula, both grabbing her upper arms, one either side.

They began to walk around the periphery of the room, moving briskly whilst holding her between the two of them and Ursula had no choice but to go at the same speed. On legs which were already aching.

'Mary,' Ursula whispered, 'why do you do this to your fellow women?'

'So it is not me in your place.' The reply was hissed through clenched teeth and it told all that Ursula needed to know. She couldn't blame her friend saving her own life. Mary must live her life unto her own beliefs, as she did.

After an hour, the two women tasked with making sure she didn't stop were replaced by others, neither of whom Ursula recognised. The walking continued.

By the sixth hour Ursula could see why they used this torture, her legs felt as though they were on fire and her feet in their ill-fitting boots were rubbing and sore. Outside, night was falling, the light starting to dim. Stearne appeared with candles and then sat down to watch. He'd tire of this before she did, she thought, however long it took.

Twenty-four hours later Ursula could barely put one foot in front of the other, mostly being dragged by whoever was holding her arms although she no longer knew which of the three pairs of women who'd been walking her it was. She hadn't been allowed to stop and use the pot and consequently her hose and shift were wet and smelled rancid. Nor had she been given food or ale, and she was dizzy with fatigue and hunger, desperate for a mouthful of ale. The soles of her feet were burning, her feet slipping in her boots where they were rubbed raw, the blood occasionally seeping from the hole in the front.

Eventually, Stearne indicated to the two women to stop as they drew level with him. He stood in front of Ursula and with his hand under her chin he lifted her head, which was lolling against her chest, so she could see him.

'Are you ready now to tell the truth, witch?' he said.

'I have told you the truth,' she croaked, her tongue stuck to the roof of her mouth. 'Many times.' Her body was vibrating with the fury and power that only she could feel, and tipping her head back she brought it down sharply against his face. There was a satisfying crack as his nose spurted crimson blood down his jacket and white collar. Droplets sprayed across her clothes. With a roar of rage his arm swung round and smacked the side of her head, the force of which knocked her out of the grip of the two walkers and threw her across the room where she landed in a heap on the floor. She was too exhausted to do anything but lie there.

Her mouth filled with blood and she spat a tooth out. She didn't care, she could hardly be in any more pain than she already was. At least now she had the satisfaction of Stearne running from the room, his blood dripping across the boards. As he left, he screamed, 'Keep walking her!', and the two women did as they were bid.

Yet more hours passed, Ursula marked the laps as they went past her tooth which still lay on the floor in a pool of blood and saliva slowly sinking into the boards. It reminded her of the bloodstain on the hearth at home. However much she'd tried to scrub it the mark was always there, as dark as the day her mother's blood was spilled. She knew the same would happen with hers, blood spilled in anger, forever left to stain the souls of dangerous men.

The walking didn't stop. Ursula no longer noticed, her head now drifting away to a place where she couldn't be reached. She was too exhausted to think, a low buzzing in her ears now filling her head, a swarm of bees caught inside. One of her eyes wouldn't open, she could feel how tight the skin on one side of her face was, and the sight from the other eye was now so blurry there was no point even trying to use it. Just the swinging around the corners of the room gave any alteration to her movement. Her lips were dry and cracked and bled if she accidentally moved her puffy mouth.

Finally, as the windows were beginning to grow light again in the first whispers of another creeping dawn, Stearne walked into the room, banging the door back against the wall.

'Stop now,' he said. Ursula couldn't see him but she recognised his voice although even through the fug in her head, she was pleased to hear that he sounded different. Nasally. The voice from a person who was unable to breathe through his nose. She was too exhausted to smile, she wasn't sure her own face could move even if she tried to.

The two women let go of her arms and she fell to the floor

and lay in a heap. She could feel the boards bounce slightly as Stearne walked across them, followed by a sharp pain in her lower back as his boot made contact.

'Sorry, are you yet?' he asked. 'Ready to confess your pact with the Prince of Darkness?'

Ursula couldn't dredge up any energy to refute yet again what he was saying and she lay with her face against the rough floor. The manacles around her wrists were digging into her skin and she tried to move her arms but couldn't. She needed the last threads of energy she had left to simply breathe in and out.

'Take this one back down to the cell,' Stearne shouted and immediately the floor shook as other heavy booted men arrived and pulled her to her feet.

'Come on, witch.' She recognised the voice of the gaoler who'd brought her upstairs hours, maybe days, ago. She had no idea how many though. Hung between the tall men the tips of her feet dragged as she was taken back down beneath the building to the cell she'd been in before and thrown in.

'Who is there?' a voice reached out from the darkness. Not Amy's though, older. Ursula didn't think she'd ever be able to speak again but she managed to croak out her name from between her inflamed lips.

'Amy told me about you, I am her mother, Lizzie,' came the reply. 'She is sleeping now, and barely with us but it makes no odds. They made me declare our guilt even though we are innocent and she and I will swing in the morning. With my confession I have signed my daughter's death warrant. My sweet Esther died before they had a chance to do the same to her. The gaoler took her body and that of Maud last night.'

Despite her pain and exhaustion Ursula felt a surge of solidarity, of anger, burn deep within her. These women had done nothing wrong. They were just poor and trying to earn a living, just as she was. Their sex defined where they were placed in society. But men who wanted to do so, could crush them.

Lizzie shuffled over to where Ursula lay and helped her to the wall where she'd sat previously with Amy, and holding a flask to Ursula's lips, she dribbled a small amount of ale in. It burned as it trickled down her sore throat, but Ursula was able to move her tongue enough to whisper, 'Thank you.'

'I kept it for Amy,' Lizzie explained. 'But I do not think she will need it now. Her breathing is as shallow as Esther's was. I think they will carry her to the gallows in the morning.' Her voice broke as she spoke the words and Ursula moved her hands, still shackled together, to hold onto the other woman's.

Exhaustion finally overcame her, although every time her body twitched or moved in her sleep, she woke with a start. At one point she realised she'd been crying, her cheeks wet with tears, but almost immediately her head fell forward once again as she drifted back off again.

She was awoken by a loud clattering as the gaol door opened and a man's voice shouted, 'Time to go!' Beside her she heard a thin piteous wail from Amy with Lizzie trying to comfort her as the two of them were pulled from the cell and the door slammed shut. A trencher had been left beside the door and for a moment Ursula wondered if she had the strength to crawl across and get it. She'd hoped Amy wouldn't have been awake sufficiently to know where they were taking her, but she knew the two women, mother and daughter, would be strength for each other. There was no one for her, but she'd never needed anyone else, she was strong enough to bear whatever came next.

She found the wooden slab containing pieces of cooked turnip and a jug of ale and slowly she sipped at the drink and pushed small chunks of the vegetable into her mouth. Feeling around she found the flask that Lizzie had kept for Amy, which was still half full. She'd be able to eke out what she had for a couple of days if needed, she had no idea how long she was going to be left in this foul-smelling cess pit.

Despite being underground she could just hear the crowds outside gathered for the celebration that a hanging created. There were few opportunities for entertainment in the hard lives of labourers, and this was considered distraction indeed. There was jeering and shouting followed minutes later by a large cheer and she knew two more innocent women had departed this world. She wondered if Katherine, her only real friend, would travel to the assizes when Ursula was tried or even to see her hang when her time came. It would be nice to see a friendly face in her final moments.

Ursula was left for several days, although she couldn't have said how many, given that she could see neither the sun rise nor set. She spent most of the time asleep. A small chunk of bread arrived, so old she could feel a weevil moving about inside as she bit into it but she couldn't afford to be fussy or she'd be even hungrier than she already was. The swelling on her face had gone down but she lost another tooth whilst trying to eat the dry bread. Her feet still throbbed as did her wrists where the irons had rubbed the skin off continually opening the weeping, oozing wounds. The place where she'd been kicked in the back ached with every movement.

Eventually the door opened once more and a gaoler entered, holding up his lamp and looking around.

'Get up,' he sneered. 'Master Hopkins wants you.' Ursula's heart fell, but she'd expected nothing else. What hideous torture had he in mind for her now?

Once again they walked along the dark corridor, slimy with water dripping from above and slippery underfoot. Ursula stumbled on the uneven stone flags, her feet still sore and her thighs burning with the effort of having to put one foot in front of the other. If they were going to make her walk again, she thought, then she'd drop to the floor and die. And be pleased to do so.

When she entered the small room Oliver and Hopkins were waiting for her once again. In the corner of the room sat Mary Smith. She looked up once at Ursula with pity in her eyes before resuming her knitting. Ursula knew she looked a terrible sight with her bruised face and bloodied clothes which now hung off her, she'd lost weight since she'd arrived.

'You do not look as pretty as you once did,' Oliver said, smiling grimly. 'But that is mostly just temporary. Perhaps now is the time to confess. Or agree to all I offered you and you shall be free to go.'

Ursula assumed that it was either a trick, or Hopkins knew she'd been brought in under false pretences, because he didn't question what Oliver said. She lifted her chin up, a shaft of pain shooting through her neck, stiff from the angle at which she'd had to sleep for days and looked him in the eye.

'Never.' Her voice was croaky still and she cleared her throat. 'You ask too high a price. I value my freedom and, if I cannot live with that, then I have no desire to live at all.' Oliver's eyes narrowed and he blew out his breath through puffed out cheeks. Turning to Hopkins he nodded, before leaving the room.

Hopkins stood up and took a step towards her, looking her up and down. 'If you have been cavorting with the devil, he will have left his mark on you, and we shall find it. Where you have suckled him.'

'I do not know the devil,' Ursula protested. 'All this is because I will not agree to being Bruton's whore. He knows I am no witch, he wishes to grind me down, as if I am the mortar and he the pestle, until I concede to his demands. And I will never do so.'

Hopkins clicked his fingers and Mary lay down her knitting and came over. From a pocket in her apron she produced a small wooden instrument with a long spike. A bodkin. Despite her defiance Ursula felt her stomach churn and acid bile rise up in her throat.

'This will show us truly if you are a witch,' Hopkins said. 'Mistress Smith will look for marks upon your body; if she finds any then she will prick them. If you do not bleed 'tis because you have been kissed there by the devil and you are one of his disciples.' Turning to Mary, he added, 'You know what to do.' He left the room and Ursula heard the grind of a key being turned in the lock. The windows were small, too small for her to climb out of and it was a long drop to the ground. And doubtless there were guards outside. Even if she had the strength, there was no escape.

Mary pushed her into the chair Hopkins had just vacated. Forcing up one sleeve of her dress and then the other, Mary examined her for marks and occasionally pushed the bodkin into her skin, puncturing it and making Ursula want to scream. She hadn't heard Hopkins walk away from the door and she was certain he was crouched the other side like the obscene coward her was, listening. She bit down on her lip and stopped herself from crying out.

After her arms had been examined Mary pulled open Ursula's bodice baring her breasts. Here the stabbing bodkin was even more painful, the blood running faster than the tears which trickled down Ursula's face, but still she remained mute. Eventually her skirts were lifted and her legs exposed. She knew what Mary would find there, she had a small mark on the inside of her upper thigh which had been there since she was born. With her skin darker than other people's it was barely noticeable and she found herself hoping it would be missed, but she was wishing in vain. Mary looked her in the eyes and mouthed 'sorry' as she pushed the bodkin against the mark. Ursula stiffened ready for the searing pain, yet it didn't come. There was nothing. She waited for her to do it again, but she felt nothing. 'Master Hopkins and Master Bruton were right. If the pricker does not draw blood then you be a witch and see here, no blood when I prick this devil's teat.'

Ursula didn't understand why she wasn't bleeding from it nor felt any pain, but everywhere else on her body was on fire and her hands and chest were stinging as warm blood soaked into her dress. Drips pooled on the floor. Was there to be no place in this building not scarred with her blood?

'I forgive you Mary,' Ursula whispered, her voice breaking. For a moment her fellow midwife, her erstwhile friend's eyes met hers in regret. She had no option than to do what the men bade her to, they both knew it.

'Master Hopkins,' Mary called out, 'you may return now.' Immediately the door opened, confirming Ursula's suspicion that he'd been hovering outside. Oliver wasn't with him. Maybe he'd finally become ashamed of what he was putting her through? Although she doubted that.

'Well?' Hopkins asked, barely looking at Ursula. 'Are we in the presence of a witch?'

'We are, Master,' she replied. 'She has a devil's teat near to her privy parts and when I pricked it no blood came forth.'

'That is all the proof we need.' Hopkins couldn't hide the satisfaction in his voice, he was almost laughing in delight. 'There are assizes here, in one week's time. You shall be tried there and thereafter hung by the neck as you deserve to be.' He called for the gaoler who came running, his keys clanging against his thigh as he hurried, and Ursula found herself being taken back down to the cells.

This time she was thrown into a different room. Just as dark as before, but smaller. It smelled of stagnant water, decaying vegetation and the putrid scent of rotting meat. She missed having Lizzie or Amy beside her, just the touch of another body. Her mind crept towards where they were now, swaying back and forth on the end of a rope, their faces purple and their eyes bulging. She hoped that someone had run forward to pull on Amy's legs to hasten her demise. Would someone be there to do the same for her? It was unlikely, only Katherine would give her that kindness now. She'd wanted to live on her own, to keep herself safe but now she was in more danger than she could have imagined. And all created by a man.

47

2024

Adrianna received no other communication from Rick until she received a text at 8.30 p.m. saying he'd be at King's Lynn in twenty minutes. Cursing under her breath she grabbed her bag and ran out of the house. If he'd told her which train he was coming on a bit earlier, she could have ensured she left in plenty of time. Now, as previously, she may well be late and it would start the weekend off on a sour note. Again. She could picture the way his mouth turned down at the corners and his eyes narrowed when he was cross, and she didn't want that.

Pulling up outside the station, her eyes scanned the people waiting for lifts or taxis, heaving a sigh of relief when she couldn't see him there. She must have arrived just in the nick of time. Then out of the darkened doorway, Rick stepped out. For a moment Adrianna wondered if he'd been standing out of sight inside the building, hiding, and watching.

'Hey,' she said as he threw his bag onto the back seat and got in beside her. 'You should have let me know which train you were on when you left London, I had a mad dash to get here in time.' She paused for him to give her a kiss but after he'd done his seat belt up, he stared straight ahead and she realised one wasn't forthcoming. Although she was desperate to ask him about the slew of vile messages she'd received, she needed to wait. Just like with the conversation about her bank card, timing was of utmost importance. Concentrating on driving, they travelled home in silence. Even having to slow down for a muntjac to trot across the road did nothing to break the icy atmosphere. Adrianna was surprised she couldn't see her own breath crystallising in front of her to cling onto the windscreen.

As soon as they pulled up in front of the cottage Rick jumped out before the engine was off and taking his bag, he marched up the garden path and waited beside the front door. He knew Adrianna only used the back door now and ignoring him she walked around the side of the cottage. Behind her, she could hear his footsteps as he followed.

Once they were in the kitchen Adrianna left the kettle, her usual first activity when she arrived home, and instead took a bottle of white wine from the fridge and a glass from the cupboard.

'Do you want one?' she asked, holding the bottle up and giving him a smile to attempt to break the brittle, frigid atmosphere. Rick shook his head wordlessly and instead went to the cupboard where he'd previously left a bottle of whisky. She passed him a glass and he filled it halfway before taking a large gulp and topping it up again. Adrianna felt her insides curdle. Rick who was unhappy about something was one thing, but Rick who was unhappy and drunk was a whole different problem. She'd seen his mood turn sour if he thought he'd been slighted and he didn't care who got caught in the crossfire. It hadn't ever been her. Until now.

'Food?' She continued with her light tone as if she hadn't

noticed his mood. 'I was going to make some pasta, it won't take long to prepare.'

'No thanks.' Rick took another slug of his drink before walking through to the lounge and flopping down on the sofa. Adrianna followed him. Despite the warmth outside, the room felt uncannily cold, it prickled at her face and made the hairs on her arms stand up. Shadows in the corners shifted and spun and she flicked the light on, but it made no difference. The cold was creeping down her throat every time she breathed in, settling in her lungs. Whatever was occupying the cottage with her was as tense as she was, it could feel the danger.

Sitting on the sofa next to Rick, eventually she grew tired of his silence. 'Well? Are you going to explain those messages I received? And how you guessed I was out again with Jess?' His behaviour since she'd collected him at the station had made her doubt her initial suspicion that one of his so-called friends had sent those texts. And she'd had enough of appeasing his fragile mood.

'I didn't need to guess.' His voice came out in a deep snarl and she shifted away along the sofa so she was sitting in the far corner. It barely even sounded like him. 'I know you were out partying. Again. Supposedly you came to stay here for some peace and recuperation, and yet you've been running around with that tart from the pub and probably dropping your knickers at every chance you got.'

'Whoa, where has all this come from? I've been into Norwich twice and this week it was to see a show that Jess, who incidentally is *not* a tart, had a spare ticket for. And you haven't answered my question, how did you know? Do you have one of the villagers spying for you?' She laughed as she said it, the idea being so ludicrous, when he wouldn't even meet her friends.

'For someone who's supposedly very intelligent, you really

are surprisingly thick at times.' His voice had a whining sneer to it. 'I don't need a spy, as you call it, not in this day and age. I just needed to be a bit cleverer than you, which isn't hard.' Rummaging in his pocket he took out his door keys – her door keys – and rattled them in her face, before pushing his face against hers and laughing loudly. She could smell the sour whisky on his breath and she tried to lean away from him, the arm of the chair digging into her back.

At first she couldn't see the significance, but then she realised what he was showing her. He'd been excited when he'd first bought his AirTag so he could track his keys when he inevitably left them somewhere.

'Wait, did you put an AirTag in my car?' As the realisation dawned on her, she didn't wait for an answer, running outside, snatching up her keys as she went. Where could he have put it? And when, because he hadn't been in the car on his own for ages. She pulled open the glove box but as usual it only contained the service book. The pockets in the backs of the seats and doors were all empty. Suddenly a memory, fleeting and insubstantial, stopped her racing thoughts. Rick had lost his phone and he came back to the car and found it down the side of his seat. Sliding her fingers down the narrow gap they caught hold of something small and round and closing her hand around it she pulled it out looking at what she was holding. Rick had indeed been tracking her.

Locking the car, she turned towards the cottage expecting to see him at the window watching her, but instead she was surprised to see his outline still sitting on the sofa, seemingly unperturbed. Her shock made her feel nauseous and her hands were shaking, but above the disgust she felt an overwhelming wave of fury. A huge crash of anger which left her breathless.

As if unravelling in front of her like a wobbling home movie, she thought about all the times she had stopped herself questioning Rick's behaviour. When she'd accepted his excuses for upsetting her and believed his claims that she was in the wrong.

The time she thought she'd lost the bracelet he'd bought her for Christmas, he hadn't spoken to her for over a week, and yet she'd found it later in his bedside table. He'd told her she must have put it there and she'd believed him. If she was losing her mind at work, then of course she was at home too. Now she knew differently. And her beautiful handbag – she was certain she hadn't sold it, but she could guess who had.

After what James had told her, she now realised in a moment of clarity her breakdown hadn't been caused by her incompetence to do her work, but because she was continually questioning her own abilities, despite her previous exemplary career record. And those questions had grown in her head after being planted there by Rick. As she thought back, she realised that her anxiety had begun within months of dating him. He'd begun a campaign of manipulation and she'd allowed him to.

How could she have been so stupid? His so-called considerate behaviour had always been to his own advantage. Because he only cared about her when it affected his life. Even though he was living off her like a leech.

No wonder he'd been so horrified when she had intimated that she was thinking of not returning to work and selling the flat in London. He didn't want to go back to his own little bedsit, he enjoyed the kudos of living where they did. Everything he wanted he expected her to acquiesce to; she was simply a chattel to him. The realisation of what was happening, of history repeating itself hit her like a sledgehammer. Women had been used by bullying men throughout history and now she must fight back. For herself, for Ursula. Finally she understood what the journal was trying to tell her.

She walked back round to the back of the house, the AirTag feeling hot in her hand as she gripped it. Her mind was turning over so many of the scenarios of the past year. Rick agreeing with her when she began to question her decisions, encouraging her feelings of worthlessness. Taking her phone out of her pocket she logged into a credit reference website, knowing already what she'd find. She should have realised immediately. There it was on the screen, a new credit card taken out in her name. The letter she'd torn up at the flat believing it to be simply a circular had been confirmation that someone – because it wasn't her – had fraudulently applied for a new card.

She sat down on a garden chair and looked out at all she'd done since she'd moved to the cottage, creating flower beds and an herb garden where there was none. It was an oasis of peace, despite finding a dead body – which was the last thing she'd expected when she'd started clearing the ground. Now she was going to have to do something incredibly difficult and her heart was beating a tattoo in her chest as she braced herself.

Getting to her feet she walked back into the living room and tossed the AirTag onto the sofa beside him.

'Why, Rick?' she asked. 'Why did you feel the need to track me?'

'Because you could be in trouble somewhere and not able to contact me.' He shrugged his shoulders as he replied. 'I need to know where you are at all times, you're safer that way. When you were just here in the village it didn't matter, but once you started going out God knows where and meeting up with other men, I needed to protect you.'

'I wasn't meeting other men!' Adrianna had given up trying to talk sensibly and she shouted at him. 'And you sent those vile accusations calling me all those dreadful things. You had no right!'

'Of course I did,' Rick said as he got to his feet. 'You're mine and I need to know you're safe, you know that I'm doing it for you. Because I care about you. You're just getting yourself into a state, like you always do.'

'I'm not *yours*. I'm not a belonging, I'm nobody's person but my own,' she spat. 'I see you for what you are now, manipulating and controlling me. Spending all my money and, I suspect, forging my signature to get a credit card in my name.' His expression wavered for a moment and for a split second his eyes flicked to his watch.

'Get out now.' She spat the words. 'And don't bother going back to the flat because I'm ringing a locksmith the moment you've gone. I'll leave your belongings at your office when I next get down to London.' Her heart was racing, but already she felt the heavy shroud of suppression begin to lift. Her fingers were beginning to tingle as she held her arms out. There was a wind starting to build in the room and she saw Rick's eyes flick to each side as he tried to work out what it was. The power that she'd felt growing within her since she arrived at Church Cottage was spilling out, it was unstoppable and nor did she want to stop it. Ursula was here, manifesting herself through Adrianna's physical form.

'You can't throw me out, I live there too.' He stepped forward until he was almost standing on her toes and pushed his face into hers. 'See where your choices have brought you, Addie.'

'No,' she replied through gritted teeth, 'you are nothing to me now. Your words are empty. If you have no more to say then take your threats and leave!' As her voice began to rise there was a crash as the ornaments on the mantlepiece began to wobble and fall before another flew across the room and smash against the far wall. The wind increased and Rick's eyes widened in fear. 'Leave. Now,' she hissed. It didn't sound like her own voice.

She didn't see the sudden movement until it was too late. Rick's fist caught her jaw, throwing her across the floor to land with her head on the hearth where it gave a sharp crack. She tried to get to her feet again but her vision was blurred as blood began to flow down her face and to drip off her chin. When she managed to rub her eyes, she could see that he was gone, as were her car keys. Crawling to her phone still left on the coffee table, she called the police.

48

1646

Ursula lost count of the days in her cell. It was only large enough to walk ten paces before having to turn around and although she tried to do that several times a day her whole body felt so broken that finally she only got up occasionally to stretch her limbs. She sat in the dark waiting for the one time a day when some bread and ale appeared. Often nothing came.

When eventually the door was flung open and Oliver came in carrying a candle flickering in the draught from the corridor, Ursula covered her eyes from the light. She didn't see who her visitor was, but she could tell by his scent who deigned to come down to this pit.

'What do you want?' She could hardly sound the words, her voice having almost disappeared after being unused for so long. Her matted hair was stiff against her face, tendrils stuck to the dried blood. She'd been bitten by numerous fleas living on the rats who occupied the cell with her and she knew she was now contributing to the dreadful stench.

'It isn't too late to change your mind,' Oliver replied. Ursula noticed that he'd taken a step backwards as if to avoid the smell that arose from her.

'So you would still wish for me, when I'm like this?' she answered with a laugh which caught in her throat and made her cough.

'This can be changed,' he said. 'With good food, clean clothes, hot water and soap, you would soon return to your former beauty. And be thankful to me for helping you to avoid what shall be coming to you.'

'You put me here in the first place,' she replied softly. She was too exhausted to be angry. 'After all that you have caused, surely you do not care what happens to me any more?'

'Oh, but I do,' Oliver replied. 'I always get what I want eventually. I can give the gaoler enough silver to let me take you home. Or I can let you come before the judge who is putting on his robes as we speak. Your neighbours are waiting to give their evidence and the jury have been selected. Is this how you wish to end your life?'

'Being put to death by a man? Because I would not do as he wished? Despite all that I have worked for and all my efforts it has come to this, that which I strived to avoid. Let it be so.' Ursula felt a thread of anger, liquid mercury buried deep inside began to twist and turn, binding its way around her heart and turning to steel. Giving her the energy she was accused of possessing, that which she believed she'd lost. 'I shall say my piece to the judge and let him decide my fate, not you.'

Behind Oliver came the sound of the gaoler with his clanking keys and as he stepped away from the open door, she heard Oliver say, 'I am finished here, you may take her to the courtroom.'

Ursula felt the gaoler grab her beneath her oxter and haul her to her feet. Barely able to move her legs, she was pulled along the corridor and up the stairs, from which they entered the hall which was full of people. She heard an intake of breath, and looking over, she saw Ruth and John Blacksmith standing with Rebecca. Their eyes burned into her and Rebecca pulled her skirts away as Ursula staggered past. To her surprise behind them stood Anne Bruton, who seemed to be trying to tell her something as she caught Ursula's eye, and Katherine, no longer pregnant, her eyes swimming with tears. She was grateful to have some friends in the crowd even though they couldn't openly display their allegiance.

The courtroom itself was even more crowded. A dozen men were stood in a huddle to one side, away from the general mob who called and jeered. A stone flew and struck her on the shoulder but she cared not. Her body was broken, what was one more injury?

The room quietened down as the judge entered from a door across from the dock in which she had been put. In the pit in front of the judge stood Matthew Hopkins, Stearne and of course, Oliver. No surprise he was there to watch the culmination of all that her refusal of him had put into place.

Hopkins stood up and relayed the incident with the whirling column of water and the destruction it wrought. It seemed the jurors had already heard what had happened, Ursula suspected news of the event had reached London and was now on leaflets being distributed around the country. Denigrating her as the witch who'd summoned whatever it was that had been created that day.

One by one, Hopkins called forward the witnesses, those whom Oliver had convinced of Ursula being a witch. Ruth tearfully recounted how Henry had been born and John interjected words like 'burden' which made Ruth flinch and cry even more. Couldn't the jury see that she was being manipulated by him?

She looked over at Ursula once and seemed to be mouthing something, but as soon as John had finished his piece, he hurried her back out.

Then it was the turn of Rebecca who relayed the results of the palm reading, the discovery of a poppet in the well and Samuel's hideous death. There was a lot of murmuring amongst the jurors. She turned towards Ursula. 'Murderer!' she screamed, her hand pointing across the room. 'You killed him, you sorceress!'

'No, no I did not, I could only tell you what I saw. I did not make the poppet either, I swear.' Ursula had been told not to make a sound but there wasn't going to be a point in the proceedings where she could deny the allegations, she realised that now. The gaoler who was standing beside her on the platform squeezed his hand around her upper arm and told her to shut up. He was squeezing one of the places where Mary had pricked and a sharp stab of pain caught her unawares. With a slow hiss of breath, she quietened down again. The jurors had barely even looked across at her, nobody seemed to care what was being played out before them, their decision already made.

She couldn't imagine that Hopkins had anything else he could produce as evidence, but then, to her surprise, Daniel Hooke's wife was brought by a guard into the space designated for witnesses. Ursula's heart fell even further. She'd heard that one of the witches in Lancashire had been tried for causing the palsy in a man, and that woman had gone to the gallows for it.

The jurors muttered amongst themselves as the woman cried and wailed, barely able to get her words out describing the devastation that not having Daniel's earnings was having on the family. Apparently, they'd been saved by Master Bruton the physician, who was not only treating Daniel but also giving them money to buy food.

'Of course he is,' Ursula thought to herself, 'and the minute this trial is over and I am swinging from a rope your usefulness will be over and he will leave you to starve. He cares only for himself and what he wants.'

Inevitably, as he had presumably planned, the jurors were now glancing over at Oliver with smiles on their faces and small nods of approval whilst he looked benevolent, his shoulders back and a bashful beam on his face. The man could do no wrong, it seemed. He strolled to the witness stand as Daniel's wife stepped down, still sobbing into a rag until Oliver whipped out a pristine white linen handkerchief and passed it to her, earning yet another murmur of appreciation from the crowd.

'Are you able to confirm what this lady has relayed to us?' the judge asked. 'In your profession as a physician can you tell us what you believe Daniel Hooke is suffering from, and the likelihood of him returning to full health?'

'I can,' Oliver said. He addressed the whole courtroom as if he were the judge and they had all come to listen to him. Ursula could see he was enjoying every moment of what was going on. The court room was a stage as far as he was concerned and now finally, he was the centre of attention. 'I was called to Daniel's home on the night of the fifteenth of June. He had been innocently walking across the fields twixt the village of Finchingham and the sea, which lies approximately three furlongs away. The accused, Mistress Beal, came out of her cottage and set upon him verbally accusing him of watching her for nefarious reasons.'

'That is because he was doing it at your behest,' Ursula shouted, hurting her dry throat and causing another coughing fit. Oliver was deliberately leaving out the reason why Daniel was there in the first place.

Turning to the judge, Oliver said, 'I can assure you, he was not. Before I was called to his cottage, I had never before met the man.'

If any of the jury had their wits about them, they'd have seen through this, Ursula thought to herself. A physician wouldn't attend the rundown cottage of a peddler where he had no chance of being paid.

Oliver finished telling the assembly about the state he'd found Daniel in and ended his statement with the grim prediction that the man would never regain his previous abilities and would die at some point in the next few months. Ursula knew that was not necessarily the case, unless he was left lying on his pallet to get sores. The judge nodded slowly, making notes on the parchment in front of him.

Oliver remained standing where he was, and looking up the judge said, 'Do you have anything else to add, Doctor Bruton?'

'I do have one last piece of information that I believe is pertinent to this case, yes. I would like the jury to know that – as well as the evidence we have laid before you and that which Master Hopkins has discovered when the accused was pricked – I wish to inform you that Master Stearne and I have seen, with our own eyes, Mistress Beal's familiar.'

Ursula's eyes grew wide. She knew immediately what fabrication he was bringing to everyone's attention. Wicker, just a gull, was now tarnished with the same dark lies as she was. She listened to Oliver as he described how he'd been attacked by a huge sea bird when he had visited her cottage after she'd been taken away and he'd instructed Stearne to have it killed, but it had vanished into thin air. At that, Ursula breathed a sigh of relief, the bird was far shrewder than he was. His evidence given, he stepped away from the witness box.

'I believe we have heard everything we need to hear,' the judge intoned. 'This is a foul litany of events.' He turned to the jury. 'You may now make your deliberations and come to a decision.'

'No, wait!' A shout in the courtroom made everyone turn towards the perpetrator. Anne was on her feet waving her arms, her coif falling back from her head. 'What my brother has told is not true. I have met and talked with Mistress Ursula. She is simply a lone woman, wishing to live a solitary and peaceful life. It is not right that she cannot do that without attracting the attention of men who wish to use her.' She turned towards Oliver, whose face was now puce as he pushed his way through the crowd towards her. 'Yes, brother, it is you to whom I refer. Your carnal desires have led you to violence and murder.' Her final words were lost to all, other than those closest to her as, with one hand wrapped around her hair and his other arm across her body, Oliver pulled her from the room.

Everyone looked towards the judge, but as if the interruption had not happened, he merely turned to the jury and repeated his directive to them.

The men clustered into the corner of the room, their heads together. The room was hushed, until a rotten apple flew across from the public watching gallery and hit Ursula in the chest. Juice and pulp spurted out and sprayed across her face. There was a bark of laughter from the crowd but she didn't reward them with a reaction, letting the juice roll down her face and drip off her chin.

Within minutes the jury returned to where they'd been standing. It hadn't taken them long, but before the head juror announced the verdict, she knew what it would be.

'Guilty, you are guilty of being a witch.' The judge repeated what had just been said. 'You shall be hung in King's Lynn market place in two days' time, with the other felons who shall be tried at these assizes.' He nodded to the guard who was standing next to her, also covered in flecks of apple pulp. Taking hold of her arm he dragged her out of the room and across the hall to the door which led to the cells. It all happened so quickly Ursula had barely been able to take in what had been said. That she was to be executed. Where she was going now would be her last place before she was taken outside to the cart which took the condemned prisoners to their fate.

By refusing a man, he had pulled her down and would end her life. Because she would not agree to what he demanded. That she would not allow herself to be oppressed. What hope was there for any women when this could happen? As if by thinking about him could conjure him, he appeared at her elbow and flicked his hand at the guard indicating he should stand to one side.

'Are you happy with the tale you have told?' she spat at him.

'This is of your own doing,' he said. 'I gave you many chances to change your mind and now you see that your choice was wrong.'

'Never,' she replied, 'I still stand by my choice. You know I am no witch, every piece of evidence you brought has an explanation, events that were sent by the Lord, not created by me. How do you think a single person could conjure up a pillar of wind and water to rip across the countryside?'

'A powerful witch could do it, and now your neighbours have seen it with their own eyes. You would never have been able to return to the village, even if you had been found not guilty.' He shrugged his shoulders. 'But you would not listen to me and see now where it has found you.' He nodded to the guard who was standing a step away as if she would make a dash for freedom. After the tiny amount of food she'd been given during the time she'd been in gaol and the torture and beatings she'd endured, she could barely move. She let the guard take her down the stairs, her foot tripping on a raised slab and only his hand holding onto the manacles, which still clamped her hands together, stopped her pitching head first to the floor below.

She was thrown back into the cell from where she'd been taken two hours previously. A minute later a bowl of cold watery porridge was pushed in through the door. It was disgusting and needed some of the honey she had on the shelf at home, but she ate it anyway. She had to scoop it up with her fingers which she wiped down her skirt when she'd finished. There was no point having any pride in her appearance now, her dress was covered in bodily fluids and filth and that would be the lasting impression people would have of her when she was taken to the gallows in two days' time.

49

1646

The time crawled slowly on. No more food or ale appeared and Ursula had no idea how long she'd been waiting for the gaoler to arrive and take her outside for the final time.

Eventually there was a grating as the key turned in the lock under the dim light of the gaoler's lamp. Ursula shielded her eyes and staggered to her feet. Wordlessly she left the cell and made her way along the corridor and up the stairs, keeping her eyes barely open as she waited for the brilliance of daylight to scorch them. But it didn't come. When she got to the top of the stairs, she opened her eyes properly and looked around. It was still dark outside.

Although executions were customarily held first thing in the morning it was usual to wait until daylight for the crowds to arrive. The events were an excuse for festivities and the pie sellers and peddlers would be expecting to make a good purse of silver. Ursula turned to the gaoler.

'You have chosen the wrong time,' she said, even managing a splutter of laughter. 'Do you not see that it is still dark?'

'He has not, for it is I who have had you brought out of your cell.' Oliver stepped out from the shadows.

'You cannot have more trials for me,' she said. 'Surely you are done now?'

'I am giving you one final chance to change your mind. I do not like to be thwarted in obtaining what I desire,' Oliver replied. 'The guard here has agreed to look away while I take you somewhere.' There was the chink of coin being passed and to Ursula's delight the guard unlocked the manacles and released her wrists. They suddenly felt so light she imagined they would begin to float away from her sides. The cool air on the weeping and bloody abrasions was a relief.

Oliver took her arm and pulled her outside. Despite being night, the air was warm and soft and after so long being incarcerated Ursula couldn't pull enough of it into her lungs, breathing deeply for the first time in weeks.

A snort from Oliver's horse tied up close by reminded her that she wasn't being taken out of the gaol for a pleasant reason, of that she was certain.

'Why have you had me released?' she asked. 'I thought you were looking forward to seeing me swing?'

'As I said, I shall try and persuade you one final time. But first, we have a journey on my horse, we will have to ride slowly as it is dark.' He lifted her up and almost threw her onto the horse's back. She was so thin now she knew she must barely weigh anything and she wrapped her fingers in the mane hoping she didn't slide off and under its hooves. Although perhaps that might be a better way to die. Mounting behind her, Oliver put one arm around her waist as if he'd also considered how weak she now was. It seemed that, even at this final hour, he didn't want to lose the prize that was never his to claim.

The horse trotted along a track. Ursula had no idea where it was taking her, the usual waypoints, trees and cottages she recognised, all consumed by the darkness, as black as the ink which was hidden beneath her floorboards. Who would find her notes in years to come? She hoped that they'd finally exonerate her.

Eventually the clouds above them cleared a little and a sliver of moonlight illuminated the countryside around them. It began to look familiar and within minutes they rode past a church. Her church, the one she'd looked out upon every day of her life. Oliver pulled the horse up outside her cottage and dismounting he drew her down beside him. Ursula had no idea why he'd brought her back, but never had her home looked so welcoming and tears welled in her eyes at the familiar sight. It was her sanctuary, her refuge.

'What are we doing here?' she asked, but Oliver didn't reply, instead he looped his arm in hers and pulled her close to him. She could smell the soap on him and a visceral excitement which emanated from his pores. Walking towards the back of the cottage she wondered if they were entering through the scullery. She could hear a scuffling and the rush of bird wings in the air. Wicker was there with her, to witness that which was about to happen.

Instead of going inside though, Oliver continued to walk her across the garden and through the wooden posts which separated her land from the former common land. The ground was wet, she had no idea of the weather having spent her time below ground but it seemed the heat had been broken by the tempest. Land so close to the sea did not drain well. Her feet and legs, still sore and weak caused her several times to slip and almost fall as Oliver hurried her across the uneven mud. Looking back at the cottage bathed in moonlight she thought about the bloodstain which had never faded, her mother who had lived and died there. Years of terror outweighed by the calm Ursula had enjoyed. Despite her resolve, violence would indeed bring about her end.

'Where are you taking me? I do not understand why you have brought me here,' she said again. They were almost at the church wall when they stepped through the undergrowth into a clearing. She could see where the bracken and grasses had been trodden down, a gaping hole in front of them. It hadn't been there before; this was land that she was familiar with. Her land, even though Lord Mayling might disagree. There were rabbit warrens in this area and she'd hit pigeons roosting in the trees which overhung them. Beside the hole was a large pile of earth, pieces of flint sticking out.

'What is this for?' as she spoke the words, it dawned on her what she was seeing. 'Do you mean to bury me here tomorrow? In un-consecrated ground within sight of my home?' It was the final act of a man made mad by desire and the need to dominate and abuse. To hold the power, not just to end her life but beyond, to ensure that her resting place was somewhere which would hurt her. Even after her death he would continue to control her.

'See here,' he dragged her to where a piece of stone with a flat top was sitting. She could see it had been cleared of lichen and moss. Oliver pushed her head down and in the dim moonlight she saw symbols carved on the top. She reached out and ran her fingers over them.

'I do not understand,' she said. 'Is this a gravestone? I cannot tell what is engraved here.'

'Witch marks,' he replied. 'To prevent your soul from rising and continuing your witchcraft from beyond the grave. And your initials, UB. A reminder forever to your neighbours of what you really were.'

'Only that which you have told them I was,' Ursula said. 'You know I am simply a herbal woman, a midwife. A wise woman, that is all. But not *your* wise woman. So, you have arranged for a cart to bring me back here tomorrow? I am surprised you would go to the expense when you could see me buried somewhere on the outskirts of King's Lynn, thrown into an unmarked grave with the other criminals who will be hung tomorrow.'

To their left, in the distance above the sea, the sky was beginning to pale slightly, a new day waiting in the wings. Ursula knew it would be dawn within a couple of hours and that today was the day she would die.

'I have not organised any such thing,' Oliver said. 'It is my wish that you perish here without the rector praying for your soul. The guard has been paid well to tell anyone who may ask that you died during the night and your body has already been taken away. The judge will not care and those who go to watch shall have plenty of other hangings to enjoy. No, you will die now, at my hand. See here,' he pointed to the ground beside the grave, 'I have witches spikes to keep you tethered to the ground so you may not rise again.'

Ursula had heard of such things, pushed through a witch's limbs. He truly meant to humiliate her, even in death. She hoped it came quickly.

'And how do you intend to kill me?' she asked, her voice quiet.

'I will not sully my hands taking your life,' he told her. 'You can rest below the earth until the worms consume you.'

'Alive?' Ursula gasped as she realised what he was saying. 'You will put me in there whilst I still breathe?'

As Oliver began to laugh wildly, he threw his head back and

momentarily unbalanced himself, his feet slipping on the sticky mud which surrounded the hole. Ursula lifted her arms straight out in front of her, her fingers burning with the force she had always kept hidden. Her body an instrument, channelling from the ground beneath her feet, the strength it had always offered her. His eyes wide, he stared at her as his arms flailed, swinging around like the sails on a mill as his stocky body unbalanced and slowly, he fell backwards so his torso was overhanging the hole. He lay for a moment, winded. Ursula could see his eyes were open and blinking slowly as if he couldn't understand what had just happened and silently, keeping her eyes on him, she stepped away and bent down to the pile of earth waiting to be thrown on top of her body. Fumbling around her hand closed around a large, sharp, fragment of flint.

Oliver attempted to push himself up onto his elbows but dazed, he was moving haltingly and with one swift moment she brought the rock down as hard as she could on the back of his head. It made a sickening crunch and blood splattered across her hand as he fell backwards again, groaning. Lifting the flint again she smashed it down once more and finally he lay still. She dropped the stone and bent over, her hands on her knees as she gasped for breath and retched. There was nothing in her stomach to bring up.

She had no idea if she'd killed Oliver or if he still breathed, but she knew there was only one outcome that could now save her own life and gathering up every last ounce of energy she had, she pushed his body until it rolled over and into the grave.

Climbing in beside him, she leaned back out to take the spikes before pushing them into his arms and legs as he'd intended to do to her. At least he wasn't conscious as she'd have been, indeed he may well already be dead, and she felt no shame for what she was doing, not now. She'd long ago realised that there was only one way the situation was going to resolve itself, either he would be the victor, or she would. Neither of them had expected it to be her, but it was just and right that it was so.

Even though he couldn't hear her she let out the hate she held for him in whispers, filtering out beneath her breath. 'To prevent your body from returning from the dead.' She pushed the spike in. 'To stop you resurrecting to curse all women, we who hold the power.'

Climbing back out of the grave, she began to push and throw the mound of earth back into the hole. She started with his head, not wanting to see his eyes if they suddenly opened.

Finally, the only evidence that they'd been there was the uneven, trampled down earth, but she knew that nobody ever came to this tucked away spot. She dragged the bracken and brambles surrounding her over the fresh earth until it was no longer visible. Then there was one last thing to do.

She found the large lump of stone that Oliver had shown her, the gravestone he'd clumsily engraved. She rolled the rock over, her arms burning with the weight of it after already having been strained moving Oliver's body and she pushed it on top of his grave.

She picked up the piece of flint with which she'd stoved in his head and leaning over the stone she felt around for where her initials had been cut into it. It took just a few hacks, the stone in her hand sliding about with the blood still covering it as she completed the U and made it an O. Not the gravestone for Ursula Beal, but the one for Oliver Bruton.

Wiping her hands on her skirts she made her way on shaking legs back to the rear of her cottage. The back door was open and when she walked in, her feet crunching on the broken glass still on the floor where the windows were broken in the storm, she could see that every stick of furniture, her work bench, and her cooking utensils were gone. Ransacked by those she used to call her friends.

Going to the cupboard beside the cold fireplace, she pushed her fingers under the loose floorboard and pulled it up. The parchments she'd hidden were still there and she heaved a sigh of relief. Pulling them out together with her quill and ink she knelt over them as she added a final codicil to her story and a warning to those who came after her.

Always look for that which seeks you out, to do you harm, for it watches you. Harness that which is concealed deep within you, as I have. Our strength and might shall overcome evil.

She would have liked to take the papers with her, but she knew how dangerous they'd be if she were caught and searched, so after taking out her purse of coins, she pushed them back into their hiding place, wedging the floorboard back in place. There they could remain, there was no need for them to be discovered. Not unless another woman in another time needed to draw strength from her power.

In the scullery there were a few dried herbs still left hanging from the ceiling. Possibly her neighbours were frightened lest they were poisons but she knew what they were and gratefully she took them down and pushed them into one of the pockets in her skirts.

Creeping out of the back of the cottage she moved stealthily as dawn was now breaking, she couldn't risk being seen. Once she was clear of the rough ground around her cottage, and keeping her eyes averted from where she'd just buried Oliver, she ran as fast as her weakened, wobbly legs could carry her towards Peddars Way. If she was able to stay out of sight and get to King's Lynn port, she could find a boat to take her across the seas. She had enough money in her pocket to pay for her passage and she'd make a new life for herself elsewhere. Wherever she ran to she'd never be safe though. For there would always be men who chose to assert their power over women. But there were always women, like herself, who would fight back to save themselves.

50

2024

The police came promptly, as did most of the customers in the pub once they saw the flashing lights of the ambulance which arrived soon after. Between them Jess and Roger managed to get everyone to go back to their drinks whilst letting themselves in the back door to look for Adrianna.

'Don't worry,' she laughed shakily as she saw their shocked faces. 'It's just a bang to the head. Well, a punch to the face which ended up with my head bouncing off the hearth. It appears I've added to the bloodstain.' She pointed to the pool of darkening blood which was beginning to congeal. Behind her the paramedic, who was holding a handful of gauze to the side of her face, told her not to move.

'What? What happened?' Jess asked. 'Don't worry about this,' she pointed to the floor, 'I'll deal with that for you.' Another bloodstain made in anger to remain forever, reminding the world of the violence of men. Adrianna guessed that it wouldn't disappear, however much scrubbing Jess did.

'I discovered Rick has been tracking me, that's how he knew where we'd been and it was him who sent those awful messages.

We had a row and I told him we were finished. He turned nasty and,' she indicated her head, 'got violent. I've been sitting here thinking of all the times he was supposedly looking out for me, the times he'd twist my memories until I didn't know what was true or not – he was just controlling the narrative to his own advantage. Telling me I wasn't able to do my job even though I was completely capable. And then tracking me, so he knew where I was at all times. Just like you said, Jess. I should have listened to you.'

'Where is he now?' Roger asked, perching on the edge of a chair and holding her hand. 'You aren't safe here, come and stay at the vicarage.'

'She'll be going to hospital with us in a few minutes,' the paramedic told him. 'This needs looking at and, I'm sorry to say, some stitches.'

'Rick drove off in my car,' Adrianna said. 'So heaven knows where he is now. I'll quickly call the porter's desk in my building. They know me well so they can stop Rick if he turns up there before the police do. And they can organise for my locks to be changed.'

By the time Adrianna was sitting up in a bed in A & E with fifteen stitches in her forehead, and her eye starting to close up as it turned purple, a young female police officer had come to find her and let her know that her car had been found outside King's Lynn station with the keys still in it.

'Our colleagues in the Met will be waiting for him to arrive either at your flat or his own, and he'll be arrested for assaulting you and for stealing your car too.'

'Thank you.' Adrianna managed a shaky smile. She could still hardly absorb everything which had happened that day. It was as if a veil had been pulled away from her eyes and she'd finally seen Rick for who he was. She'd been so stupid and she could feel tears welling up. Even the bruised eye still seemed to be able to produce the hot salty tears which stung her cheek. Their whole relationship had been a lie. He'd manipulated her, and she'd allowed him to do it. Her crisis at work wouldn't have happened if he hadn't been so supposedly caring, whilst at the same time telling her she couldn't cope. He enjoyed living in her expensive flat but his ego couldn't cope with a woman earning more than him. More successful than him. Even the way he'd moved in with her without them ever having a discussion about it. He'd been so loving – almost too loving – never letting her go anywhere on her own, other than to work. And the times she had made him angry but he wouldn't speak to her so she never knew what she'd done wrong. It had just made her more anxious. She hadn't known that abuse could be so subtle, so deadly.

He didn't want an equal relationship, he wanted to be the dominant one, the master. She remembered his failure to pay rent. Another way of abusing her by making sure she wouldn't have enough money. Her missing handbag, the credit card and the shining Rolex on his wrist, she was sure that the watch was actually what had caught her face when he hit her. And clearing her bank account with her card. She never wanted to go back to the flat, she knew that now. It was tainted.

After she'd reassured the doctor several times that she hadn't lost consciousness, he agreed she could go home. When she walked through to reception, she found Jess waiting for her.

'Don't tell me you've been waiting all this time?' Adrianna exclaimed. 'I was going to call a taxi to get home.'

'I've got your door keys,' Jess explained. 'And I think Roger, Tom, Mum and goodness knows who else are watching your cottage in case that git returns.'

'Little chance of that,' Adrianna said, relaying the information she'd been given. 'The police brought my keys back so I need to go and collect my car.'

'Not now, you don't,' Jess admonished. 'With one eye working and probably a horrific headache?'

'It is a bit sore,' Adrianna said, nodding and then wincing at the stab of pain. 'I think I need some painkillers and to go to bed.' She followed Jess outside and sat silently as they drove home.

The next three days passed quietly with a steady stream of visitors who arrived with meals. The fridge was stacked with various pasta dishes and cottage pies despite the still unwavering heat outside. She'd had a call to say Rick had been arrested and charged with assault, and that the locks had been changed at her flat.

Sitting outside, Adrianna closed her eyes, enjoying the warmth of the sun on them. Finally her bruise was turning yellow and didn't look quite as violent as it had. She had an appointment in a couple of days at the local doctors to have the stitches removed. She'd had to change her GP practice from the one in London but somehow it felt like the right move and had begun a train of thought in her head as she considered her future. Close by, a bee droned as it flew around the lavender. As the sun warmed the flowers, the gentle scent surrounded her. The fragrance of yesteryear she thought to herself, here in the garden for hundreds of years.

Opening her eyes, she looked across the fields. The air was so still she could hear the distant waves as they scattered across the stones on the beach. An ancient soundtrack to the village and those who lived in it. Going back into the house she picked up the last page of the journal. This would hopefully allow Ursula's story to finally be told. She now knew the basics about what happened with Oliver and that Ursula had been accused and found guilty of witchcraft. And yet she was certain that wasn't the end of the story. Whatever was occupying the cottage with her was not yet at rest. She was aware that she hadn't explained to Jess the strange happenings when she'd argued with Rick, but she didn't have the words.

'Hello? Are you there?' Her friend's voice called through the open back door.

'In here,' Adrianna replied. She waved the piece of paper in her hand. 'I'm still trying to decipher this final message that Ursula left. I've got so much other stuff going round in my head I need a diversion.'

'Well, I have one for you.' Jess flopped down on the sofa and Adrianna saw that she was grinning widely. 'I've heard back from our chap examining the bones. And it's not a woman.'

'Sorry? Wait, what do you mean?' Adrianna said, her face creasing in confusion.

'The skeleton you found in your garden is that of a man.' Jess showed her an email on her phone. 'So your assumption it's Ursula is wrong.'

Adrianna leant back in her chair and rubbed her fingers across her forehead as she tried to absorb what Jess was saying. 'I can't believe it,' she said. 'I need to understand this last message more than ever.' She started to read it out, her voice getting slower the more that she went on.

My story does not end here, for it will creep on through all time. From mother to daughter, sister to sister. Woman to woman, our fight shall go on. When my end did approach, I turned to harness the dark side and called to the powers I have been convicted of working with, to battle the evil. To assist me with that which I had to undertake and I placed him where he had thought to put me. I hope my god will forgive me. Now I leave this place forever and may those who come after me honour my fate and that which we will always fight, forever.

'Harnessing the dark side,' she whispered. 'Perhaps she had more powers than she would admit, those that I channelled when I needed to. I'm certain the evil she talks about was Oliver. I thought she'd been hung for being a witch and then buried here as a final act of revenge because she wouldn't consent to his demands, but what if, in actual fact, she killed him? That he ended up in the grave he'd dug for her?' Getting to her feet she ran out into the garden and across to where the witches stone still lay. Behind her she could hear the crashing of undergrowth as Jess followed shouting ineffectually, 'Don't run, you mustn't trip and hit your head again!'

Kneeling down in front of the stone, Adrianna ran her fingers over the grooves which were etched there, slowly tracing the UB. 'Of course,' she gasped, 'these initials aren't UB. Feel here, it's an O, not a U. OB. Oliver Bruton. That's what the final message is trying to tell me. For some reason, she left the gaol in King's Lynn and he brought her here, perhaps to kill her himself. He must've made all these witches marks on the stone beforehand, and it explains why there's no record of her hanging. But somehow, she got the upper hand and killed him instead. Those spikes must've been intended for her corpse, not his.'

'And then what happened to her?' Jess asked. 'We don't know that.'

'I think we do, the last line, *now I leave this place forever* is surely saying she escaped. We may even be able to find her on a passage list for one of the ships leaving King's Lynn, they still have some records I think.'

'What will you do about Oliver's bones? The man was a brute. Do you really want him putting back in your garden?' Jess said.

'No I don't. I'll let Roger give him a Christian burial in the churchyard. Perhaps then Ursula will find some peace.'

Getting to her feet she brushed the dry dirt from her knees and went back inside to email Jason and let him know the end of the tale, it was his garden after all. Although not for much longer. Because she'd decided to take him up on his offer to buy the cottage. The four walls were her sanctuary and already, her home. She could continue to live amongst her new friends and within a community who cared about her. Who loved her.

It was the end of one chapter of her life and the beginning of the next. She'd hand in her notice and sell the London flat. The degree in forensic archaeology that Jess mentioned was starting in September and she'd already emailed to enquire about a place. It was time for a new start. She realised that what she'd thought of as a curse was in fact a warning for her.

Always keep watch for that which seeks you out, to do you harm, for it sees you. Harness that which is concealed deep within you, as I have. Our strength shall overcome evil.

Her strength had indeed overcome the evil in her life, as Ursula's had. Two wise women. From the witch stone the herring gull flew up, spreading its wings and flying towards the sun.

ACKNOWLEDGEMENTS

The idea for this book came about, as they often do, when I was so far down a research rabbit hole I couldn't remember how I'd got there or what I was supposed to be looking for. I read about a skeleton of a supposed witch being found in a garden in Essex and from there I began reading up about Matthew Hopkins, the Witchfinder General, and his persecution of innocent women whose only crime was to live a simple quiet life. I was hooked and I wrote the book in record time! As always though, my contribution is only a part of everything that happens to bring a book to publication so I have a lot of people to thank for their help.

Firstly, a huge thank you to my editor Isobel Akenhead who has used her magic to bring this book to be the very best that it can be. I am so, so grateful for everything you do Isobel! And also thank you to the rest of the amazing Boldwood Books team, copy editor Debra Newhouse, proof reader Candida Bradford, and Jane Dixon-Smith for the stunning cover.

And this time I have to thank not one, but two agents. To my agent Ella Kahn at DKW Literary Agency thank you for all that you do and for having my back. And also, a massive thank you to another DKW star, Camille Burns, for your fantastic unstinting work on this book and on my behalf; you were incredible.

I couldn't do what I do without the support of my very special authorly friends. My virtual office colleague, Jenni Keer, who is the ultimate cheerleader and maker of top-notch virtual cappuccinos, thank you for all that you do. Keep checking in. I also need to mention a special bunch of people (yes, yes, you know who you are!) who keep me sane when I want to throw the manuscript through the window. Your friendship, your support, the mad photo shoots and the belly busting laughs you bring mean everything to me.

I could not do all this without my husband, my one-man fan club. He uncomplainingly plays golf every weekend so I can work, visits places I want to go for necessary research and provides endless cups of tea when I am locked in my writing cave. Thank you, Des, you are the very best.

And finally, thank you to my lovely kids who are an amazing bunch of international cheerleaders!

ABOUT THE AUTHOR

Clare Marchant is the author of dual timeline historical fiction. Her books have been translated into seven languages, and she is a USA Today bestseller. Clare spends her time writing and exploring local castles, or visiting the nearby coast.

Sign up to Clare Marchant's mailing list for news, competitions and updates on future books.

Follow Clare on social media here:

facebook.com/claremarchantauthor

x.com/claremarchant1

instagram.com/claremarchantauthor

tiktok.com/@claremarchantauthor

Letters from
the past

Discover page-turning
historical novels from
your favourite authors
and be transported
back in time

Join our book club
Facebook group

https://bit.ly/SixpenceGroup

Sign up to our
newsletter

https://bit.ly/LettersFrom
PastNews

Boldwood

Boldwood Books is an award-winning fiction publishing company seeking out the best stories from around the world.

Find out more at www.boldwoodbooks.com

Join our reader community for brilliant books, competitions and offers!

Follow us
@BoldwoodBooks
@TheBoldBookClub

Sign up to our weekly deals newsletter

https://bit.ly/BoldwoodBNewsletter

Printed in Great Britain
by Amazon

49929793R00183